Over The Wall & Beyond The Rim

A Double Novella Offering by

Thomas James Taylor

Contents

OVER THE WALL

BEYOND THE RIM

OVER THE WALL

1

— I Thought I Had an Answer —

Perched atop a prison wall after dark, the plan, as sketchy as it was, was to scarper towards the car park where, with any luck, the pair of us would find an easy vehicle to hot-wire and drive away before security guards began pouring out of the main gate, keen to test their marksmanship in our direction.

A bolt of hot pain shot upward from my right ankle as I hit the unyielding ground at the foot the ten metre high wall crowned with razor wire. I could not believe it. How many times had I scoffed at distressed movie actresses in some B-grade movie when they turned an ankle while fleeing pursuers?

'Give me a moment,' I hissed to my friend in humiliation. 'My goddamned ankle,' I explained, grasping the offending body part. 'If I'm not up shortly,' I told him, 'best you press on without me.'

I willed the paining joint to mend itself immediately, while Abe crouched patiently beside me. To my immense surprise and relief some flexibility did soon return. I was able to stand and put some weight on it, gingerly testing reliability.

'Good to go,' I confirmed, and we moved off, keeping to the shadows, pressed against the wall, all the while hoping the guard in the corner tower had not glimpsed our rapid ascent before launching into the darkness. There was no light within the tower but that didn't mean it was unmanned. From behind the glass any outward vision would have been severely hampered by interior illumination, which would amply explain the lack of any.

The haphazard escape from C-Division had been a hastily planned affair on the day. A rush of blood to the head had been of sufficient impetus for this and many, alike, seemingly illogical escapades I had initiated in my time. In defence of this particular exploit, I could only reason to myself that it was my in my nature to test the boundaries of logic and convention and even reality, to mess with the rules of predictable, future events. For this argument to lend reason to my actions, there had to be an observer; someone or something attempting to predict events along the time line. The only possible observer that could be, I conjured, was God, should such a being exist. I was gambling then, that God, or at least something approximating the designation, did exist. I cannot say there is a god. Then again I cannot categorically say there is not. There are arguments either way, but on the off chance of there being an omniscient, omnipotent entity overseeing, attempting to predict future events for the purpose of stitching together some vast, eternal plan, it gave me immense satisfaction to think I may be causing *Him/Her/It* some measure of irritation, affecting the flow of ordained, future events. Perhaps, at the root of this odd psychological itch I had issues with the concept of an inflexible, immutable reality. I need to know that reality, so called, is fallible and can be messed with, even by the likes of little old me. It would, to my mind, make the cosmos a little more user friendly. Who knows? It may simply have been some weird, inbuilt mechanism I was born with, to poke at something as big, dangerous and uncompromising as the cosmos. There was at work that *'What would happen if?'* scenario going on, testing the bounds of *What is.* A compulsion to experiment with the orderly; that which is seen by most as the natural, logical progression of events. As long as the option to meddle with *what is* continued to present itself, I would ever feel challenged to tempt fate, just to see what happened. And the bigger the occasion— the more portentous it be; the stronger the compulsion to poke; the greater incongruence the decision to poke creates, the more tempted I am to test God's patience and disrupt His notion of perfection and stability by messing with those things he would consider steadfast and predictable, and, therefore, forgone conclusions. It's only fair after all, I figured. We human beings are forced to deal with exactly that sort of unpredictability for all of our lives. Whenever has anything in our struggling, mortal existence been predictable, reliable, dependable?

I have to admit that in attempting to explain this, even to myself, it does sound quite mad, and perhaps it is. But, hell, the cosmos is a strange place, and existence, no less so. Whatever our nascent, puny minds are able to make of it all can only be as sophisticated as our intelligence and our ability to understand allow. Despite the great opinion we have of ourselves, we have a long, long way to go before we achieve anything close to understanding what we call reality. And that, only if there is such a thing, because, as far as I can tell, it's all little more than unsophisticated perceptions and illusion. A separate reality for all.

As for my own, possibly aberrant take on reality, I can say only that it's more interesting than some, and no one has ever been hurt by it. No one but me, but I can take it, and it's not without amusement value. I make sure of that. Never a dull moment.

I first met Abe in D-Block. D for detention. Described as a prison within a prison, the cells are bereft of any creature comfort, unless a wooden bench and a toilet bucket are considered creature comforts. A thin padding, which serves as a mattress, and a few cotton blankets are brought into the cell each evening to sleep on. The rest of the time there is only the four concrete walls, the bench and the bucket. Each morning, at precisely eight o'clock, after toast and porridge is served as the morning repast through the steel trap in the door, the inhabitants of D-Block are summoned to the opened doorway for inspection, counted and asked by the keeper if there are any requests or complaints. That is about the sum of human contact for the day. The rest of the day is spent alone, and it was during my first thirty day stay in D-Block that I experienced something revealing about the perceptions of the mind, with particular regard to its relationship to the fourth dimension, being time.

Living with units of time that are separated into twenty four hour segments can create within the mind an illusion very like the frames of the old style celluloid film; each frame representing one day.

Living in a strictly regimented environment, where everything occurs according to an inflexible schedule governed by the clock, during my extended isolation within solitary confinement my mind began to comprehend the past, and even the future, as simple, isolated frames within the moving picture of the world I live in. The effect was particularly evident during my stay in isolation, where every day was almost the exact replica of that which preceded it, and hence my mind extrapolated so that I saw the future as being just the same as the past. The effect was interesting. I began to see myself replicated, standing, sitting, exercising, whatever my position, within superimposed, transparencies representing individual days; slices of time stacked, one atop the other ad infinitum, stretching backward into the past, and likewise into the future. It got to the point where my cell was populated with many selves crowding the one small space; overlapping transparencies of twenty four hour time periods. My cell became full to the brim with layered doppelgangers from days future and past, with the experience causing me, forevermore, to view time in an entirely different light than was the case prior to my introduction to detention.

Abe inhabited the next cell along from mine. We eyeballed one another while standing to in our cell doorways during morning muster. Conversation was impossible throughout the day, but in the middle of the night, when the guards pulling night shift mostly stayed at their post at the end of the corridor, some exchanges were made by hoisting one's self up to the high window in the outer wall, and talking quietly.

Having made one another's acquaintance in this way, after being introduced back into general population, we occasionally played a game of handball together, in three-yard. I figured him for a stand-up guy who kept mostly to himself, much as I did, but there was a quality about him. People have an aura about them, and this guy was interesting. Mostly unassuming, he could put anyone who tried it on with him on the back foot in short measure; zeroing in on an offender's weakness with unerring accuracy, able to disarm the most threatening of them with a few, quietly spoken words. And his manner; radiating an ineffable quality which could make it impossible to get a read on him. Everyone knows an unknown quantity is best treated with caution, even a prison yard bully.

Putting one's trust in a fellow inmate is not advisable, and it went against instinct doing so myself. But *no man is an island*, as the pithy adage correctly advises, and as time passed I learned that he was not your average scoundrel, cutting out time for some horrid, criminal act. The circumstances landing the man in prison were of a tragic nature, and to be raised later in this account, but to my immense delight I came to realise that he was at least as weird as myself when it came to his own, personal take on life.

~

Before long my awkward gait and the dull, throbbing which accompanied, had very much improved; almost miraculously so, I pondered some time later, and I was again a fully functioning criminal on the run. *Criminal.* It was ludicrous that I should be labelled as such. The word,

I was certain, was not something to be applied to me. When, a long time later, I learned that my mug was plastered across newspaper pages along with the offensive description, I was appalled. To my mind I was nothing more than an energetic, if occasionally erratic, perhaps even misguided but adventurous liver of life, searching for I knew not what, exactly, but it was important and I knew that it would never be found without risks being taken and by experiencing everything possible on the journey of life.

Nothing I did was ever carried out with anything even approaching ill-will. Not a soul was ever harmed during my brief apprenticeship as an outlaw, and only fully insured, unscrupulous enterprises were targeted. I may have taken advantage on the odd occasion, though only as an agent of karma in evening the score as far as the scales of cosmic justice was concerned.

Times were tough back in '77. Well, for me they were, and in view of the then situation I considered the basic imperative of survival as a good enough excuse for my oft spontaneous, occasionally questionable behaviour. Truth be told though, it was all just a harmless game. Life back then was little more than that, despite surrounding circumstances. From where I stood any young man attempting to get a handle on life while negotiating the 1970's and into the early 80's had a job cut out for themselves if they were looking for answers to the big questions.

I saw that many appeared satisfied simply to hold down a steady job, to get married, settle down with kids, a dog, a car, a house and a forty year mortgage. Seeing those same people twenty years later, their satisfaction had not lasted. There had to be more to life, I figured, and understanding what that was became my sole propose. I would do whatever it took to achieve enlightenment. Experiencing life to the full was the surest way of achieving understanding that I could think of. Extracting knowledge and wisdom from all this was the only goal I could see. If it took a lifetime in the doing, then so be it. If it took several lifetimes and all were full of effort, disappointment and countless barriers, I was prepared for that, too. There was nothing to equal the immense wonder of existence; of being an intelligent being amid it all while blundering about on the surface of this rare and remarkable planet which is poised and vulnerable, out here on the outer spiral arm of one of billions of galaxies, and all hurtling at enormous speed through the intergalactic corridors of the cosmos.

Drug addiction is a nasty affliction. It torments the victim without letup, leaving not much time to slow and contemplate the crazy, hell-for-leather ride one is strapped in to. Clear, objective thought is difficult while cognitive functions are overridden and impaired by the urgent demands of the demons of imminent withdrawal. Waking in the morning with that horrible, creeping feeling of impending illness and incapacitation, the mind immediately becomes occupied with the problem of identifying the simplest route by which to procure more of the very same stuff which waylaid you in the first place.

Perspective can eventually seep through, though. It begins to emerge after a time, if one allows it. Especially when a fleeting glimpse of the stranger reflected in the mirror causes one to flinch in response. A jolt of reality is what it takes. When it finally comes, one knows, *absolutely,* that unless steps are taken one's future is likely to be a foreshortened, ignominious affair. The aftermath of addiction involves being deposited back to the exact, selfsame place of departure, considerably more tarnished and worse for wear than was the case prior to departure.

~

The vehicle fired up and away we sped, headed for we knew not what or where and exceedingly glad to be going there. We were free spirits once more. No more having to march to the dreary beat of someone else's drum. We were young, healthy, fully fuelled and primed, ready for action, with adventure in our hearts and endless horizons stretching out before us. We were in all kinds of a hurry to commence adventuring right away, contemptuous of prison walls, ill-fitting social mores, a system less concerned with remedy and improvement than it was in retribution, and stamping out endless replica people; citizens modelled and shaped by indoctrination; behaviourally modified entities whose education prepares them for nothing more promising than conceptualized, perfunctory positions to meet with a future where they are to live out orderly but misshapen lives as taxpayers, consumers and producers of excess everything; where the fruit of their restricted minds and trammelled labour combined was to be obfuscated, the purported future misrepresented by those privy to power, wealth and control of information by manipulation of elaborate, far-reaching creations of advertising and social propaganda, all designed to continue the contemptible charade until the inevitable consequences of the vast and terminally invidious deception is too near to fulfilling its destiny for there be any time left for contrition and desperate acts of course correction.

We were bent on nothing other than forging ahead. Inertial forces were in play: life forces. We were caught in a powerful current, being swept along by the capricious, irresistible pull of the future; a tidal force against which there was no counter measure, taking us wherever it would, entailing whatever it entailed, and happy we were to be caught in it's liberating, intoxicating, embrace.

~

Abraham stands at around five, eleven tall, solidly built with thick, black, curly hair on top and a thriving beard on the underside. His smile, when it was employed, beamed out from the growth in unison with the light of those blue bright eyes; a transforming effect which, when I first witnessed the man expressing true merriment, put me in mind of a lighthouse emitting something uncommon but radiant and fascinating across deep and mysterious waters. I had no idea why the odd vision impressed itself on me, but that was the impression I received, and as our association with, and our acquaintance of one another grew in the fullness of time, I learned the allusion was not so very far from the mark in describing the true nature of the man.

I am a few inches taller, less bulky, clean shaven whenever a razor blade is at hand. My hair, usually tied back from the face, is light brown, framing, I have been told, slightly hawkish features, with hazel coloured eyes, and emitting an overall easy demeanour. As to why we gravitated toward one another, I cannot say for sure. The rule of attraction usually involves opposites, and while that was mostly true in regard to us, in time it became obvious that, at the core, there lay something indefinably familiar; a thread of commonality which not once throughout the duration of our confederacy was questioned or otherwise alluded to.

~

The little car, we abandoned, leaving it parked beside a toilet block near a suburban nature reserve from whence we legged it along a nearby railway line for an hour, before emerging at the seaside. It was a sultry evening. We sat on the cool sand, under a low ceiling of cloud, listening to the rolling surf we could not see. Enveloped in near total darkness I attempted to let dissipate the surplus excitement generated by the flight to freedom.

'When I woke up this morning, I can't say I expected to be sitting here on this beach tonight,' I told Abe, the note of amusement in my voice.

'You didn't see this coming?' he asked after a moment.

I considered the question. It was the type of question only Abe would ask, a big part of the reason I had befriended the guy in the first place. The question caused me to identify something I had not considered until now, and I had to chuckle.

'I guess I'm not so surprised to be sitting here,' I admitted. 'Life has always been full of unexpected twists and turns. What about you? Have you always been so... impulsive?'

He looked somewhat taken aback by the question. 'You see our action as impulsive? Without forethought?'

'Without *much* forethought,' I amended.

'You already said you're not so surprised to be sitting here. How much forethought does it take?'

'It takes *some*.'

'What was taken into consideration?' he quizzed further.

'The repercussions,' I answered immediately. 'How much extra time I would get for this little caper.'

'If you're so concerned about that, I'm surprised you came.'

'I wasn't, I guess. I'm here because I'm annoyed they took so much time off me. I get that I crossed the line, but after serving a year and a half for swiping a few grand from a supermarket, with only three weeks left to go, they dropped another year on top: A suspended sentence I had from years ago, which ought to have run concurrently. They waited 'til my time was almost up. I was all set to go home next month!

'I mean, I'm a believer in justice, but this ain't that. Truth be told, if I hadn't been stopped when I was, I might well have destroyed myself. I needed something like prison to save my life... but justice it is not. If they won't dispense justice, I decided I would dispense some of my own, and grant myself this holiday.'

Although I could barely see his outline in the darkness, I knew he was looking me straight in the eye. 'And having said that, you expect me to believe, for you, tonight was *spur-of-the-moment?* And what of everything that now follows? The remainder of your life?'

'It's the way I've always lived it,' I answered, following my own brand of logic, and, '*No!* not a single regret,' I preempted.

I sensed his humour, as if he were entertained by my response. 'What?' I snapped in protest. 'I've come to live life according to my own values, with my own sense of justice, of what's right, wrong or unfair. What I see of this world is not what it ought be about,' I found myself arguing, surprised by my agitation for his amusement.

'And just what do you think it's all about?' he returned, his voice gaining an edge.

'Learning—learning as much as we can in the time available to us. That, for one. And when we have gained as much wisdom and knowledge as we are able, applying it to answering that very question.'

He held me in that steady, probing gaze of his, which somehow pierced the darkness, and as I watched, the corners of his mouth appeared to curl upward, a quizzical expression emerging.

'Did you mean to do that?' he asked, curiosity now evident.

'Mean to what?' I replied, for the moment affecting a look of innocence, but I could not maintain it for long; or, at least, I did not wish to, and broke with a smile of my own. 'I'm not sure,' I told him. 'It's a tough question. Perhaps the toughest of all.'

His attentiveness did not waver as he repeated, 'Did you mean to do that, David?'

'No,' I answered honestly. 'I thought I had an answer, 'til I realised a lifetime is likely not long enough to learn the answer.'

He nodded. 'Any answer cannot be more than conjecture. Ask a thousand wise men, *What's it all about?* and you may get as many differing answers. There can be no definitive answer, unless, of course, one were to ask *the creator* himself. But is there *a* creator? And would he/she/it, *if* they exist, be able to provide the answer? Perhaps they would say, *There is no real point. I did all this simply because I can and for no other reason than that. I was bored and needed something to occupy my time.*'

'Well, that would be an answer, would it not?' I countered.

'Is it? Such a response only says there was *no real reason* for it. We're left with nothing definitive, still. No good reason other than "*because I could?*" It's not the answer anybody wants, is it? It hardly makes all the pain and effort and strife worthwhile. What is to be gained by it?'

The train of thought was beginning to wear on me. I did not like that Abe would fain to accept an argument such as that, and I was sure he was toying with me. What was it he expected of me? I wondered. If there was another, more salient answer to his damn question, was he expecting me to unearth it? I was miffed for being maneuvered into a position of failure to come up with an answer.

'Don't trouble yourself,' he expressed amiably, and chuckling amusedly, which annoyed me all the more. 'Some solutions are so plain obvious, we never see them for want of getting out of our own way. People make a habit of it.'

That he was amused by my increasing consternation angered me. 'Have it your own way,' I said, rising. 'Let's get off this beach before someone comes along a finds us dressed in these prison toggs. Where's your friend's house from here?'

~

Upon waking in Abe's friend's tiny seaside rental, the next morning it was decided we needed to make ourselves scarce. I had, before laying my head down that night, contacted a friend of my own; a staunch and trusted ally whom I had grown up with during my happy but rather wayward youth. He was a member of the brotherhood of motorcycle riders, Inc. His name was Henk, *aka* Evo. The moniker, an abbreviation of *evolved human being,* had been bestowed on him during his initial, sponsored days with the brotherhood, when it was discovered that he possessed the skilled and useful ability of being able to talk his way through almost any situation; a trait much valued whenever the eruption of violence seemed unavoidable but not the preferred method of resolving an issue at that juncture.

Evo negotiated a useful option for Abe and myself, a destination where we might evade detection by the authorities for a time while they buzzed around like angry bees, looking for us. We would *go bush*, it was decided. Evo's associates had some acres of fertile land needing cultivation, north of Adelaide, beyond the Mount Lofty Ranges, near the irrigation plains toward the Murray River. We travelled there in a lovely little Cessna 182 Skylane, a trip taking a little over ninety minutes, taking us over some of the most gorgeous countryside. We circled an expanse far from any access road; bushland, with mallee scrub and a few, stunted acacias growing in a depressed, sloping swathe of grass-covered ground where the watertable seeped to the surface, made visible by the more lush undergrowth thriving for the availability of as much moisture as it could possibly need.

The Cessna touched down on flat, virgin ground which availed itself to the purpose. Evo, our pilot, Abe and myself unloaded the equipment we had brought along, including a good sized tent, food stores, pots and pans, drinking water and bedding. The rest of the equipment had already been stashed in among bushes and covered by camouflage pattern tarpaulin; a useful collection including fuel, a small generator, assorted tools. Not far from where we were to establish our campsite lay scores of shallow, timber crates containing marijuana seedlings. I estimated well over a thousand of the little plants, placed in circular fashion under the dwarf acacias, and representing the manner in which we would be making ourselves useful over the following few months, while the law tired of looking for two escapees who will have appeared to have vanished from the face of the Earth.

Other items of interest wrapped in hessian were retrieved from the aircraft's rearmost storage compartment. A satellite phone was provided, with instructions to use it only in event of an emergency such as the arrival of the police drug squad unit, or interlopers looking to steal the produce. Also wrapped in hessian was an automatic twelve gauge shotgun, a triple two rifle with telescopic sights fitted and a large capacity magazine, useful for hunting in order to supplement our rations, and a forty-four calibre handgun, all of which came with ample ammunition.

After being told that someone would drop by once every few weeks in order to restock supplies and to see how things were progressing, the two of us stood, watching as the aircraft return to the sky, banked hard to the south as it climbed steeply, eventually disappearing from view amid the vast, blue, summer sky.

'Well, here we are,' I uttered, without quite knowing why, and turned to amble off toward our yet-to-be-constructed campsite. With our tent strung out between the low branches of a pair of bent and twisted mallee trees, a campfire area with a cooking area set out, a good supply of wood was then gathered from around the site. Enough clean burning mulga to last a day or two. By the time the odds and sods were attended to, such as the ground sheeting, insect netting, camp beds snapped together and positioned, clothes sorted and stowed, firearms inspected, cleaned and made ready, supplies unpacked, sorted and evaluated, it was already getting on towards evening. Planting would begin after a sound night's sleep, we determined. Until then, we figured we would slap together a simple meal before turning in: canned steak and kidney pie, canned potatoes, canned carrots and canned peas, washed down by a copious amount of instant coffee.

Tin cans were buried before dragging our camp beds out from the tent, near to the warming influence of the campfire, the smoke of which we hoped would dissuade buzzing insects. The evening temperature would drop quickly, but neither of us could pass up the chance to enjoy a night under the stars—stars which, as prisoners, we had not seen in far too long a time. We lay, exhausted but content, under the rapidly darkening sky, looking up at the dizzying depths of eternity that is an outback night sky, and my mind began to swim as our adventure began to replay at speed in attempt to catch up with the now.

'Long day,' Abe observed, his voice manifesting the weariness we shared.

'Long day,' I agreed, and without further exchange we allowed the small sounds adrift on the ocean of surrounding silence to steal our thoughts away.

~

For the past year and a half I had been having a reoccurring dream. It makes no sense and yet it keeps coming back. I'm walking through the streets of a city where I come upon a huge memorial. The memorial is in memory of the sacrifice made by all who went to war to preserve peace in the world. The statue denotes a guy following a plough, pulled by a pair of draft horses. Close by there's the figure of a soldier in uniform, wearing a slouch hat and with a gun slung over his shoulder. Two similarly dressed soldiers in front of him are kneeling, looking up in awe at the angel Gabriel, shining resplendently, emitting the light of omniscience and unsurpassed power. I then find myself joining a short procession who are passing by. I fall in behind them, pulling behind me on a short, golden rope at the end of which is connected a miniature golden cannon. At the head of the silent procession leads a woman—a woman of great wisdom and majesty—a beautiful, holy woman. My impression is that she is a female version Jesus Christ, dressed in white, flowing garments and wearing a radiant crown. Behind her, following in step, come three wise men types, silent and solemn, reading from sacred scripture held before them as they continue purposefully forward. At the tail end of the line I am now following, feeling ridiculous but knowing I fill a position which must be filled, dragging behind me the miniature, golden cannon connected by the golden rope. The dream feels terribly portentous, charged with powerful prophecy but lying just beyond my reach, to leave me grappling desperately for understanding as wakefulness drags me reluctantly from the otherworldly and into the next new day.

My eyes opened. The bright world of my next new predicament crashed over me as the inscrutable damned dream lingered on awhile longer, and vanished.

2

— Bushed —

The day consisted of digging and planting. Watering in was unnecessary. The ground held plenty of moisture rising up from the shallow water table beneath the surface. It was good, honest labour, but repetitive drudgery none the less, and in short time I was over it.

By the time the sun had reached its zenith we had dug two hundred seedlings into the moist earth. It was hot and the air had become still; not a breath of air moving over the landscape which now shimmered through the encompassing heat haze, lending an otherworldly, surreal quality to the landscape we alone inhabited.

We dropped our tools where we stood and made for the campsite where we quenched our thirst from a water barrel atop a rickety, folding table. Lethargically we dragged a couple of camp chairs under the shade of a gnarled and twisted flowering wattle, to sit in silence for a time.

I found myself drifting, my eyes drawn to the few brilliant white clouds sailing in the sky, and I realized how utterly at peace I felt for the first time in an age.

The digging and planting had put to work muscles not usually employed in the prison metal working shop, and the mild ache to me felt good, and was welcome, reminding me of earlier times when, as a boy, I worked beside my grandfather in the fields and orchards on the family farm.

From a distance the familiar cawing of a lone crow released me from my reverie, and I looked over to my companion, eyes closed, a smile upon his face and breathing rhythmically in sleep. It occurred to me in the moment that I was as happy as I had ever been in my entire life; and realized, too, the moments of my life when I experienced such joy had been moments of stillness such as this, surrounded by open countryside and far removed from the influence of others of my kind.

With eyes still closed, Abe said, 'It's peaceful here. It reminds me of Shin Chen.'

'You're awake then. I thought you had fallen asleep.'

Shin Chen, I thought, recalling him mentioning it in the prison yard one afternoon; how he had sought knowledge in a secluded monastery near to the Tibetan border. A Buddhist martial arts academy where he had spent eight years of his life, reaching twelfth dan level, the highest ever level attained by a westerner. He had become estranged from his family in that time. They had hardly recognised him when he eventually returned, hardened by the physical training and so different from the young man who had departed as little more than a boy. After barely two weeks back in Australia he had accidentally killed a pedestrian in the Adelaide mall. The man had emerged rapidly from a department store. Abe's reflex training had kicked in when the guy emerged, seemingly from nowhere, to startling him. He had lashed out reflexively from the indoctrination of years of training, killing the poor fellow with a lightening fast blow, and, at the age of twenty five years, landing himself a life sentence.

Reflecting on what he had told me, I asked, 'What did they teach you there?'

'How to breathe,' he replied languidly. I figured he was employing sarcasm, deflecting from a conversation he did not want to engage in.

'How to breathe,' I repeated. 'Yeah, breathing can be tricky to master. You forget to do it and. . . Yeah, dangerous.' I waited for something further from him, but nothing. 'How to breathe,' I repeated again in dismissing it, and in a minute I had nodded off in the shade, while listening to the many small sounds around us.

~

When I awoke, the angle of the sun told me it was about two in the afternoon. Abe was on his feet, stretching, as if he too had only just awakened.

'I spotted tobacco amongst the supplies,' I said to him as he walked towards the water drum. 'Do you know where it is?'

He splashed his face and neck with the water before answering, 'In one of the boxes in the tent. But why not leave it for now? We can get another stint of work done and knock off for the day. With all this clean air around you to breathe, why would you want to poison yourself?'

The remark, like most Abe was capable of, stung just enough to make me think better of the decision, and we did as he suggested, returning to the field.

The soil was deep, rich and fertile; the abundance of natural green growth already around us bore testimony to that. It required nothing further of us than to push a spade into it, pop in the seedling and replace the damp, aroma rich earth around them. It was certainly a prime spot. From the air, and aircraft generally flew at high altitude over this part of the country, more green growth on this naturally irrigated patch would attract zero undue curiosity. I imagined the brotherhood of motorcycle riders, Inc. would catch a pretty penny at the end of the growing season, their only expenses being labour and living expenses supplied by a couple prison escapees.

Abe arrived carrying a fresh box of seedlings. His mind, like my own, had obviously been wandering as we applied ourselves to the task.

'What would you say is the most important thing you have accomplished in your life?' he asked me, as he kneeled to separate a single seedling from the others in the crate.'

Nothing came to mind. Not a solitary thing could I isolate from the multitude of things I had done in my time. When I tried to think of a suitable reply, all that came to mind was the string of ill-considered decisions and non-productive episodes of my adult life, preceded by the long period of time wasted which constituted my teenage years; a time of confusion, filled with emotional turmoil manifesting itself in substance abuse and an array of failed attempts to identify anything to which I might earnestly apply myself in attempt to gain approval by my father.

But for the numerous short term jobs, all of which had ended in frustration, dissatisfaction and a sense of futility, not a thing came close to being described as worthwhile.

Without looking away from planting, he continued: 'Is the question so difficult to answer? Name something you have accomplished which gives you a sense of pride.'

'In primary school I once won a wissing contest by clearing the top of the urinal wall.'

'As impressive as that is,' he replied, 'I was thinking more along the lines of academic achievement. An athletic accomplishment or maybe a distinguishing act like saving a life. Anything at all which might have brought a feeling of satisfaction and accomplishment.'

'Nothing,' I told him, embarrassed.

'Nothing,' he repeated straight back at me. That's interesting.' 'Is it? Why?'

'Never mind. Let's get this lot finished, shall we?' he deflected.

We can talk when we're done.'

Not for the first time he had set my mind to contemplating something discomfiting. No one but Abe could mess with my mind that way, and for the remainder of the day, though I tried everything to resist the process, I anguished in reviewing every bit of my life in hope to recollect a single moment of feeling anything akin to pride.

The question should have been why was he doing this to me? But I knew the answer already. We had assumed the roles we played a long time ago; a tacit agreement made in which he would instruct and I would glean from it what I could. Much like what he must have experienced in that Buddhist, martial arts monastery he attended, I imagined. The man was, after all, someone who had been following the path to wisdom far longer than I. At first he had refused to play the role I attempted to cast him in, telling me that the attainment of knowledge on the path to wisdom was a journey to be taken by the individual, and that the journey was necessarily different for everyone. But in the end I had worn him down. I told him that I would likely be dead, long before attaining anything. I had already wasted so much in this life that I would depart it with nothing learned and have to do it all again, from scratch, in the next. It sounded a lame argument to me, and it had been no more than a ploy. My allusion to reincarnation was sheer fabrication, and I'm sure he knew it at the time, but I think, at that moment, he must have recognised something I had not recognised, myself, because, the following day he approached me in the yard, saying, 'Do not question my method. Do not turn away from the path once you have set your feet upon it.'

His decision to take me on impacted me in a positive way, giving me something tangible to hang on to, and from that moment on, not only did we become fast friends, but we have very much been the master and the acolyte; and, without argument, I have followed those first two instructions he gave me, to the letter.

~

The days that followed, while being repetitious, were a joy, and I still, to this day, look back on them with great fondness. The pristine environment, the solitude, clean air and daily physical activity were, for me, the perfect ingredients, inducive to a kind of clarity I had never before known. After a solid night's sleep, we rose before the sun in the cool of the morning, to eat breakfast while sunrise painted the sky with light upon high, wispy clouds. With no-one barking orders we applied ourselves to our task with complete alacrity. The place became as a home, and ever more familiar as the weeks passed.

We shared the vicinity with foxes, kangaroos, wombats, echidnas; animals which we had not noticed before. Obviously they knew well enough of our arrival, and gave us wide berth, but as time went by and we had done nothing offensive, their guard had dropped and they returned to going about their business without too much regard for us.

One night, about an hour after sunset, as the land darkened to night, we were disturbed by the sound of a motor, far off, but steadily approaching our campsite.

'This is not good,' I observed, needlessly.

We doused the flames of the campfire and reached for the guns we had taken to keeping close at hand for just such an event as this. It was exactly the scenario we prayed would not happen. It was expected, by those who employed us, that we defend, at all cost, their considerable investment.

As the sound of an engine drew very close, with headlights intermittently breaking through the bushes to cast light and shadows across the ground in dizzying fashion, the vehicle, a sand buggy, we assumed, veered suddenly away, roaring off into the night again, from where it had come.

In the depth of the silence the machine left in its wake, the pair of us breathed a deep sigh of relief. I noticed that my hands were shaking, in them the hunting rifle we had been equipped with, cocked and ready to fire.

Abe gripped a handgun in similar fashion, and we took particular note of one another's readiness, apparently to use the weapons if the situation had called for it.

'Bloody hell,' I breathed raggedly. 'That was close. They must have gotten a good eyeful of us, crouched here with guns in our mitts, before taking off in fear.'

'It's a fair assumption.' He put down the large handgun. 'There's not a lot we can do about it, but hightail it away from here. What do you think?'

'I'm a little shaken, to tell the truth. It didn't hit home until right then, that we are criminals. . . Escapees! We're expected to behave like escaped criminals, I guess, and resort to violence in defence of our freedom. Not to mention the cash crop we're cultivating here. It got very real very quickly. What's your take on the situation?' I wanted to know.

'I think we take our chances and hang on.'

I thought about it while Abe started the fire going again. It occurred to me that whoever that had been tearing around the bushland at night, they had come upon us unexpectedly and simply hightailed it out of there, realising they had disturbed campers.

'At least they weren't coppers,' I mused aloud. 'Coppers would have rousted us.'

'True enough,' Abe replied, rebuilding the small campfire. 'There's at least an even chance they were as startled as we were, and won't be back this way in a hurry.'

'I'm for hanging on here and finishing the job we started. We have no money and nowhere to go. If we don't get paid, we're sunk.

I don't mind taking the punt that we'll survive this.'

'And if they report us to the law?' he asked, raising an eyebrow? 'Then the jig is up,' I concluded. 'But, screw it, I have a hunch

we'll pull through this one. Just a minor hiccup.'

'You have a hunch?' He was turning that scrutinising look of his on me.

'Yes, a hunch,' I told him. 'My hunches usually play out, Abe. In fact, I don't recall a hunch ever leading me astray.'

'Well, in that case...' he let the sentence hang, a mercurial, amused expression on his dial.

'So, we stay?' I asked, looking for confirmation.

'Well, of course. You have a hunch. That's good enough for me.'

I would normally allow such a comment to pass, but, tonight, I wasn't prepared to let it slide. We were discussing a course of action, the decision of which might well see us back in prison. And he was willing to back my hunch? The Abe I knew did not allow hunches to influence a decision. Certainly not something of such gravity as this.'

'I trust your hunches,' he said, as if reading my thoughts, and my expression must have displayed my incredulity. He then pulled the packet of tobacco I had been searching for earlier from his pocket, saying, 'Here. I discovered this while I was cleaning up earlier.

'The other day, the subject of pride came up. Do you remember?'

I laughed, derisively. 'That was weeks ago, but yes, I remember. I spent the entire rest of the day raking through my life, trying to unearth a memory of ever being that pleased about something I had done. *Pride.*' I pronounced the word with animus. 'One of the deadly sins. Why would you probe me for such information?'

He was smiling broadly now.

'Before I got to know you, I saw you in six yard one day. There was a new arrival. A kid just up from remand, after being sentenced. He was being stood over by a couple of knuckleheads, and he was frightened. I watched him amble over to you and ask if he could sit beside you, on the bench. You recall?'

I nodded.

'You must have asked him what was wrong, because, the next thing, I see you walk over to those meat-heads, and you knock the first one within reach on his backside with a single punch. Tell me why.'

'I have always despised bullies,' I replied, simply. 'The kid was out of his element, and scared. He had just copped a six month sentence for whatever. Unpaid fines, I think it was. I didn't like to see those jerk-offs intimidate the kid, just for sport.'

'And he asked you to do it?'

'Of course not. Why would he?'

'So you did it out of the kindness of your heart,' he continued. 'I told you, already. I cannot abide bullies. The kid was scared.' 'And you tell me you cannot think of one moment in your life to

be proud of?'

I shrugged. 'Knocking someone on their backside is something to take pride in? How's that work?'

'Even I know you did it out of principal, your own sense of right and wrong. You are, although you do not seem to recognise the fact, yourself, a man of principal.

And I've witnessed other instances. I once witnessed you face down a guard who was behaving like a little Hitler, but he was not a little anything. He was a tough S.O.B. and you stood your ground, telling him to his red flushed face, to grow up, putting yourself between him and another inmate in trouble.'

'And it cost me ten lousy days solitary.'

'Yes it did. But you're a noble son of a gun. I know that about you, as well as having a crazy streak a mile wide. What that's about, I haven't put my finger on yet. Why do you think I agreed to instruct you?'

Again, I shrugged. 'Charisma?'

The response caused him to laugh aloud. 'Yeah, right. Charisma. Truth is, I've known all types in my time. From the wisest, most knowledgeable human beings with amazing energy, to the downright crazy and unpredictable. But, you? I don't know what you are. You I regarded as an anomaly. I couldn't pass up the chance to take you on, just to understand what makes you tick.'

It was my turn to laugh. 'Well, good luck with that. You ever find out, be sure and let me know. But, we're staying put, are we?' I manoeuvred, wanting to get back to the important subject of our safety.'

'You have a hunch, don't you? Why would I argue with that? If were in agreement, we'll stay, and see this thing through. We need the goddamn money.'

3

— Thanks, but No Thanks—

We continued the work, despite feeling much more vulnerable. Whoever it had been that very nearly drove into
our camp, there was no way of knowing. Kids lairising
about the countryside at night, hunters, a curious someone who had noticed our presence and came to snoop
around? Who knew?

The real danger was, of course, that whoever it was
may have detected the freshly planted field. We followed
the wheel tracks. Fortunately it appeared they had not
come close enough to discover the crop in the darkness,
but people are strange, curious creatures; always unpredictable... and prone to talk! It would be only a matter
of time before word got around of our campsite, here in
the scrub. Still, what could we do besides trust to providence? With nowhere else to go, lacking any alternative
survival plan, and not to overlook the promised twelve
thousand dollars at the end of our tenure, there was little
option.

At the end of six weeks, our satellite phone began
to buzz while we were relaxing at the end of the day.

The president of the brotherhood was flying out in the morning in order to witness our achievements, the aircraft again piloted by my old friend, Evo. We were asked to make sure the landing site was free of debris, and to expect them at around ten the following morning. We took the opportunity to request they bring with them new clothing for us, and straw hats, to keep the sun off our heads. We had, for a time, as a means of whiling away the long evenings, and in the name of mannish self-sufficiency, attempted to weave hats for ourselves, constructed from the tall, reedy grass which flourished in the dampest depressions of the landscape. Producing a hat of just the right size was difficult, and the brims were never sufficiently rigid to keep their intended shape, collapsing in our faces. Hence the fashion fad soon lost popularity and we were forced to resort to tying shirts, strips of fabric, whatever, wrapped around our heads in order to keep the sun from baking our noodle.

In the morning we declared a holiday for ourselves. Our first task, that of planting, had been completed and we were simple caretakers now. With four thousand healthy cannabis sativa plants growing under the hot, sunny sky, we were pleased with our achievement, and even more pleased that it was over.

In celebration, and instead of rising at the crack of dawn, breakfasting on the usual, freshly baked damper and apricot jam, and in anticipation of fresh supplies arriving with our visitor, this day we polished off the last cans of vanilla flavoured rice cream, followed by the single remaining six-pack of air-temperature beer. The nights were most always cool this far inland, and the chill air of the mornings took time to warm, making the draught perfectly palatable.

We were seated out by the fire pit, lazing comfortably, sublimely pleased with ourselves for completing phase one of the mission, when Abe's attention zeroed in on something over my right shoulder—something causing his eyes to widen enormously.

He was up on his feet and sprinting before I knew what was happening.

'*What?*' I called after him, but then saw what was occurring, and I quickly rose to race after him.

A pair of teenagers. Fifteen, sixteen years-old. They must have been spying on us, snooping out the nature of our industry here, and fast on their feet, they were. It took everything we had to run them down, and even as I was pursuing mine, I had to wonder what the hell I was doing, and, *What will I do with him if I catch him?*

Abe had his by the scruff of the neck, the boy's toes barely making contact with the ground as he was brought in for interrogation. Mine twisted and struggled with all he had, and I had to growl threateningly in his ear with the promise of a slap if he didn't cut it out, before he relented.

Reaching the campsite we sat them on the ground, cross-legged in front of us, while we *ogred* above them, silently assessing the depth of the problem, with Abe and I occasionally regarding one another, intensely aware that in less than an hour's time an aircraft would be landing, not a hundred metres away, carrying the man who held our immediate future in his wallet.

Boys, and typical teenage boys they were: brown hair, lanky, dressed in blue jeans, t-shirt and sneakers. Brothers they looked like to me.

In a mild tone I asked, 'What the hell are you boys up to, sneakin' up on us like that?'

Neither responded. Both only glanced nervously in my direction for the moment, before returning their attention to the groung in front of them.

I turned to Abe, shrugged. 'Do we involve head-quarters?' I asked— the seed of a ploy germinating some-where inside my scull.

The light of savvy instantly shone with amusement in his eyes. 'Probably should,' he responded, and rubbed hard at the back of his neck, as if considering the gravity of the situation. 'What's your names, boys?' he demanded.

The names, Bobby and Davey Johnson, were given.

'Where you come from? Who sent you?'

To that, the boys turned a shade paler than they had already been.

'Sent us?' Bobby replied, his voice quavering slightly.

Inspiration struck me then, and I asked. 'It was you two the other night, on the quad bike.'

The boys glanced very briefly and very nervously at one other.

I had guessed right.

'Your parents know where you are? What you been doin', thieving?' I continued.

Heads shook in denial.

'This is a restricted area. A government project... and you come barging in, unannounced? You might have been shot, did you think of that? We have guards posted all around. I can't believe you made it through.'

'We were just curious, is all, mister,' Bobby submitted.

I turned to Abe. 'I want corporal Smith put on report. He must be asleep out there. No one is to be within a two thousand metres of the facility. Are you boys properly immunised?'

'Yes,' Davey answered reflexively, and obviously lying. 'That's good. Then you're safe, for the moment.'

Abe cleared his throat. 'A private word, captain?'

'You boys wait here,' I instructed, and followed Abe for a few metres until we were out of earshot.

'Where are you going with this?' he wanted to know.

'I'm not sure. I'm playing it by ear. Any ideas? If these boys let on we're out here... but there's little we can do. I was thinking to put the fear of God into them and set 'em loose.'

From far in the distance came a low, steady drone; the sound reaching us intermittently, muted by distance and the eddying breeze.

'And here comes the boss,' Abe observed. Judging by my friend's visage, it was evident to me he was extracting an inordinate amount of amusement from our present situation.

We did the only thing possible. After impressing on the lads the ramifications of divulging our presence to anyone; that it was a matter of national security, and a breach would precipitate a personal visit from the Bureau of Internal Affairs. It was the best I could come up, and anyway, in life, shit happens. Again we found ourselves trusting to chance, something I very much doubted our employers would approve of. I had them scamper away, keeping to the thickest vegetation to be sure of being well out of sight of those who were, at that very moment, touching down, barely a hundred metres away.

Abe and I remained at the campsite while we viewed the arrival from a distance. The moment the aeroplane came to a standstill, from it alighted two men: porters; both stocky, wearing cut-off riding jackets displaying club patches on their backs, although indiscernible from where we stood. They went to the storage compartments to begin unpacking the stores and supplies we had requested.

Next to alight, Evo: five ten, dressed in track pants, zip jacket and sneakers, and still very much resembling the young man I remembered from all those years ago. He seemed not to age at the same rate as the rest of us.

Evo came around to the other side of the plane to open the door for his passenger, and out climbed a man of considerable size.

We popped the tops of two fresh beers and sipped as we waited for the president and his entourage to approach, but keeping an inconspicuous eye on the man as he came within proximity.

The president of the Brotherhood of Motorcycle riders, Inc: Large, sporting a Genghis Kahn style chin beard and mustache, dark hair tied back into a pony-tail, face recently shaved, wearing blue jeans, a sleeveless denim jacket covered in badges over a colourful, Balinese print shirt. I noted the weathered features of his face as the man drew nearer, and smiling now, he halted before us, removed the sunglass to reveal piercing, blue eyes.

How's it going fellahs?' he asked, extending his hand.

As we exchanged the perfunctory manly greeting I took greater interest in the badges adorning the denim jacket, all denoting various international gatherings of the brotherhood.

'We got a view of the planting as we flew in,' he said, without preamble. 'You guys have held up your end. Shall we take a closer look?'

The president, with Evo beside him, accompanied Abe and myself for the tour. Four thousand thriving young plants stood to attention for inspection, every last one looking fit and healthy.

That is some primo, A-grade, kick-ass, mind-altering variety of bhang, gentlemen,' he told us. 'That seed stock is something special, imported only after considerable, complex negotiation, and at no small expense.'

'Is it to be processed?' Abe asked, taking great interest.

'Absolutely,' the president replied. 'This is medicinal. I'm sure you fellahs thought you were a involved in some kind of organised, criminal enterprise, aimed solely at the accumulation great piles of cash. Not so,' he expressed with an expansive hand gesture, and halting our progress. 'This is an organised criminal enterprise, aimed at providing access to pain relief for the thousands in this country, who, because of small-minded, interfering bureaucrats, would otherwise be condemned to a life of suffering and inactivity.'

It took Abe and I a moment to digest this, our bemusement not lost to our visitor.

'I've smashed your iconoclastic stereotype,' he responded, laughing delightedly. 'I haven't disappointed you to much, I hope. If you were expecting the beer swilling, hell raising variety of biker, I'm happy to supply you boys both a good reference and an address of a likely bunch of lads I know?'

'Not necessary,' Abe replied, appreciating the humour. 'Truth is, we weren't in a position to judge what was happening here. We were just grateful for the opportunity of a wage and a place to hide out awhile.'

'Will you stay longer? he asked. 'Continue to keep watch for us?

You've already proved your worth.'

At that, I gave my friend what I hoped to be an inconspicuous look of concern.

'You might need to give us a short while to consider,' Abe responded. 'And there's the question of reimbursement to date,' he added.

'Your wages. Yes, you're right. Come on back to the camp and we'll get you sorted.'

While we had been inspecting the crop, the others had brought over the supplies and stacked them beside our tent. Fresh fruit and vegetables, canned food, extra blankets; a thoughtful array, including the special items we had nominated.

Our employer opened a zip bag containing twelve thousand dollars, cash, and to it added and extra thousand apiece.

'A small bonus,' he told us, 'in appreciation for doing a fine job. I have to leave soon. Why don't you two take a moment to talk about my offer to stay on? Three more months. Maybe four. That'll take us up to harvest time.'

'Where does it leave you if we decide to call it a day?' Abe asked.

'Those tow blokes who came with us—' he indicated with a nod toward the pair adding the last of the resupply to the pile. 'They will take it over if you decide to fly back with us today. Go on, go, talk it over for a minute while I wait,' and we did as he suggested, ambling away a short distance until we were sufficiently separated to be able to talk frankly between us.

'What do you think?' I asked.

'I think you should be the one to decide.' 'Why me?'

'This is your journey,' he responded. 'I'm here because of you, in case you hadn't noticed. It was your dissatisfaction, your personal sense of injustice and your lifelong habit of living spontaneously which has brought you here.'

I simply stood, observing him with a mixture of incredulity and exasperation.

'You must realise the reason we are where we are,' he continued. 'You say you wish to travel the road to wisdom, the longest, most demanding road of them all. Well, you are on that road, and though you do not appear to know it, you have been travelling that road since the day you were born.'

'I just want to know if you want to leave this place, now, today,' Abe. I wasn't looking for a philosophical discussion. What do you want to do?' I demanded of him.

'You're evading again, like you do. What is life if not a series of choices?' was the response I got.

'It's more than mere choices, and you know it,' I replied, knowing this was the only way I was going to get anything like an answer from the man —the man who suddenly, annoyingly, decided now was the perfect time to play the role I had asked of him.

'What more besides choices?' he asked. When an answer was not immediately forthcoming, he added, 'Oh, that's right, I had almost forgotten. Your personal one on one with God perception, and the concept of reality.

Well if you ask me, *right now*, with its imminent conver-gence of lines of possibility and diverging time lines of cause and effect, this would be a perfect occasion for you. Why are you asking me for my opinion? The universe is at your disposal. Are you afraid to wield your power, Mandrake?'

4

— Steel Cocoon—

We were on a good thing, with an income and an environment which gave a kind of peace I had not experienced since childhood. I really liked being there, and, because I could, I decided to leave. The confrontation with Abe ignited in me that *What would happen if,* syndrome, the need to challenge fate and let in a little chaos, just to see what the next allotment of time would bring.

We were on the run again. We had a good wad of cash but we were naked to the world in that the moment we were identified by the law, things would get quite exciting quite quickly, and it was just what Abe had anticipated. Had he not gotten in my face the way he did, with that "Mandrake" remark, we would have stayed on, living life free and easy because the peace I felt there presented me with absolutely no need to question my state of being and the reality I inhabited. But what was done was done, and life would return to its natural state of randomness, which, I had to admit, for me was my natural state of being.

Our benefactor offered us a commercial airline ticket to anywhere in Oz we wanted to go; but a plane ride, having to pass through a concourse and boarding gates fitted with security cameras seemed a little too chancy. A bus ticket on the other hand. That seemed reasonable. So after arriving back at Parafield airport, Adelaide, we boarded a metro bus into the city, and from there, walked over to the interstate bus terminal on Franklin Street, to purchase our tickets.

Where to? The Eastern States, especially the cities, to me represented a lifestyle I would rather avoid. Too many human beings. The West, then. To Perth, Western Australia, and all that lovely open space, south, north and east. Yes, it felt right, but it was early in the afternoon and our ride to Perth did not depart until seven thirty that evening. Hanging around a bus station for that amount of time was neither pleasant nor a particularly intelligent thing to do. I've never gone into it, but it occurs to me that monitoring bus stations for drifters, outlaws and vagabonds was a likely practice employed by police. I would have to engage my highly developed sixth sensory organ to the advisability of entering the bus station and boarding the bus at seven thirty. Until then, though, we needed somewhere to park ourselves and kill time. A comfortable somewhere, where we could shower, don our new, clean clothes and treat ourselves to a decidedly well deserved, first-class meal.

The Wayfarers Inn. The name was perfectly apt and the rooms, perfectly acceptable after so long living and working in the dirt. The long, hot showers and fresh, clean clothes made us both feel like new men. Abe had spied a barbershop downstairs, on the street, and not far from the Inn. By the time we were given the treatment, with a haircut and a shave, we hardly recognised ourselves in the mirror.

With clothes and personal grooming attended to, the feast was next, and much anticipated. A steak, well done, covered in butter fried mushrooms with black pepper, steamed silverbeet, lightly salted, and a serve of fried, chipped potato and green beans likewise salted, all chewed thoroughly and washed down intermittently with a good claret, smooth but with just the right amount of acerb aftertaste. Compared to what we had been eating for the past few months, it was a sublime experience, bringing extraordinary satisfaction.

We returned to the Wayfarers feeling wonderfully sated, and with nothing more on the agenda until the bus departure time of seven thirty, we stretched ourselves out on our beds; real beds, with sprung matrasses that, after sleeping so long on camp stretchers, felt as if one was borne on a cloud and floating in the air. In that quiet moment my mind replayed every event since we had launched ourselves into the darkness from the top of that prison wall.

This, I told myself, is why I live life as I do. The day would come when I would be lying on my death bead and I could only imagine the horror of having to look back on a life more resembling an assembly line that an artist's workshop. The thought struck me as authentic. It hit the mark, well and truly. Funny that I had never seen it before. If ever it was behoving of me to describe, or account for the way I lived my life, that description was as close to the mark as any I could conjure, and I delighted to finally be able to understand, if only in a small way, what drove me to do the things I did; what was at my core, the driving force, because I always knew that human beings were much more than mere intelligent animals, able to navigate through life, making this and that decision, following the path of least resistance in the endless pursuit of comfort and satisfaction while walking the narrow path set out by convention.

'Society.' The word slipped out between my lips without my knowing.

Abe, who I suspected had already drifted off in soporific euphoria, which was exactly what I was in the process of doing, replied, " Society?'

'My mind was wandering. I didn't mean to speak.'

'That's interesting,' he replied. 'What were you thinking about?'

'Nothing. Like I said, my mind was wandering, drifting around.

But, I just kinda realized something.' 'Oh? Do tell.'

'Life. This astounding thing we are born into. Why the hell have we imprisoned ourselves with so many rules and regulations? Who says we have to rise at eight o'clock in the morning to go work a job, pay the bills, tie ourselves to a convention which perpetuates a system, which, as best I can see, makes slaves of us all? Am I the only one who sees it? And seeing it, am I the only one who feels impelled to resist it? God, I don't get it at all. What is wrong with homo sapiens that they willingly condemn themselves as slaves? I've long observed that the human race has become slave to a system they constructed to make their lives easier, more orderly, more predictable. It's like some weird science fiction story. The weirdest and the most scariest, if you extrapolate the tendency to its ultimate destination. We serve a system we constructed to serve us. Right? The system, like any mechanism, needs servicing, else it fails and falls apart. We have, albeit unwittingly, chained ourselves to maintaining this damn monster we created, until, in a most diabolical twist, it ceases to serve us and it is now we who devote all our lives to maintaining and serving it. It's preposterous. Worse than that. It verges on the absolute insane, doesn't it?'

'Is that how you see it?'

'Is there another way? I know something about history, and about human nature. I do, and looking at the path mankind follows, from where I stand our destination is as plain as day.'

'Tell me about the destination, as you see it.' He twisted himself around to face me, his head propped on the palm of his hand.

This was easy for me. All my life I had been appalled by what I saw of my own species; the way they spread like some kind of bacteria, scouring and scarring the land with their mindless expansion while devastating the natural world.

'Are you sure you want to hear this?'

'We've got plenty of time,' he said, relaxed and attentive. 'We have a long bus ride in front of us. Sleeping is the best way of coping with so long a ride across country. Anyway, I see that your mind is high functioning right now. Make use of it while we have the chance.'

'I thought your job was to enlighten me, not engage in a session I might expect in a psychiatrist's office.'

'Can't be doing the enlightening thing until I know what I'm working with, he replied. 'Now, tell me what has surfaced in the last fifteen minutes?'

'Like I said. After laying here with a full belly, feeling totally relaxed, my mind began to drift. I wasn't thinking, just following wherever it went, you know?'

'Yeah.'

'Am I, do you think, antisocial? My prison file says I am, but it's not true at all. Like, aggressively so?'

'Just tell me what you want to tell me.'

I looked up to the ceiling, with its stained, once white paint beginning to crack and peel, attempting to recall the notion which filled my head just moments ago, and realised it was mostly gone now. Only the ghost remained; the impression it had left imprinted in its place. So I began talking, trying to conjure it again, but like a ghost resisting the attempt to communicate, it would not come.

'I've always stood outside of structured society. Well, tried to. It's difficult to fully disconnect, but my heart has never been truly connected to my kind.'

'Why do you think that is?'

The answer came in that moment. 'Destroyers,' I blurted out. 'I just realised how devastated I was, as a child, to see the family farm carved up for profit. Carved into rows of quarter acre blocks by developers, and sold for people to build their little boxes on, in which to inhabit and live out their obedient, meaningless lives, serving the machine which continues the process of exploiting, themselves included, every natural resource we, as one time free beings, inherited. I have, since the loss of the farm, seen my kind as nothing but consumers, destroyers, blundering on without forethought, heedless of where it must inevitably lead. We are totally insane to think that this is any way to exist. We call ourselves intelligent. *Ha!* what a joke. I want no part of it. And it is the same insane society which sits in judgement of people like you and me, locking us up because we infringe it's ill established mores, its puny rules and regulations designed to keep free will tied down, lest it diverge from the master plan of preserving the invisible web of control which binds us all.

'Has it never occurred to anybody that we are quite capable of evolving without being whipped into submission? We all know and understand the difference between good and evil, right and wrong, positive and negative. You know? And if we would stop playing this game of "This is mine. That is yours"—if we would only share the resources and that which we produce, instead of laying claim to *things*, what need then would there be for money, and stealing? You can't steal what is yours, and if everything belongs to everyone, there goes nearly all crime! The only ingredient needed is that of respect. Respect the needs of others, allow them to have what is needed and no one has cause for discontent.'

'You are constructing quite a world,' Abe commented. 'Perhaps a perfect world, but the reality is, human beings come in a variety of types. Not all will behave as you might expect, given this perfect environment you conceptualise. Even in this perfect world, wouldn't the same imperfections arise?'

'Truthfully? I don't know. I guess you'll always have those who want to elevate themselves in some vain, material way, but surrounded by others who agree with and comply to the new order, they would be prone to falling into step.'

Abe looked amused. 'Just like you are prone to falling into step with society?'

'But this society is all wrong, Abe. Some of us have to resist.'

'What about this lifelong feud you have going on with God? Your compulsion to derail the trend and upset the notion of determinism?'

'Do you agree with the notion that the cosmos's future is predetermined?' I found myself asking.

'Only if what we do remains relatively insignificant compared to the vast complexity of what surrounds us. And, really, I think that is a foregone conclusion. In any case, we are, ourselves, an integral part of the all. We are subject to the overriding laws of nature, the same as the planets and everything else. I guess, following my own logic, yes. Everything in existence has a predetermined end. If, amongst that determinism our actions are also acted upon by the same forces governing everything else, it is reasonable to assume that we act *not* according to free will, but according to what is dictated by fulfilment of that pre-determined future end.'

'Thank-you,' I answered, having found focus. 'I think, then, that it is the notion of freedom of choice being made an absurdity that, instinctively, I am rebelling against. I will not have my life made meaningless by accepting that freedom of thought and of choice is mere illusion.'

'*Hmm,*' Abe responded, thoughtful now. 'I can't answer about freedom of thought. We might all be on this pre-determined ride, unable to change a single thing, but I see no reason why our thoughts cannot be totally of our own devising, if ultimately meaningless and ineffectual.'

'I will not accept that our thoughts are meaningless,' I told him, passionately. There is, I think, *real power* of a kind when talking of

intent.'

'Perhaps you're right,' Abe accepted. 'After all,' the story goes that God created the heavens and the Earth merely by his intent to do so. If that is not power, I don't know what is.'

'You realise, as I do, that God is not a someone?' I quizzed. 'Of course.'

~

We boarded the bus at 7:30pm. To say we were a little apprehensive would be a vast understatement, but choices are limited when one is on the run, and we rolled out of town at dusk, with the big diesel motor of the coach roaring and echoing through near deserted city streets, caught in pale shadows and pallid illumination as the streetlights began to flicker into life. I had ridden coaches many times in my life of peripatetic journeying, and, always, the sound of an interstate coach, either entering a city in the pale light of dawn or departing in the dusk of the approaching night, has been a wistful and oddly lonely affair. As I was being carried out of town I re-lived those instances, the memory of all those otheroccasions, interposing themselves in my mind as a gallery of snapshots; a long collection of stills, arrayed, one atop the other; a haunting population through the corridors of time and memory.

It was as if the conversation Abe and I had earlier that afternoon had awoken something lying dormant. A terrible melancholy came over me: a haunting, detached unreality as I viewed the totality of my life only to see a man adrift and without connection to anything meaningful. If Abe had not been sitting a couple of seats along the aisle, I think I might have abandoned the bus right then and there, sought out a place of refuge, like a bar, and the seedier the better. In such places one can usually find what they're looking for, a means of putting at arms length, if only for the night, that emptiness which can crawl inside and rip so bad at your vitals that self-inflicted oblivion via the use of chemicals is the only defence. In such cases, waking in the morning to find you have survived the night often comes as a surprise. Sometimes it is a relief to see the next day, but not always. Sometimes the goal is to put the act of waking up to a new day in the hands of providence, to relieve one's self of the responsibility and the burden of continuing what has become no more than a farce. . . a pointless charade.

The monotonous drone of the motor took on a comforting persona, like that of the voice of an old friend not heard in far too long a time. As the city fell away behind us and the flat, suburban sprawl fanned out with its streetlights, shopping hubs, garages and creature shelters where I imagined so many families holed up for the evening, perhaps sharing a meal at the dining table, or sitting, watching television at the end of their ordered, prescribed day of obedient labour. There was something both comforting and sad in the thought. Comforting for the fact that the concept of family survived and was still in effect, bringing the occupants together in shared abjection; sad because of the long practised ritual of returning to a small, basic, mass-produced dwelling so many were forced to endure, particularly in the low income suburbs we now traversed, working for little reward after performing whatever tasks were deemed necessary in order to meet the financial burden; the never ending stream of incoming bills that would be their lot 'til their dying day; the futility of it when one considered this behaviour would continue from one generation to next, because if those on top of the heap had anything to do with it, the poor would always be poor, and this was how the battlers believed existence was. It was the way their parents did it, and so it goes on: it was just the way the world was.

The bus interior began to warm, becoming cocoon-like, insulating the passengers from the cold night descending across the land. The suburbs began to fall away until there was only the open road and surrounding blackness of the night. Like time travellers in a rocket ship now, shooting through time and space, the velocity increasing to blur separation of dimensional boundaries, and once again my mind wanted to leave the confines of hard edged reality where things were finite and unbending, heedless to the whims and desires of the human heart, to enter a realm where rules did not bind and the imagination was able to soar like a bird with wings for the first time fully unfurled, to discover a new realm where true freedom exists, limited by nothing, our dreaming reaching far beyond the confines of its own limited imaginings to transcend those borders we have chosen to construct and separate ourselves from the unknown.

The vehicle must have hit a dip in the road, causing it to lurch and breaking me free of my reverie. The visions hung there for some time in spectral form, allowing me to study the workings of my own mind; the deep seated impressions which had accumulated over the years, the things which for me had shaped the world I live in. What had occurred throughout the span of my existence to build the impressions of my own reality I did not particularly wish to delve, but I understood, more than ever, how life experiences shaped the individual and in turn the world the individual inhabited. How many times had I used the term *a separate reality* and thought I understood the meaning? Now more than ever I under-stood its meaning, because suddenly I saw that because I viewed the word a certain way it did not transpire that it truly was the way I imagined it. In that, I was no different than anyone else. The world was how one perceived the world to be and even if millions perceived a thing in the exact same way, it did not then follow that it was so. The world was how each individual saw it not only because it was how it was but because it became the world the individual inhabited. But what of the hunger, disease and poverty? Is that no less real? I had to admit then that some things were real to all who witnessed it, more so for the suffering and sick and the starving. I could not reconcile the apparent inconstancy. What was I missing? What made the difference between real and perceived? My understanding was beginning to fracture.

I woke at being grabbed by the shoulder.

'Roadhouse,' Abe explained. 'Fifteen minutes for bathroom and coffee break.'

5

— Window Dressing —

We rolled into Perth as the sun rose on the second day, weary, hungry and with nowhere to hang our hats, had we been wearing any. We had earned a good wad of cash money, enough to hold us for a while. Finding employment was something we needed to attend to, but I figured we deserved a little rest and recreation, and Fremantle, a large port town south of the capital, Abe had informed me, was an entertaining place to be.

We found a guesthouse, a pleasant, two storey building within walking distance of the entertainment district, with it's night clubs, bars, cinemas and the usual variety of establishments catering for those with money in their pocket and the desire to enjoy themselves. We weren't exactly tourists, but the town did cater for our immediate needs. The Mariner's Rest guesthouse provided clean, comfortable air-conditioned rooms, and evening meals if desired. Fremantle was an enchanting town, stretching to the waterfront and full of historical interest, with plenty open spaces and all bathed in sunshine day after day at this time of year.

After a pleasant ambulatory tour through some of the town, just to familiarise ourselves, it made sense to freshen up and rest after the unusually exhausting bus journey that had brought us here. Wending our way back through the streets, we returned to our new digs, there to indulge in a long, hot shower before retreating to the room and a siesta for a couple of hours.

With the air-conditioner running, shutters pulled and curtains drawn, the room became a cool, restful haven away from th searing afternoon sun. We lay atop our beds, my mind once again, and without leave, insisted on reviewing the journey thus far. It just would not heed my desire for pause. Like a dynamo without a means of shutting it down, it whirred and spun, unrelenting, the voltage generating multiple trains of thought at once, accompanied by a newsreel like depiction of events, seemingly unrelated, and yet there was present, and underlying within it, something obscure; a commonality which, though I pained to understand it, remained tantalizingly just beyond reach, and defying definition.

I knew the condition well enough. It was a part of that which had separated me from contemporaries during the formative years, and, later, from the rest of the world. I had come to reason it to be so. Ever since childhood there had been an ability to view the world in multiple facets: the mundane and the ordinary, the focussed and the precise, and later the vertiginous heights of superreality, where, on occasion, the world came to be viewed in its component parts, seen as a vast interrelationship of atoms and molecules combining, forming and re-forming into the most incredible complexities of nature and beyond, until the imagination faltered under the strain of attempting understanding so much. It was somewhere within the third level of understanding where I assumed God, for lack of a suitable description, dwelt; an intelligence of monumental capacity sprung into existence over the aeons as a vast interconnecting plexus of elemental particles. It was as near as I could come to a description. There was a portion consisting of faith or of intuition concerned with the ability to envision that which instinct had been alerting me to all along. To me it all fit, acting as a clarifying lens through which cognition found purchase enough and there came the recognition of an alternative, mostly unrecognised realm of existence. This realm, I knew, might well be a concept generated by thought alone, but there were so many possibilities and so many dimensions far beyond the ken of homo sapiens; and, as I have seen written, *with a word* God created the heaven and the Earth. To me it illustrated something I had long imagined to be the case, that it was a perfectly literal statement, though one which people never fully appreciated and were unable to well enough recognise its truth.

I had, many times, suspected that we simple creatures were so far removed from what reality, at its most basic, actually was; that all we had was our as yet insufficiently developed sciences and stumbling-block religions, both of which were lacking, by far, any chance to hit upon the truth. For most of my life I had experienced episodic leaps, either of understanding or of imagination, which always left me wondering about their veracity, and of the nature of what it was I was seeing during these transient glimpses.

'I cannot sleep,' I announced quietly, so as not to disturb. 'I'm going out.'

'What's wrong?' came Abe's immediate reply. 'Mind working overtime?'

My response to that was to stand and stare. How the hell did he know? I wondered, but I had momentarily forgotten, this was Abraham Akid, martial arts paladin and esoteric master, the one human being who had ever really understood what seemed to drive me; the man who, despite advising me not to go over the wall, did the amazing thing of accompanying me on this crazy sojourn leading to I knew not where; another of my *what if, anti logic, impulsive* decisions, designed to interrupt the eternal order.

'Yeah, something like that.'

He nodded, knowingly. 'Sit down a minute. I want to tell you something.'

I lowered myself to sit at the edge of my bed.

'We've done alright so far,' he began, 'and had some fun. During our spell in the bush, tending to the crop. . . I witnessed a change in you. A contentment, I think. Yes?'

It was true. I felt very much at peace out there, and I nodded in agreement.

'We've been in this town barely an afternoon and you're restless again. Mind going a thousand miles an hour? Won't slow down?'

'Look,' I interrupted, not needing to hear what I knew was coming, but he ignored my attempt.

'I have a friend. If you hadn't agreed to coming here to W.A., I don't know how I would have got you here. Perhaps we have witnessed a touch of divine intervention,' he chuckled. My friend lives south of here, on a country property. You'll like it.'

'We just got here,' I pointed out. 'What's this all about?' 'Do you trust me, David?'

'Not a jot,' I tried, but of course he knew better.'

'This city is a change of pace. If you want to spend a couple of days, no problem, but I want you to meet this guy. It's the whole point of the journey... why I accompanied you over the wall, goddamn you. You were meant to finish the term of your sentence. I was going to bring you here to meet him, but you had to play your crazy dice game with Yahweh, didn't you. I couldn't let you go over alone and that's the reason I am here. So now you know.'

'How do you expect me to respond to you telling me this?' I responded, calmly, and at this point not particularly giving a damn.

Since rising and telling Abe I was going out I had already detached myself from everything—anything to do with cause and effect. If Abe had not become the friend he was now, I would be ignoring this attempt to sway me one way or another. I would already be off down the road, watching other peoples lives play out against the backdrop illusion of affected continuity on the ever shifting stage generated within the space-time continuum.

'How do I expect you to respond?' he repeated, and I could see his mind calculating a response. 'Go. Take your walk if you must. Just do me a favour and don't do anything—' he paused, attempting to select an appropriate word.

'Crazy?' I obliged.

'I want you to come and meet my friend,' he said. 'You wouldn't wander off on me, not after all this trouble. Would you?' And the moment the words had passed his lips, I saw him abandon any expectation he may have held. 'You're an unpredictable bastard,' he lamented. 'I sometimes wonder why I—'

'Okay, Abe,' I responded, in a rare moment of empathy. 'I'll resist the temptation. I owe you that. I gotta walk awhile is all. See you in a while.'

Walk, I did. With no destination in mind I set my legs in motion, allowing the sights and sounds of the harbour city to impress their identity upon me as I meandered through the thoroughfares and alleyways, allowing the milieus to interact with me through some unknown, emergent language stemming from their enduring presence and imbued with stories of bygone lives and times.

The question of Abe's attachment had been answered in an insufficient kind of way, but the mind attached small consequence to it. Motives were not important at the moment, but an inconsistency had arisen and I would have to ask him, when I returned, at what juncture the term of his own sentence was due to terminate.

I found myself standing in front of a curiosity shop display window. Exhibited within were any number of fascinations, each with a unique story of coming into being, whether by the hand of a highly skilled artisan, such as with the exquisitely fashioned jewellery set with stones of flashing colours, mined from the depths of the earth after the passage of many millions of years of heat, pressure and the precise circumstances which had brought them into existence. As I had experienced during my period of long isolation in my prison detention cell, strata of time superimposed themselves as a layer cake continuum, impressing upon me my own fleeting moment of existence amid all that surrounded.

It was becoming more intense, I was aware. These moments of abstraction were not in any way new or disturbing to me, but never had they invaded everyday clarity to this extent, distracting me now, even from so simple an action as strolling the length of a city laneway, taking in the profusion of sight, sounds and the multitude of assorted impressions being carried in the ether.

At the heart of it lay my understanding of existence; what constituted a state of physical being. Was there really such a thing? Without the presence of the mind to witness a thing, did it exist at all? To others the subject was, perhaps, a mere curiosity to be considered in passing, but because of the many anomalous occurrences I had witnessed and personally experienced from an early age, my mind had attuned to constant, careful observation and analysis, year upon year, until cracks had begun to appear in what, for everyone else, passed for everyday life.

It was simply my nature to explore *what is*, and to delve for minute cracks and faults; inconsistencies and things which do not match with preconceived notions of the world surrounding each of us. The upshot was that there were far more errors in our perception of the world than anyone might think possible, and before too long everything becomes rickety, full of holes, allowing for the possibility of venturing into terrain commonly recognised as bizarre, far fetched, impossible or just plain insane.

Random thoughts and kaleidoscopic impressions flooded my mind, overwhelming my capacity to correlate and distinguish one item from another. The mind began to panic for it's inability to cope with the sudden deluge of what ceased being the recognisable world, but now translated as pure data, streaming at a rate which began eroding minutia and the irrelevant in favour of the more potent quintessence.

Alarm rose rapidly, instinct warning the ego it was in imminent danger of being eroded, being regarded as irrelevant, with erasure the next step of whatever it was that was happening to me.

Finding a way back to the Wayfarer's Inn and my friend was the single objective. Information, in the form of arcane and unrecognisable data, came as waves, surging, almost as a physical force, causing intermittent loss of consciousness while the world, obscured by the whirling assault, receded farther from my grasp until being entirely lost.

6

— Herbal Tea From Little Bowls —

I awoke to surroundings, strange and unrecognisable. A bed chamber. A drip-line attached to my arm leading to a solution on a hook. The bed I occupied was huge. The chamber walls were hung with rich tapestries; scenes depicting images associated with Buddhism; elephant and monkey images, golden idols and lotus blossom. A large yin yang circle adorned the ceiling.

In a moment Abe entered the room, a large smile across his face as he approached, then lowed himself on the edge of the massive bed.

'Welcome back.'

'Why? Did I go somewhere?,' I answered, meekly. 'Where the hell is–?' I would have finished the question but my throat constricted before I could.

'It's the home of my old friend… Zen master, Tenzin.'

Abe reached to the nearby tumbler of orange juice for me to lubricate the vocal cords with. 'Tenzin,' I said, easier now. 'Cool moniker. In fact, cool room. What's the going rate? Can we afford this crash?'

He didn't answer, merely continued to regard me with obvious derision. 'You caused us some concern. It took some doing to keep the law out of it too.'

'We're okay then. Thank Christ. Better tell me what occurred,' I suggested.

'You first.'

'Damned if I know. The last I remember, I was window shopping in downtown Freo. Your turn.'

He heaved a heavy sigh before beginning. 'An hour or so after you left for your stroll, I heard someone screaming like a banshee out on the road. I figured it was one of the crazies from the area. The racket continued, causing such a disturbance, and I became curious enough that I came out to investigate. And what do I find?'

'You're the one telling the story.'

'You, you crazy person. Blathering on about how it's all a deception, a figment without rhyme or reason. Until you collapsed in a heap and wouldn't wake up. You've been comatose for three whole days. I had to call Tenzin. He had his assistant drive all the way out to collect us both. And by collect, I mean smuggle you out of a hospital ward in the dead of night. It was some caper, I can tell you. How we evaded detection I will never know.'

The mental image of my friend and his assistant smuggling a body out of a hospital in the early hours brought a smile to my face. 'Exciting,' I replied.

'Exciting,' he agreed. 'How you feeling?' 'Exhausted.'

At that moment the door into the room opened. Entering, approached an old man with long, white beard and hair, a healthy, tanned complexion, and dressed in a long, red robe tied at the waist with a gold coloured cord, sandals on his feet. He moved lithely across the intervening distance, giving me the impression of strength and vitality.

'Hello, and welcome to my home, David. My name is Tenzin Yeshe Are you feeling alight after your ordeal?'

'I'm okay,' I responded. 'Tired maybe.'

'Yes. It's to be expected. When you're up to it, we have much to discuss. Are you hungry? Is there anything I can get you?'

'Hungry, yes. I didn't realise until now. I'm absolutely famished.'

The old man chucked. 'I bet you are. You have burned an enormous amount of calories. The drip in your arm is glucose, but I will have a suitable meal prepared. Would you be able to join us at the dining table in, say, half and hour?'

'Delighted.'

'Until then,' replied the old man, turned and made to depart, but then turned back to face us. 'We're not big meat eaters here, but if you like I can send out for something.'

'To tell you the truth,' I said, 'I could murder a supreme pizza with anchovies.'

'Supreme with anchovies. Absolutely. See you in half an hour, lads.'

After Tenzin departed there was an unnatural silence between us. In effort to dispel the oddness of the moment I was able to say, 'I'm sorry, Abe. Really. Something strange happened to me. I sense it. I don't know what it was but I feel kind of different somehow.'

'Don't worry about it. Not your fault. And as for the strangeness, it's why you're here. Why we're here. You're in good hands, I promise.'

We made our way to the table on time. Abe pushed me along in a wheelchair provided by one of Tenzin's house guests, Cardi, a young chap from the city of Surat with bright eyes and a smile to match.

The table was laid out with all kinds of treats; been salads, pasta, green vegetables, yellow vegetables, rock and watermelon, taco bread, chilli con carne minus the mince beef but with some kind of soy substitute: More food than I had seen in a good, long time; but the pizza I had asked for sent my tastebuds into party mode.

As we helped ourselves to the fare, people began to introduce themselves to me. There was a young couple from Germany, Hannah and Burn, another couple from Montana, USA, Mary and Jason, plus an assortment of singles; international travellers who had heard about the retreat and had to come and see for themselves. Tenzin thrived on the attention of young folk. That much was obvious, but, too, the chance to share his considerable wisdom with *the youngsters*, as he called them, was something he could not pass up. He was as happy as a bullfrog on a lily-pad.

Danny, a sturdy and fit looking thirty something year-old from Sri Lanka, seemed inordinately interested in Abe and myself.

'Have we not met before?' he inquired. 'Your face is familiar to me, sir. I cannot put my finger on it. Where have you come from before arriving here?' he wanted to know.

'Out bush,' I told him.

'What was there in the bush for you?'

'Peace and quiet,' I replied, emphasizing both, and hoping he take the hint.

'Oh, yes. I understand your desire for these things, sir. A man is reduced by the life of the city. The bushland is an excellent place to be, I know it from my own travelling. Are you sure we have not met before, sahib?'

'Quite sure', I insisted. There was something about this guy I did not like, but I could not isolate what the something was.

'But you will find whatever answers you are looking for in this place, he continued. *Yeshe* is the finest master. Whatever you are looking for,' he finished, and at last the man relented, leaving me in peace to enjoy my pizza.

'Yeshe?' I quizzed, turning to Abe.

'It translates to holder of light,' he obliged. 'But one of the titles our esteemed host has earned.

I had thought it to be his last name. He had introduced himself as Tenzin Yeshe. . . Tenzin, keeper of light, I mused.

'And if you're wondering,' Abe continued, the name Tenzin is in relation to Tenzin Gyatso, the fourteenth Dalai Lama, and means 'Upholder of teachings."

I put the two together, coming up with, 'Holder of light, upholder of teachings. Impressive name. What does David mean?'

'The name David has deep biblical roots, translating to 'beloved." 'Beloved, eh? What about you, Abraham?'

Tenzin overheard our conversation. 'Abraham is also a biblical name. The Hebrew meaning is 'exalted father.' Well suited, is it not? You are fortunate to have such a friend, David.'

'I never knew there was so much in a name before.'

'The name Daniel,' announced Danny to all, 'means God is my judge.'

'Really,' I muttered, unimpressed, finishing by pushing the crusty remains of my supreme with anchovies away.

After the meal, feeling decidedly better, Abe wheeled me around the grounds. The site straddled a permanent stream, with a temple and bungalow accommodation on the opposite side of the fifty acre expanse, with Tenzin's home come community house on the other, accessed by the long driveway off of the unsealed country road, some two hundred yards distant.

'Wow, this is some place,' I commented, as I was propelled along a track beneath a stand of massive pines, headed towards the stream at the bottom of the slope. 'There must be big money in the guru business. Where does it come from?' I asked Abe.

'Donations,' he told me. 'Of course, rich folk pay good money for spiritual guidance.'

'I've heard that. This place is obviously worth millions. We've been in the wrong game all along.'

I was joking, of course. Ripping money from people, even rich industrialists and fat cats, for spiritual guidance was not sporting in my view. Honesty was my adopted way, and had been all along. I just kind of got turned around when I was young, but when I started to take hold of the reins for myself, I returned to the principles and self evident truths I felt in my bones to be right; those things which were taught to me as a child but were seldom adhered to by those who purported them to be standards to be adhered to. If people from whatever background and walk of life wished to elevate their spiritual existence in effort to make themselves whole, it was not the kind of situation to be taken advantage of. There was a principal at work, but then, maybe Tenzin, keeper of light, or whatever it was, thought their vast accumulation of lucre could be put to work for the greater good? I guess I could see the logic.

At the bottom of the slope a timber built, arced footbridge spanned the stream, the trail continuing toward the ashram. Off to the side, on a stone ledge beside the stream, presented as a comfortable spot to sit and ponder, under the shade of an elm tree.

'Perfect,' Abe declared, parking me and finding a prominent ledge to sit on, and there we lingered, listening to the orchestra of crickets, the many finches chirping while scouring the grass for insects, the light breeze rattling the leaves above us, the occasional choral of magpies and call of a lone crow on the wing passing overhead, its almost arrogant cry resonating over the landscape. We remained silent, reluctant to break the spell while soaking up the serenity of it all. This for me was joy personified; a feeling unsurpassed; as good as it gets. Such moments come and go, but they are never forgotten. They come, infrequent and interspersed throughout a life, like pools of translucent beauty, too beautiful by far to be expressed by mere words, and for me the passage of time ceased, holding me suspended to witness how perfect the world could be if we had a mind just to view it and leave everything alone to do as nature is want to do. If only we took more notice of the world without, instead of allowing our messed up internal world to inflict itself on physical surroundings. All it took to preserve this beauty was simple forethought, something we humans are well able to do, but in scrambling for our prize it matters not, the damage wrought in the process.

I could stay here forever, I was thinking.

'It is beautiful,' Abe agreed. 'A powerful beauty—' and I laughed at the apparent incongruity.

'What's funny? I was agreeing with you.' 'Agreeing with what?'

'To your comment, *I could stay here forever."*

'But I didn't say a word."

'That *is* funny,' he responded. 'You sure?' 'I was thinking it, but I didn't speak it.'

His face expressed puzzlement, transformed to surprise, followed by bemusement, but he remained silent, allowing the oddity to pass without further comment.

'That's exactly the sort of clue people overlook,' I was compelled to point out. 'Incidents such as that direct towards something other, something incredibly important, and everybody shrugs it off as if it's of no consequence.

'How do you let something like that pass without notice? Life is full of hints of something powerful at work, just beyond our knowing. It's a tiny clue, but I tell you, Abe, the reasons behind such clues are immensely important. It's a case of not seeing the forest for the trees. Am I the only one who sees the forest?'

'That seems to be the case,' he replied. 'And that's a part of why we're here. Tenzin suspects. . .' but he let it trail off, as if he had accidentally entered a proscribed topic.'

'Oh,' I responded. 'So that's what it's all about. And you can't tell me more?'

'Tenzin wants to broach the subject, himself. My instructions were to get you here safely, and I've done that. We must let the master handle this. He says its important it's done correctly. Is that okay with you?'

'Yeah, sure. Why not? It feels to me we got here not a moment too soon. There's something going on I'm not understanding. The last few days have been getting a bit. I don't know. Intense?'

From behind us came a voice. A girl I had been introduced to as Claire. 'I'm sorry to disturb you. The master asks if you wouldn't mind coming to the ashram. He is there, now, waiting for you.'

We crossed the bridge, followed the path the hundred metres or so to the tall, dome-topped, white building with large, double doors of carved oak, beyond which opened into a massive chamber. It was a lavish interior; a polished stone floor with a circular, mandala type pattern in orange, red and gold at its centre. There were wooden lattice partitions near the rear, and more tapestries of the type I saw back at the house. Claire beckoned us toward a lattice partitioned room at the rear, which we entered by pushing between purple drapes edged with gold, there to find master Tenzin, kneeling upon cushions at a low, dark wood table, the surrounding interior festooned by yet more tapestries with arcane symbols woven into them.

'Welcome,' he said. 'Come, sit—' motioning to the cushions nearby. He reached for a large pot with a spout positioned at the centre of the table. 'Tea, gentlemen?'

We sipped tea from little bowls. Not terribly pleasant, but, when in Rome. . .

'How are you feeling now, David?' 'Very much better,' I answered.

'Good. Are you enjoying the surroundings?'

'How could I not? This is some place. Beautiful. I envy you having all this.'

'You are welcome to come here any time you wish,' he answered. 'It is a haven for anyone in need of rejuvenation, or simply as a place to escape the tribulations of the outside world.'

I nodded. 'Thank-you very much… *um*. How should I call you? Master? Carrier of light?' I asked, with some amusement in my tone.

'My name is Tenzin, but call me as you wish.'

The preliminary chit-chat over with, I figured it was time to get down to it, asking, 'What the hell am I doing here, Tenzin?'

'Allow me to tell you a story,' he responded, and he took a quiet breath, steadied himself while accessing what I learned later to be a formidable memory.

'In 1817, Trinley Gyatso was the twelfth Dalai Lama of Tibet. His period coincided with major upheavals, political unrest and wars among Tibet's neighbours. His short life ended at age eighteen, on the twenty fifth of April, 1875.

'The thirteenth Dalai Lama, Ngawang Lobsang Thupten Gyatso Jigdral Chokley Namgyal, abbreviated to Thubten Gyatso, born twelfth of February, 1876, succeeded Trinley Gyatso. Thupten was, of course, the reincarnation of Trinley Gyatso. His second death occurred in Lhasa on the seventeenth of December,1933, at the age of fifty seven. One of the major reasons for–'

'Whoa there… padre. Give me a chance to catch up here. Thupten was Trinley Gyatso reincarnated, and this Ngawang Lobsang guy was Gyatso, and … ?'

Tenzin's lips curled at the edges, a wry smile emerging. 'Quintessential transmigration, David. Reincarnation, in simpler words. I'm sure you've heard of it. The Dalai lama is the Dalai lama, from reincarnation to reincarnation.'

'Yes, I've heard of it. Just, was that really necessary? My head began to swim for a moment there.'

Claire, the girl who had escorted us here, entered with a large bowl of dates held in front of her. Setting it before us on the low table, she departed as quietly as she had come.

'Have a date,' Tenzin suggested.

Abe, who appeared to be having no trouble at all in following, piped up with, 'The succession of the Dalai lama has been an unbroken chain for fourteen generations. It has been suggested, by *His Holiness*, himself, that the succession finally cease. His view is that it has created a hierarchy similar to a feudal system, which, oddly enough, is the condemning description given by communist China over the decades.'

I had always greatly admired the old guy in an orange sheet. He had championed human rights for his own people and others around the world. 'Political interference? Strongarm tactics?' I offered. I cannot believe he would cave in.'

'His reason for saying so does actually hold water,' Abe argued.

'Maybe, but it obliterates the reincarnation lineage. God only knows how many years of tradition!'

Tenzin was nodding his head in agreement. 'It does, but we are close now to why we have gone to so much trouble to guide you here.'

I regarded the old man with renewed suspicion; and Abe too. 'I don't much like where this is headed, fellahs.'

'You're going to like it even less in a minute. The story is not over.'

I was getting one of those feelings. Similar, I considered, to how a fish must feel when a fisherman begins to draw the ropes on the net, cutting off the one and only escape route to open water and the vast free range of the open oceans.

'The line was broken, said Tenzin, again taking up the tale. 'Thubten Gyatso was not the next transmigration. The next incarnation could not be discovered. The line skipped generations, coming up one hundred and twenty years hence, give or take.'

'Where did it emerge?' I asked, both enthralled now and resisting the panic rising from somewhere deep in my being. There was no need for a reply, and the two men with me knew it.

'Why the hell didn't you let me know what was going on before this, Abe?'

'Are you kidding? What do you suppose your reaction might have been?

He was right about that. Their carefully laid plan would have been blown all to hell. I could only shrug. Whatever my reaction, I definitely wouldn't have been sitting here, sipping tea and chatting rationally about missing Dalai Lamas. But there was opportunity here, I realised. I would milk the rest of the story for every iota of information I could, and with it attempt to assemble my life story in some new and meaningful way. Perhaps the re-assemblage would provide the insight needed, if I ever I were to make sense of the way I had always found myself at odds with the universe.

I chewed on a date as Abe recommenced:

'Our organisation has become exceedingly far reaching and well organized over the long period of time it has been. All or our members know of the missing link, if I can put it that way, and we work in every sector of society, worldwide. I'm telling you this so's you know how we happened upon you.

'It was your police and medical records. Quite unique, really. We noticed that you were unusual, the kind living with existential concerns which caused you upheaval, revealed by your track record for quite bizarre behaviour. Such people are not so uncommon, but instinct, on the part of the parole officer who is a member of the order, urged him to take a little extra notice, and, turns out, he was right.'

'I need you to say it,' I said to Abe. My mind is dancing the mazurka and I cannot gather my wits. You're going to have to say it, because it's just too insane.'

Able looked across the table, silently deferring to Tenzin.

'It's not straight forward,' Tenzin warned. 'But, then, these things hardly ever are. It would appear, David, that you are, with one or two anomalies, the missing reincarnation of a past Dalai lama, named Chapoc Nir-'

'No!' I stopped him. That's enough, do not tell me. I don't want to know his name. My name is David Aaron Harrison and I do not need another identity, if it's all the same to you?'

'As you wish,' Tenzin agreed. 'There is no need for you to know the name, but what happened to you, that is of great importance. You are an anomalous human being, David. There are reasons for that. It might even be said that you are an enlightened human being living in a world which is anything but, and it is causing you considerable distress. It is our desire to put that to rights, and to understand what has happened, if you will allow it?'

My logic circuits were close to overloaded by this time; a condition not lost on either Tenzin or Abe. The old man said, 'Perhaps we should leave you to absorb what you have learned, thus far. We can reconvene at a later time, if you wish? Meanwhile, why don't you continue your tour of the property? Take Abraham with you. Having him at hand will be important during this time. Allow your mind to quieten. Tonight I will perform a ceremony which, I hope, will help with your realization.'

A hiatus was a good idea. I was unable to accept a word more of what was being told to me.

'Yes,' I responded. 'I need time for this to sink in. It has left me feeling kind of... I'm not sure. Off balance, perhaps. A walk might be a good idea right now.'

7

— Mud In Your Eyes—

'I'm confused about our association,' I said to Abe. We strolled beneath overhanging trees, beside a grassy embankment next to the stream. 'Our meeting was no coincidence, was it.'

'It was, in a way. I had already made your acquaintance in the prison yard when I received word they were interested in you.'

'Another hand-of-God occurrence?' I had trouble buying it.

'Perhaps so. I was given the task of suppressing the—' he searched for his next words— 'the more spontaneous side of your nature, before we lost you.'

I had to laugh at that, commenting, 'Good job, Abe. Jumping the wall alongside me seemed to you the solution?'

'The only solution, in fact. Knowing you as I do, I knew that dissuading you from your intention was pointless, serving only to make you suspicious. Do you have any idea of what an unpredictable son of a gun you can be? No, coming with you was the only solution.

Especially in view of the fact that I sensed an impending, accelerating influence coming over you. I had established a psychic link, and although I was doing my best to assert a calming influence, I felt something was about to occur. Letting you go alone was simply not an option.'

'And now you're an escapee, too. Worse than that, an escaped, convicted murderer who was not so far from release on parole. That's one hell of a sacrifice. But I was, at the time, under the influence of something irresistible. Now, though, I'm able to see things more clearly. I'm not without guilt for causing quite the situation for you. I'm humbled, actually, and thank-you is such an inadequate expression. You've been a real friend. How can I ever make it up to you?'

'By forgetting it. You have far more pressing concerns.'

I could think of no response, letting the subject slide for the moment. I would find a way to balance the equation, if ever given the chance.

'There's the subject of what occurred while you were wondering around Fremantle town on your own.' he said. 'I should not have allowed you to wonder off like that, but after living in each other's pockets for so long, I figured a bit of alone time was warranted. What happened, that day?'

'Not now,' I told him. 'I don't much feel like discussing it. Let's just enjoy the afternoon and keep it light, okay? I do love this place. If ever I trip over a few million bucks I'm going to have a place like this, and live out the rest of my days, peacefully. It has always annoyed me that unless one spends their life accumulating financial wealth, they never get to have the things a person needs to make life the joy it was always meant to be. We've made such a mess of things, Abe. This world is so messed up and self defeating.'

By the time we returned from a most enjoyable wander through the countryside, I was tired and went to lie down and take a much needed nap. If I had feared my mind would not obey, I need not have. I was asleep inside two minutes, and peacefully so. The kind of undisturbed oblivion I had not experienced in a far too long.

I was woken late in the day by the girl, Claire. The landscape beyond my window was already steeped in shadow, signalling that the sun had already set.

'We didn't want you to miss the evening meal,' she explained.

'We've all eaten, but there's a plate made up for you on the dining table, if you're hungry.'

I nodded in response, and righted myself to sit on the side of the bed. I noticed she was in no hurry to leave.

'Is there something else?'

She smiled demurely. 'They say you're special.' 'Do they?'

'Is it just a rumour?' She appeared suddenly to think better of it, saying, ' I'm sorry. I shouldn't pry,' and moved as if to hurry away.

'No, it's fine, really,' I answered, halting her. She was just a curious girl and it was an opportunity for me to talk to a normal human being.

'In answer to your question, Claire, No. Not really. I don't want anybody thinking of me in those terms. I'm no more special than anybody else. No more important. No more unimportant, if that makes sense.'

'It makes perfect sense. But. . . why are you here?' Again she looked as if she had let her curiosity get the better of her, reflexively raising her hand to cover her mouth; an action so guileless and childlike, it made me smile.

'Why am I here?' I shook my head slowly, ruefully. 'Why am I here,' I repeated. The question suddenly struck me as being immensely hilarious. I began to chuckle and found I had to struggle to keep it down to no more than that; on the verge of exploding into ragged laughter, and fearing that if I let it go, I would never be able to stop.

'The eternal question,' I barely managed to answer in an even tone. I'm sure everybody asks themselves the question sometime in their lives. When I know the answer to that, I'll let you know.'

I was very glad to find the dining table devoid of others. There was indeed a plate left for me, covered in cling wrap, under which a cold chicken salad awaited my attention. Meat. The accommodation was not lost on me.

I ate slowly, pensively, surrounded by the silence of the large space. Through a large window I watched as twilight deepened to nighttime, but there must have been a full moon in the sky; a full moon bathing every-thing in that soft, milky light the way a full moon does. Why are you here? Yes, it was *the* question alright.

I realised I was glad to be here and I wondered why that was. It wasn't at all like me to be glad of being around people. I was a loner to the core. I had learned that much about myself early in life. Even as I child my favourite place to be was somewhere away from everybody else, very often deep in the countryside, roaming exploring; *communing with nature,* my mother used to call it, and it was likely the truth. I loved everything about wild, unspoilt places. There is an energy in it, from the sun and the wide, blue sky, to the swaying of branches and rustle of leaves on a transient breeze. The buzz and hum of life as every creature went about its imprinted routine, filling every niche and contributing the whole, interconnected weave that was the tapestry of life on planet Earth.

And there was that feeling, a most powerful feeling, which told me there was an unseen, much greater depth to it all, lying just below the surface. Invisible, perhaps, but it was there alright. There were layers to existence I learned as I grew; a membrane barely separating one realm from the other, and another, and another. How I knew this, I don't know, I just did. The mind of a child is unhindered by conventional thought, is open to all that touches it, accepting every experience and including them to the ever growing understanding of that which surrounds.

Once coming into contact with that larger understanding, the limited world that human beings have constructed for themselves is instantly recognised as the inferior model it is, lacking depth, lacking the natural flow of energy that binds and includes, one to the other—that which was the true universe, and which most knew very little, if anything about. I did not want to live in the wold of human beings, with their shortsighted, destructive and selfish take on it all. Perhaps I should have tried harder to fit in, saving myself from living life on the fringe of society all this time. But I did not want to deny my true nature. To do so would have been no more than a betrayal, seeing me living in denial of who and what I truly was. Who can do that? And what is, *is!*

But, here, at this retreat, I was forced to admit to myself there was a different feel. The outside world felt distant, now, allowing me a re-connection to that broader, more peaceful something which made all the difference. These people were easier to be around. Maybe it was their philosophy? Buddhism was something I knew little about, but from what I had observed it illustrated to me that not everyone accepted the dog eat dog, produce and consume, win at any cost way of life.

Of its own volition my mind switched to the more disturbing subject at hand. The weirdness which lately had been encroaching with such unnerving force; the way I had been picking up on strange notions, images and reflections, lake a radio receiver picking up electro-magnetic waves, only, whatever it was my antenna was attuned to, it was something primal... Yes, something primal, I realised suddenly, and it was daunting. Had my mind finally begun to fail? Where would it lead? Tenzin had laid that crazy story on me, but I wasn't so far gone that I was going to swallow it whole without looking for flaws. In my experience there were always flaws. What was the game being played by this orange wrapped, superannuated wise-guy? and why had I not protested and told them both, *That's some tall story, fellahs. I'll be leaving in the morning.*

But, hell, something *was* going on with me and I had little clue what it was. I supposed it couldn't do any harm to see where this unlikely tale was leading. It was an adventure, after all, and I lived for adventure. Life itself *was* the adventure. Why had I become afraid? Me, who defied the universe's penchant for order, Mr Capricious!

'David!' Abe's voice carried from the doorway, putting a halt to my cockamamie musings. 'Yeshe is waiting for you.'

'Yeshe?' I replied. "Who's that?'

'Master Tenzin,' he answered, making beckoning gestures. 'Come on. It's time to begin your. *Therapy*'

We made our way to a building set aside, nestled in a copse, perhaps thirty metres off the trail between the main house and the footbridge we had visited in the afternoon. I had obviously missed it the last time I walked this way. From the outside it looked much like a small, stone cottage. Inside I found a sparsely furnished room, again with the tapestries, and at the centre, a low, circular divan on which many large cushions were strewn, and with a short legged table beside it.

Master Tenzin was standing, working at a long, wooden table against the far wall. He was mixing solutions poured from glass bottles; some sort of concoction being mixed in a bowl. He ended the procedure by powdering dried mushrooms between the palms of his hands, garnishing the finished product before turning to regard the two of us.

'Ah, good,' he said, more to himself that to us, I thought, and waved a hand toward the divan, where, on the far side, two short stools had been parked beside it. 'Come, sit.'

Abe moved to retrieve the bowl from the table while Tenzin ushered me to the divan, where he seemed to think it necessary to physically assist as I lowered myself to sit on the thing.

Abe arrived with the bowl, a pungent aroma emitted from it, along with a tin mug, both of which he placed on the nearby table.

'This is looking ominous,' I voiced concernedly. What's the caper?'

'Have you ever heard of regression therapy?' Tenzin replied, dipping the tin mug into the concoction and wiping the drips from the bottom.

'I have,' I told him, 'and I must admit it has always intrigued me, until now. I think we had better talk this through, don't you?'

'Of course.' He placed the mug aside. 'Does the name Chapoc Nirdahl ring a bell?'

'Should it?'

'Not necessarily. We. . . that is to say, *The Order*, have every reason to believe that you are he. The reincarnated soul of the missing Dalai Lama, the man we have wondered about for generations. So much of your history and your apparent discomfiture with the world agrees with what such a being would be experiencing in life. But, of course, the diagnosis, if it can be called such, is not a certainty. Tonight, with your permission, we will test that theory, and you will, perhaps, have the answer to your own psychic disturbances. We have been doing this for a very long time, my boy. You have nothing to fear. For you, the result may be just what you have been searching for, all of your life. Is that not consolation enough?'

I considered this: A missing link of a Dalai Lama; a puzzle solved for *The Order*, but what the hell did I care for a cadre of Buddhist Sherlock Holmes's on the scent of a hundred years mystery? On the other hand, though. . . Whatever it was messin' with my head did display signs of ramping up, and to who new what? Living out my life in a padded room, drool running down my chin? Not a pretty picture.

I eyed the tin mug suspiciously. 'What exactly did you put in that stuff... What was the name you called him by earlier, Abe?'

'Yeshe?'

'Yes, and what does that mean? Doctor, perhaps?' 'It means, *holder of light*,' Tenzin obliged.

'A man of many hats,' I jibed, attempting to delay what was beginning to appear as being inevitable.

'The ingredients,' continued the *holder of light*, 'include various herbs and things which will induce drowsiness. A relaxant, little more. It will allow you to enter a state of relaxed receptiveness, where we can endeavour to delve the secret places of your mind.'

'A relaxant?' I repeated. 'Receptiveness, you say? As in meditation or attempted hypnosis, right?' This was ridiculous. I was attempting to convince myself that this was fine; that it would maybe resolve the question of what was happening to me and lead to a resolution. There was no choice and I knew it. I was just stalling for time—time to do what? I had no idea. It was either time to bite the bullet or stand up and depart, leaving me no closer to resolution.

I shrugged, studied the pair of expectant faces before me. 'What the hell. I wouldn't want to be a party pooper. And you guys have gone to so much trouble.'

I reached for the mysterious brew. 'Mud in your eyes, guys—' and I drank the lot down in one go.

It was likely the most disgusting thing I had ever drank, and that is no small statement. I had drunk beer dregs the morning after a party that tasted better, and that's including the missed cigarette butts at the bottom of the bottle.

'Now what,' I asked.

'Just lay back and make yourself comfortable,' Abe directed. 'It might take a little while.'

I did as suggested, packing cushions about me, making a comfortable nest for myself.

Tenzin raised the question of me losing my grip, the day I had left Abe and wandered off on my own around Fremantle town.

'Some kind of seizure, was it? Hallucinations, perhaps? Abraham says you're not exactly forthcoming on the subject, but now would be the perfect time to describe what occurred.'

'I'm not sure what happened,' I began. 'Something crept up on me, sneaky like. It's not something I would normally volunteer information about, you understand. It was the weirdest thing, and overpowering, too. Rubber room material.'

'Go on,' he pressed.

'Freo is an old town, right? A lot of history. I was walking through and older section of it when the time line seemed to reach out for me to glimpse into the past. Okay, look, I'll tell you honestly how it was.' I took a breath and waded in.

'It was like standing in a corridor of time. A translucent corridor, with like openings coming off of it, reaching into specific moments. Am I making any sense?'

They both nodded, with Tenzin saying, 'You paint a vivid picture.

Can you describe more?'

'It started to feel ominous then. Heavy, foreboding even. It began to scare me. The sky opened up. Actually rent apart, opening up a great, dark gash across the breadth of blue, summer sky. Can you imagine? But then there was the feeling of being singled out, becoming the focus of something inexplicable, and terrifying. I've never. . . It was like. . .'

I could not find the words to describe what it was I experienced at the core of me with all of that going on. I looked from one face to the other, wondering if they had any idea of what I was trying to impart to them.

'Was there, do you think, a hint of intent? Of intelligence at work?'

'Yes, yes. Intent, yes,' I began to blather. 'There was! That's what shook me to the core and seemed to overload my capacity to deal with it any further. But. . . God, there was an awesomeness about it, you know? It might be called a religious experience, but it was intellect crushing and powerful. If ever a psychiatrist got wind of what I am telling you, I might never see daylight again. You understand?'

I was studying their faces to discover if they had any inkling of the gravity of what I was telling them. That kind of crazy scares people. They revile from it, wanting to decry the person relating the experience, in an instant judging them to be of unsound mind. Anyone finding themselves being judged in this way, their future being decided by a psychiatrist with the power to snatch one's life away from them in an instant, would know, exactly, the fear I carried ever since that traumatic event.

Tenzin reached across to put his hand on my shoulder. 'You experienced something profound,' he said, reassuringly. 'I know that you did, and I believe that you have been dealing with a great weight, all of your life.'

He turned to Abe, saying, 'It's time.'

Abe rose to fetch a book from a lock-up cupboard in the corner of the room; a heavy looking tome, leather bound, the pages gold edged. It must have been very old, I guessed. And valuable, too, perhaps.

I was beginning to feel a little odd. Laying there on the divan, with cushions all around, I felt as light as a feather; as if the slightest breeze would float me off of the divan, into the air. The feeling made me laugh.

How are you feeling,' the old man asked.

'Good. I feel good,' and as I said it, the air around me quivered as a mirage, making the whole scene within the room quiver with it.

'Oooo. Did you see that?' —and being suddenly, unaccountably filled with mirth, I began to giggle without any reason for doing so.

'You going to read me a bedtime story?' I asked, as he pulled opened the pages of the ancient tome where a bookmark had been placed.

'Something like that.'

8

— Eternal Law of the Cosmos —

Abe fetched a candle to place on the little bedside table and lit it, mumbling some kind of incantation in the process.

'Now, David,' said Tenzin. 'I want you to thoroughly relax. Detach yourself from this room. Close your eyes and listen to my voice as I read.'

'What is it?' I asked.

To which Abe replied, An ancient manuscript, my friend. The Dharma. Meaning, roughly, eternal law of the cosmos. Now do as Yeshe asks. Free your mind. Close your eyes and just listen to the sound of his voice.'

I did as instructed, and in a moment Tenzin began in a low, steady voice, a kind of a drone as words completely foreign to me rolled from his tongue. The concoction I had imbibed was now working on me in a most agreeable way; the sound of his voice, deep and lyrical, transformed within the mind, becoming dancing points of light, colours blending and separating, recombining as shimmering waveform in a delightful manner.

I was being carried away, wrapped in a warm cocoon. The experience was not entirely alien to me. I had encountered similar many times over the years, as I drifted off to sleep at the end of an especially tiring day.

The end of each passage was punctuated with a word spoken with emphasis, as if a command were bing given. It went on and on, an ululating drone, drawing me in, deeper and deeper, rising and falling until I sensed that the emphasised command at the end of each passage acted to disengage something, as if the tumblers of a combination lock were dropping into position; a locking mechanism being systematically disengaged; safety latches on portals being deciphered with words in predetermined sequences, readying the complex virtual mechanism for a final command which would, in unison, force open the last remaining door to allow entry into the unknown domain; a place forbidden to the uninitiated unless accompanied by a powerful advocate, like a magician. . . like Yeshe, the holder of light.

It happened with a burst of energy: light so bright and intense in its power, yet so ethereal that it passed through me without harm. I had experience such a light only once before. It was the awesome radiance emitted by what I perceived as the angel Gabriel within that perplexing dream which had plagued me for so long. But this was no angelic radiance; the quality of it had not the same benevolent ambience. This light was ferocious; fierce in nature, and dangerous beyond understanding. Why I was not incinerated in the moment, I did not understand, but I stood within it, watching. There was an elegance to it: white undulating ribbons of energy dancing all around, both harmless and eminently destructive, with a mood to swing either way in a second; whimsical, erratic, controlled, full of purpose; both eternal and ephemeral; a menacing and unsurpassable beast balanced and so delicately poised at the edge of reason and madness.

As I watched, mesmerized by impossible power, I was drawn inward of myself. A place of calm quintessence and possibility, where, at the heart of my being merged the inter-dimensional intersections of my many selves—*my many possible selves, perhaps*—and in that moment I glimpsed the impossible. For the briefest moment I caught sight of the meaning and purpose of it all; a vast web of complexity which, for the briefest time crystalized within my mind; a snapshot of perfection like a fabulous and eternally fascinating jewel with a thousand names. The beginning and the end at its point of intersection, caught in a moment of time at once endless and fleeting.

What happened next was beyond the intellect's ability to grasp, and to attempt an explanation would be an entirely ludicrous endeavour. There had, though, somehow been a transmission of something I was able to snatch from the brink of oblivion in the instant before the whole incongruous experience blinked out of existence, taking me with it.

~

I am told that I remained unresponsive to Tensin's attempts of waking me. Tenzin had, in a manner, accompanied me on the journey into the more primal dimensions of the cosmos, but even he had been forced to relent, leaving me to voyage deeper into the unknown realm alone. The effect on him was a few minutes of disorientation, and short lived amnesia. For me, upon recovering a full twenty four hours later, I too was disorientated, but far more so, to the point of not knowing who I was or how I had come to be in the care of those who tented to me, bringing me back to health.

I had been exposed to something beyond understanding, and of which I could only relate as impressions, for the most part instinctive. As for the remainder, I was convinced that something of the order of a vast, conscious plexus had touched me, initiating a deluge of incomprehensible data which my mind had no defence against. I had, either by accident or by mysterious design, been made privy to something which, to the puny human intellect, ought to remain out of reach in the natural order of things. Making contact with it was tantamount to a complete overload of cerebral capacity, the mind reacting in the only way it could, by attempting to sever communication and compartmentalising what was perceived, leaving me unable to access what may well have been the secrets of existence and of the universe as a whole.

For weeks I functioned on a very basic level. Complex though was beyond me. Attempts at conversation were clumsy and awkward, seeing me stalling midway through a sentence, searching for the most basic of words. My past I feared had been totally purged from memory, leaving me to experience life as if from the prospective of a new-born baby. It was frightening, to say the least. I had ventured too far and been burned for my ignorance.

By the fifth week, some small improvements began to emerge. I knew who I was again, making contact with my old inner self for the first time since the purge. I made personal contact again with Abe, Tenzin and again began recognising members of the small community. Everyone was overjoyed at the signs of my improvement; none more so than Tensin who had been, these past weeks, overwhelmed by feelings of guilt, *as well he should have.*

By the time two months had passed I was approaching all the signs of being my old, incorrigible self, but there was, I felt, something hidden and unreachable, as if a partition had been installed in the old noodle, disallowing me from accessing something of exceptional worth. The feeling of its existence, there, just beyond reach, was infuriatingly ever present and it near drove me crazy for want of knowing what it was.

Tenzin had assigned Abe and myself a cabin at a corner of the main compound. The arrangement gave me the ability to seclude myself, if I wished, and with Abe sharing, he was never too far from sight and could lend assistance anytime, should it be required. The peace and quiet of the place; the unspoilt countryside and the access to a number of walking trails began to accelerate my return to the normal…whatever the hell that meant. It was only the lingering memory of that crazy incident and my inability to access whatever was locked inside my head which cast a shadow over me. But life needed to go on, and, as difficult as it seemed at this juncture, I refused to allow this thing to lay me low any longer. As it turned out, I had more immediate concerns to worry about.

I had just finished my remedial wander over the landscape and paused on the embankment beside the stream, to sit awhile in the shade. A typically beautiful autumnal day, I took advantage of the moment in attempting to still the mind in hope to access any trace of what was locked away. As I did so, I was reminded of the days on the farm as a child. The images were so clear as I closed my eyes. I was transported back through the corridors of time to be immersed in a memory so clear and so complete I might well have been that seven year-old boy once more. It was such a perfect recreation and so intensely felt, without warning emotions began to swell and rise as a torrent, and before I knew it I was sobbing for joy at experiencing again what it was to be so innocent a creature as the boy I once was, wrapped in the wonder of nature and with the future as yet unwritten.

Opening my eyes again, I was amazed to discover my immediate surroundings illuminated by a golden, pre-ternatural light. Everything around appeared intensely defined, with a clarity far beyond the usual. My depth of perception outstripped anything I had ever before felt or seen or heard. The world had become super-real, super-defined, and not just that. Instead of being a mere observer, I was so much more immersed that there was now no separation between myself and that being observed.

Suddenly everything became even further height-ened and intense. The entire view began changing from shape, colour and defined outline into what appeared as mathematical formulae; computer code, I imagined, the universal code of a program defining the entire cosmos. It floated and streamed about me like swarms of insects but it was nothing so existent as that. It was ethereal and I at once understood that I was seeing reality for what it was. It was all code. Cosmic code, generated by what or whom I could not know, but I was seeing the universe for what it was. The cosmos, ourselves included, at our most basic level were nothing more than data within, perhaps, a vast, organic computer the size of which I could not possibly guess. Perhaps the universe itself was a colossal, organic, quantum computer? Perhaps the universe was, itself, part of the program?

So powerful was this revelation, I sat, transfixed by the awe of it. But was I actually witnessing reality in its most fundamental form, at its core, or had my mind at last broken; had it always been broken; had I been wondering through life these past thirty three years as a defective unit, totally dysfunctional, with nothing but a warped view of the world, myself, everything I had ever experienced included? Was I as insane as it was possible for a human being to be?

After the apparition had passed, it was surprisingly difficult to break myself free of its spell. Instinctively I retraced the route back to the hose to seek the counsel of Tenzin Yeshe, the only person in the world I could possibly feel comfortable with in relating such an event.

I came across Sri Lankan Danny and his female companion, Kali, standing in conversation just inside the entrance. Each did a double take upon observing me enter, and followed my progress. Tenzin would be in his private study, I figured, and that was where I found him, as usual, pouring over ancient transcripts behind his desk.

'Can I help you?' he asked without looking up, but then he did, and without further preamble came from behind the desk to guide me towards the nearest chair and lower me into an armchair positioned alongside the desk.

'What has happened?' he asked, moving lithely to a long ribbon, weighted at its end, reaching down from the ceiling, and tugged twice on it.

I was still trying to ascertain what had happened, myself, and could only shake my head, slowly.

In a moment, Claire, the pretty blond haired girl, entered the room in answer to the summons.

'Juice?' Tenzin asked, to which I nodded.

'Juice,' he repeated to Claire, and she went to fetch it.

We waited in silence. Tenzin allowed me time to compose myself and my thoughts, and in a minute or two Clair returned with a large tumbler of orange juice for me to sip.

When she had departed, Tenzin dragged a chair for himself close to me, sat and leaned in to place a hand on my knee. 'In your own time.'

'It's difficult to put into words,' I answered, at last.

'It usually is,' was the response. 'You have had a vision,' he correctly guessed. 'Nothing else could account for what I see in your countenance. I was expecting something like this after our session. Do the best you can,' he soothed.

'The world is an illusion, Yeshe. It's *all* illusion.'

He laughed it this. Not in amusement, nor was it one of mocking my present state at this personal realization. It was a laugh conveying great pleasure.

'You have indeed had a vision. It *is* an illusion. The dharma tells us about life: *'It is the dream of Reality. Life is an illusion, a dream, a bubble, a shadow. Nothing is permanent. Nothing is worthy of anger or dispute. Nothing. . . !'*"

'I don't think you quite understand, Yeshe. I saw the world as a transparency, a veil of what appears to me as complex algebra, formulae, computer code. It is nothing more than an equation. I saw it and understood it to be the truth. Our whole universe is pure fabrication, but fabricated by what? What is responsible for creating it all? I've lived almost my entire life believing that it was no more than illusion, but, just a moment ago, it went beyond mere belief. It became fact. I saw the world for what it truly is.'

Out of respect for my depth of affectedness, Yeshe checked his obvious enthusiasm. 'Yes. It is a powerful thing when belief becomes knowing. It is a paradigm shift within one's own perceptions, and ultimately within one's self.

'The dharma: cosmic law, the eternal and inherent nature of reality. To we Buddhists it is the nature of reality and a universal truth taught by the Buddha, and yet, still only an *aspect* of truth. One of the many faces of reality.

'It is illusion. It is the dream of reality, and if I may add, because of the creatures we are at this point on our evolutionary voyage, it is all it can be. Life, illusion, a waking dream, a bubble; a shadow of what is. Understand, too, that nothing is permanent. Nothing is worthy of anger or dispute. *Nothing!* The Buddha tells us, *Every choice we make in life has consequences,* and that necessarily includes what we choose to believe.

'Listen to me, David. This is important. The problem is that so much of reality is driven by fear. Do you understand? Doahsim, Chinese philosophy, tells us that everything is serving our path of consciousness; we are co-creating everything of what's in us and around us. What we say to *someone*—what we say to *ourselves,* has a consequence. And, truly, it is Newton's third law of action and reaction: For every action there is an equal and opposite reaction. These are the fundamental laws that govern our life.'

I was absorbing every word, checking it against all I had gleaned throughout my self-education, and it very much resembled my own instinctive impressions. The difficulty lay in the thing I had always known: Each of us inhabit the world we construct for ourselves. 'How, then, do we share a world we have separately constructed?'

'With great difficulty—' came the reply to the question I did not realise I had voiced.

'But. . . If that be so, and I accept that it is, there also appears to me an overriding creation,' I contributed. '*The world we share!*'

'Very good,' Tenzin responded. 'There are many facets to the world we share, and a separate version of reality for all.'

'I saw reality as mathematical equations,' I reminded him. 'I am not so naturally mathematically minded that my mental construct interpreted my glimpse of *what is* as formulae. Why would I see it in such a way? I am not sure I didn't see the *absolute* truth, if such a thing exists. I saw *the all* as a mere program, and it's as good an explanation as I have ever perceived. If that is so, where does it leave Christianity or even Buddhism with their brand of *truth*?' I am left with my own revelation. But who or what in truth creates and maintains it all? Who is responsible for the formulae, the code, the equation of life? We are?'

'Your mind is working well,' Tenzin responded. 'I listen to you and hear the ancient teaching. I guess you can be forgiven for missing the answer within your own rendering. You said it yourself, but a moment ago. There is, for us, no *absolute truth*.'

'I am not content with that, Tenzin. And neither should you be. How can you accept such a thing? There must be a one-size-fits-all truth. The real truth. It can only be the world of the programmer.'

'And that is what you have been searching for all your life?'

'Yes. I will not live in another's version of the truth. Life is too precious a thing to live under falsity. I've long known the self-deception employed in this world, and how most seem happy to live with it, even sensing instinctively the deception, but allowing it. I've been too busy battling mankind's self-serving, narrow version of reality. It was difficult to swallow, that there could be a single, all encompassing truth. What had consumed– *No*. . . What had *distracted* me, and much angered me, was mankind's willingness to continue deceiving and getting in the way of itself from the attainment of a higher path, while single-mindedly accelerating along the path of least resistance, destroying the beauty and symmetry it is so blind to while chasing falsities and illusions. Financial wealth for one. The allure of which has become the greatest destructive force ever misconceived within the mind of man.

'In all honesty, Yeshe, I am ashamed of what mankind has become. Perhaps we have always been greedy, selfish, oafs. I don't know, but we must achieve a higher state of being. We have intellect and logic as allies. We have, as far as I can see, the two tools enabling the attainment of that higher path, and yet... Well, just look at what we do. Look at it!' I railed angrily.

Tenzin seemed to study me for a long moment, at last saying, 'You have come a long way in a short time. But free yourself of the frustration and anger which is holding you down. You will not reach your full potential until these things have been removed like the cancer they are.'

He consulted his wristwatch then, saying, 'I have a group to talk to in a moment. I must get to them. Think about what we have talked about and we will talk again, soon.'

'But, Yeshe...' He was already walking towards the door. 'I have not addressed the most important thing. The missing link Dali lama!'

'I must go,' he called over his shoulder, and was gone.

9

— Survival Mechanism—

I was pleased with the headway made by talking with Yeshe, and *Yeshe* was how I would be continuing to refer to the old fellow in orange garb from now *on*.

"Holder of light," the name felt most applicable to the man. Now, more than ever, I had the feeling he held a depth of insight and knowledge I had only guessed at, and I could only benefit by spending time in his company. Of course, I could not spend too much time here. I was not the sort to stay in one place for any real length of time. The feet would begin to itch again anytime. I knew I would wake one morning with the deep urge to strike out in one direction or another, ever wondering what was around the next bend in the road, over the next hill or beyond the visible horizon. *Wanderlust,* it was called. It was something I had been born with, and with it accompanies another of physics' curiosities. Inertia: the tendency of a moving object to continue moving, and likewise the reciprocal, the tendency of a stationary object to remain where it is. The second description worried me. I had never, with the exception

of prison time, remained stationary for long. I had seen the effect take hold of many old friends, and once it struck, it stuck. Married with children, jobs and responsibilities, before they even realised it they had put down roots which would hold them motionless to the end of their days, until, one day they were put into a hole on the ground. Life was meant to be lived to the full, and to be treated as the great adventure it was. Perhaps my biggest fear was to lie in my deathbed with little to recall in the way of exciting and interesting times. A wasted life. I could not possibly imagine a worse fate than to look back through the years to see nothing warranting the great gift I had wasted.

The grounds, buildings and outhouses of this quiet refuge, although being so beautiful and restful, were already beginning to become commonplace. The one spot I liked to spend time was down by the stream, sitting or lying on the embankment by the bridge. I could stretch out there, soaking up the warmth of the sun and allow my thought to wander wherever they willed. It was likely the most pleasant place I had ever been, especially if one was in need of quiet contemplation.

I didn't know where Abe had gotten to. I had not seen him since breakfast. Perhaps he had gone into town with some of the others, I mused. Not for me, although he might have asked if I wanted to join in. But then I probably would have declined, taken the opportunity to stroll down here beside the stream and stretch out exactly like this and allow my mind to drift of its own volition as I enjoyed so lovely a day as this.

That was the worst of prison, to be deprived of natural surrounds and be caged by concrete, steel and brickwork; moved like cattle from one area to the next; told what to do and when to do it, the entire day, weeks, years being controlled to the point where some found, upon being set loose one day, they suddenly could no longer deal with open space and freedom of choice. Institutionalization: the loss of self; all initiative having been eroded away until only the hollow shell of the human being remained. I had seen it. It was shocking and confronting. I had briefly befriended such a man, and been shocked at his telling me how he did not want freedom returned; that if ever they set him free he would be as lost as a child, unable to fend for himself. I was sure he exaggerated, but to look into his eyes as he pressed the point, I knew he told the truth and I was even more horrified by the system which allowed such a thing as this to happen. Some of these men self-destructed after being set free. Some committed crimes the moment the opportunity ariose, in order to be returned to the only life they had become comfortable with; where they were housed and fed, absorbed into an endless routine while surrounded by the safe and familiar.

The soft sound of a footfalls upon the grass reached me, releasing me from my reverie.

'Back already, Abe?' I chanced, eyes still closed against the brightness of sky.

I half raised myself, squinting in the direction the sound had come from.

'Don't let me disturb you,' came a voice. As he neared, I made out the form of Sri Lankan Danny. 'I didn't know anyone was here until I crested the rise,' he said, halting a few feet from me. 'A terrific spot, isn't it?'

'It is,' I agreed grudgingly, not looking for conversation.

'Mind if I join you?' he asked, not waiting for a response but promptly lowering himself, cross-legged, and leaning back on his arms to view the shallow gully, the sparkling stream with its grassy embankments and the undulating countryside surrounding.

I lowered myself again onto my back, eyes closed, hoping perhaps he would leave in a minute or two.

'Flowing water creates negative ions conducive to the feeling of well-being. If you stand on a beach when the breakers are rolling in, it's what gives one the electric feeling. Very therapeutic, Mr David. I am not surprised to find you here, beside the flowing of water.'

I grunted acknowledgement. I have always found it difficult to ignore anyone the way I wanted to at this moment.

'Are you finding your stay here enlightening, sahib David?' 'I am.'

'Yes? That is good. As am I. I find it is a place one can remove themself from the burly burly of life. Do you?'

'*Hurly burly*,' I corrected him.

'Ah, yes. Hurly burly, you say. My English has still problems.

Hurly burly,' he practised.

This guy wasn't going away. I opened my eyes to regard him at the very moment he was in the process of withdrawing a long bladed knife from his belt, flashing sunlight from the highly polished blade. Our eyes locked for the briefest of an instant, and in that instant I recognised murderous intent.

I was at a terrible disadvantage, supine, while he had raised himself to his knees while withdrawing the instrument of my intended demise. How I managed to twist myself away from the initial lunge, I will never know, but he had quickly recovered and was coming at me the second time as I managed to secure each of his wrists, gripping them for all I was worth.

'Your lineage ends here, *dhon ga garne!!*' he snarled through bared teeth.

'What the fuck!!' was all I could think of in the moment, and I managed to use the gentle slope of the ground to turn him, rolling us both down the incline.

Now I was on him, but I dare not slacken my grip on either wrist. 'What the hell is this about?' I bawled ay him. 'Why would you do this?'

His leg came suddenly over my head and lodged against my shoulder, and in a moment I had been dislodged and was rolling to my feet, standing knees bent, ready to pounce should he come again.

'You must not survive, Chapoc Nirdahl'

I recognised the name at once. The name of the skipped Dalai Lama; the person I supposedly was, and it wasn't difficult to surmise that this was an agent of the hierarchy who had been dispatched to nullify the threat to the current *grand pooh-bah*.

I found myself laughing, either at the absurdity of my posing any threat to the status quo, or at the sudden turn-on-a-dime nature of this bizarre interruption to my peaceful interlude, I had no idea which. But this was my theatre of action. The domain of the unexpected, of chaos and unpredictability, and I felt suddenly and completely at ease.

'Give it up, Danny, if that's even your name?

'He lunged when he noticed my change of demeanour, but I detected his own small shift of balance and evaded the telegraphed thrust with greater ease than I expected. The moment the blade passed the point at which it might inflict damage, at the full extent of his arm I chopped down at the intersection of the elbow to watch the weapon release from his numbed and now useless hand. In a moment I had him spun about and moving backward, then using that small momentum, I chocked his heel with my own and felled him as a dead weight, coming down on his chest with a knee and knocking the wind out of the fellow.

To his red and contorted face, I growled, 'If I see you again, Danny boy, or whoever the hell you are–' but he was already shaking his head enthusiastically.

I looked for and located the knife, noting its safe distance away from the disabled man before climbing off of him. 'I was having a nice, peaceful afternoon, you bastard,' I told him, and watched cautiously as he dragged himself up off the ground and stumbled away. And for good measure, so's he would tell whoever it was who sent him: 'And tell your demented controller I have no goddamned interest in deposing anyone! They can keep their big deal line of succession anyway they goddamned choose.'

Back at the cottage which had been assigned for Abe and myself, I secured the door by pulling across the wooden stock and lay on the lower bunk for a time, assimilating what had just happened. Things were definitely getting out of hand when assassins came sneaking up on a man while dozing on a grassy embankment.

A slight sting on the back of my hand alerted me to the fact that I had been cut. Not badly, but enough to cause some bleeding, and I had to rise and go to the basin, where I washed the tiny wound clean and waited for the blood to congeal, before returning to my bunk.

I had wanted to broach the subject of the missing link lama with Yeshe before he had run off to his spotty faced disciples, damn him. This was just the sort of thing I might have expected, had I been property appraised of the situation. *Screw it!* I thought, anger rising. Who was to say something like this would not occur again? What if whoever sent the Sri Lankan was not satisfied with my message and sent another?

'That will not occur,' an unrecognised voice responded.

I leapt out of my bunk, banging my head against cross member of the top bunk as I did so. 'What the hell is going on here?' I cried, turning about while grasping my paining forehead where I had banged it.

'Do not be alarmed,' the voice said calmly. 'I am Chapoc Nirdahl. You dealt skilfully with the assassin, David. I don't think you will be seeing the like of him again.'

'*Ooh-no.* Are you kidding me?' I called breathlessly, totally disheartened and retreating back to my bunk. 'Voices now? Disembodied voices? Life just keeps getting weirder. Go the hell away.'

Someone shook the door, heavily. Then came banging. 'You in there?' came Abe's baritone voice. 'What you doing in there? Come on, stop messing around and let me in.'

I opened the door. 'What are you playing at? That was you just now, wasn't it?'

'At the door? Yes of course.'

'No, just a moment ago. You playing silly games?'

'I don't know what you're talking about. Here, I have something to show you.'

He shoved a newspaper under my nose as he pushed past me to sit at the small table against the far wall.

I fumbled with it for a moment, began turning pages. 'Page five,' he said impatiently.

I found what he was talking about. It covered half a page. Our two mug shots and a heading:

MANHUNT CONTINUES.

Police are back on the scent of the two escapees who fled from Yatala prison sixteen weeks ago. A review of CCTV recordings at the interstate bus terminal in Adelaide confirm that convicted murder, Abraham Badash, and accomplis, David Aaron Harrison, crossed into Western Australia, unchecked by border patrols, shortly before Christmas, riding a Stateliner bus. Their current whereabouts is unknown at this time. Western Australian Police say it is only a matter of time before they are recaptured. "They always make a mistake,' Captain Sawyer commented. . . .

I had read enough and threw the newspaper aside. 'Well good for them,' I snarled irritably. 'They have narrowed it down to any one of half a dozen population centres and hundreds of thousands of square miles. It won't be long now. Perhaps we had better hand ourselves in and hope they take it easy on us?' 'What's up your arse?' he wanted to know.

'My mug shot,' I told him, moodily. 'It makes me look vulpine.' Not satisfied with the answer, he sat there, studying me closely.

'Don't worry about it,' I responded irritably. 'Where have you been all day? I'm getting tired of this place. Maybe it's time I moved on.'

'I went into town with a couple of the others, if you must know. As to the second part of your dummy-spit... *Maybe it's time you moved on?* What's that about?'

I had been nervously pacing the floor, I realised. I checked myself. I was acting ridiculously. What the hell was going on with me?

'Sorry, Abe,' I voiced contritely. 'Not one of my better days, I'm afraid. I came over to sit at the table, opposite my friend. 'I wanted to talk to Yeshe today, about the—about the succession thing. The Dalai lama thing, you know? He had some group or meeting he had to attend and there wasn't time. It's kinda been on my mind a lot, since learning about it.'

'Yeah,' he answered. 'I bet it has.'

'What, if anything, can be done about it? What are you guys thinking of? Experimenting on me or something? Because I'm tellin' you, right now. I don't like it, the idea of having a lama inside my head. Can't we like, you know... exorcise it? The whole thing is really beginning to creep me out.'

'Relax, buddy. The whole reason you're here is so we can sort you out. Yeshe it was who, once he heard that there was likely a dude walking around with the unrealised incarnation of–' he paused, trying to recall the name. 'Chapoc Nirdahl,' I obliged.

'Yeah… the unrealised incarnation of Chapoc Nirdahl in his skull, he felt real compassion, and that was before we even knew who you were!'

'Compassion, eh?' I echoed, feeling the word out. 'Affinity even?'

'I wouldn't doubt it,' he agreed. 'I've known Yeshe for a long time, David. He's like, I don't know, an old soul or something. He is unlike anyone I've ever come across before.'

'And you trust him completely,' I added.

Instead of answering, Abe paused, again with that penetrating look of his. 'You tellin' me you don't trust him? Yeshe? Are you joking?'

'I'm not saying I don't trust him, Abe,' I was quick to assert, but somewhere in the back of my mind I suddenly realised that was exactly my concern. I hadn't told anyone about the altercation with Sri Lankan Danny, and I figured I would keep that little chestnut to myself awhile, in case it proved useful. The nettling notion struck that the wonderful Tenzin Yeshe may not be all he appeared to be.

'It's cool,' I told Abe, appearing to lighten up. Just a dose of the collywobbles, I guess. What's the time? Dinnertime can't be far off. I'm so hungry I could eat the arse out of a rhinoceros.'

~

There were two people missing at the dinner table. My friend, Sri Lankan Dan and the girl I often saw him together with. No one commented on their nonattendance, which I found slightly unusual, and I had no intention of doing so.

The young couple from Germany, Hannah and Burn were there. So too were the couple from Montana, Mary and Jason, a stray named Brendan from the Riverland, South Australia, and Yeshe, as always, sitting at the head of the table, with Abe on his right and myself alongside him.

I began loading my plate with green beans, buttered, seasoned corn, cheese and lettuce—not exactly the meal I was in the mood for—and was just reaching for the sliced, tinned corn beef which had been placed there especially for me, when it happened again.

'No,' the voice uttered; the same voice as I had experienced back at the cabin.

I immediately turned to Abe, eying him suspiciously. 'No what?'

He was chewing on a corn cob, butter running down his chin. His eyes pivoted sideways, the animated eyebrows contorting into a taciturn response: *What's up with you?*

'It wasn't your friend,' came the voice again. I had done my utmost to write off the first experience as something anomalous, though I knew the way my luck was travelling, it wasn't going away and I was definitely in trouble. It was Chapoc Nirdahl, the phantom missing link lama.

'I do not like corned beef,' the voice told me. 'Could we have some of that tofu instead?'

I would have left the table but I really was hungry and stuffed food into my mouth as hurriedly as I could.

Only then did I stand to depart, but with everyone taking far too much notice.

'Not terribly hungry,' I explained rather lamely, turned and took my leave as insouciantly as was possible.

I went straight to the garage round back of the main house. There were two vehicles parked within; a jeep Cherokee and a piece of shit utility with the key in the ignition.

'Where are we going?' asked the voice, but I was in no frame of mind to respond.

I had, weeks ago, awakened at the retreat with no knowledge of even where this place was, except that it was southeast of Perth, somewhere around the vicinity of Margaret River, I imagined. I roared along the track, out onto the road and planted my foot. It was one of those hillside roads, unsealed, with unpredictable bends and with only the occasional signpost warning of dangerous curves; in the dwindling light of evening navigation was not too cleaver.

'David,' the voice persisted. 'Don't lose your grip. I'm not any more please with the situation than you are. The rite performed by Yeshe. I've been thinking about it. It must have awakened me fully. I had been lying, mostly dormant until that time. Where are we going? You're driving rather fast. I think you need to slow down before we get hurt.'

I rounded a tight bend at speed, planted the boot again and allowed the rusty crate to accelerate to top speed while I squinted through the windshield trying hard to observe the road ahead.

'Get out of my head,' I bawled. 'Now!' 'I cannot,' the voice replied.

A yellow and black signpost reading *30mph* neared, and whizzed by. "Get out of my head!' I repeated at the top of my lungs. 'If you do not, we are going over. I will not live like this.'

'David, you're upset. I sympathize, but I cannot leave. I do not know how to. I think your body was meant to be my body, but something happened during formation and maturation of the foetus. A fluke of nature, David. The rite performed released me from—Fox!!!!' the voice yelled out, and we almost killed a large, red fox with a very bushy tail under the wheels of the ute, now travelling at almost eighty miles an hour.

'David?. . . David . . . *Da-v-i-i-i-d!!!'*

I discovered, in that moment, that no matter how intent one is on driving a motor vehicle into a 30 mph bend at eighty three miles an hour, ones survival mechanism, the instinctive will to hold on to the most precious of all things—*one's life*—will always have something to say about it. Ignoring my boneheaded, bloody-minded desire to take myself out, the ego responded with *"Fuck you, Jack,"* and stomped on the brake pedal at the last possible moment, bringing the crazily oscillating vehicle to a stop in a cloud of dust within a few inches of the steep gully directly ahead.

We sat there, staring ahead, waiting for the great plume of dust to dissipate. And when I say *we*, I mean *"We"*, because it appeared to me that it was inevitable, and, according to *him*, unalterable. I had an uninvited hitchhiker and there was, apparently, not a goddamned thing could be done about it. How much more messed up could my life get? I wondered.

10

— Bliss is the Goal—

'What is the meaning of "*dhon ga garne*", I asked Yeshe.

It was the early hours of the morning. Around two thirty. Sleep seemed to be evading me with malicious intent. Over the last three days I had managed perhaps four hours of that most vital of diurnal necessities; that which soothes jangled nerves, replenishes vital energies and can, with a brush of Morpheus's cool hand, reduce the most mountainous terrain of concerns to far more manageable molehills.

'*Dhon ga garne*,' the old fellow pronounced, making it sound way more eloquent. 'It means *traitor*. Why do you ask?'

'No reason.' It was the phrase employed by my by Sri Lankan friend. At last I felt I had a piece of a puzzle that I had been sensing the presence of, but could not quite grasp. I had piqued Yeshe's interest, as I was sure I would. His response to my asking was going to tell me a lot about what might be going on here.

'It's not a common expression,' he added.

'No, I guess not,' I replied coyly. But I had the answer I needed; why my nemesis wanted me out of the way. Or should I say "us"? The emergence of Chapoc Nirdahl would cause a nasty power struggle amid the ranks, back in Tibet. A power struggle they could ill afford with the struggle going on between common boarders and the upper echelons of the Chinese communist party hierarchy.

Boy, was I ever in over my head. When a world power is connected to one's current position, a man knows things are getting complicated. But right now, that part of the equation was not the issue. The issue was, how to I rid myself of my new up-stairs roommate and figure out what was Yeshe's real role in all of this. Was he the ally he was wanting me to believe he was? It seemed likely, but was his real motivation human kindness? If only I could get a popper night's sleep, this jumbled mess spinning around in my head might begin to make some sense.

'I can help,' Chapoc spoke up.

'You keep out of it. You're not helping.' Yeshe regarded me askance. 'What?'

God, I had forgotten he was right here next to me.

'Sorry, I've not been sleeping too well,' I replied. 'I've got an internal dialogue going on with myself. Pretty weird, right? I've got to get some shuteye,' I told him, finding a way of excusing myself.

Christ, that was close, I considered, making my way back to the cabin.

You've got to look after yourself better than this, said Chapoc. *This will never do. Allow me to assist you in getting the sleep you need and I will allow you the alone time you need to better think things through. Deal?*

'All right then,' I acceded. 'I'm so beat, I can't think straight. And let me alone 'til I break the news of your arrival to Abe, will you?'

Are you sure that's wise?

'I trust no-one more than I do Abe,' I argued. 'Just let me do the deciding around here. But, one thing before we turn in. How did my would-be killer know about your presence? Answer me that!'

I would have thought the answer to that was obvious. Who in this place would have any possible inkling of my emergence? In fact, what do you assume was the intention of the ritual performed by master Tensin?

'I was afraid you were going to say something along those lines,' I said with a heavy sigh. Come on. Let's sleep on it.'

~

It's not unusual to be inundated by weird dreams after a long spell without sleep. When the noodle has been coping with the weird shit I had been coping with lately, I had no reason to be surprised. But surprised I was.

I dropped off inside a minute after collapsing into my bunk, or rather, I was swept off in an all consuming darkness, more like oblivion than ever I had experienced before, and I was nothing but grateful for the respite. The aches and pains of existence were replaced by absolute comfort; any worries were gone, and only the bliss of being accompanied me. After a timeless period, Chapoc intervened:

Better?

Much, I replied. My mind was alert, as clear as clear could be.

Good. You see, then, I can be of some service to you. Don't get too please with yourself.

We have a puzzle to solve, David. You have landed yourself in quite a situation.

Tell me about it, I jeered. *Am I correct in assuming I was to be hit because someone up top of the heap got wind of what was occurring here?*

You are correct. The world of organised religion, which, by the way Buddhism in its purest form is not, is filled with serpents. Power, the attraction of perceived power, has been a corruptive agent since the beginning. Someone, I suspect, among the Dalai lama's entourage, or perhaps within the rarified atmosphere of the immediate group surrounding his holiness, is behind the attempt on your live. A cabal exists. I know, myself, the potent forces at work just below the calm exterior. They have long suspected that I, Chapoc Nirdahl, have survived the culling.

Culling? I repeated, surprised.

Yes. You thought I was merely lost or overlooked? No, David. It was not that way, at all. Word was put out, a directive, that I should never be found. And if, of course, I was found, that I was not to survive.

The idea of such a thing I found shocking. Blood letting within the Buddhist faith was, to me, unthinkable. I remembered what I had been told, just weeks ago, that after years of searching and not discovering the reborn soul of the Dalai lama, a new candidate had been elected to take Chapoc's place. Perhaps a measure of skulduggery had taken place in the choosing, bringing into the fold someone's family—someone most likely already high up in the hierarchy, and with the resources and political clout to. Political

clout. *Politics?* The inclusion of politics would point towards–

Yes, the Chinese Communist Party, Chapoc interceded into my thinking.

I had suspected something of the sort already, but how likely was it? Was I allowing my imagination to run away with me? Fact was, this was far beyond anything within my sphere of control? No way was I going to involve myself in anything of this ilk. Staying off the radar occurred to me to be the smartest move I could make.

Too late for that, Chapoc observed. You have been on the radar for some time. Allowing that knife wielding ferret to escape with his life may prove a pivotal error.

I know, I responded ruefully. *But, I mean, even though he was there to take my life, one thing I am not is a killer. The thought went through my mind in the moment, but it repulsed me. I had incapacitated the man and it would have been like slaughtering an animal. Human beings are not animals.*

Animals are innocent, Chapoc argued. *Human beings act with intent. The man's intent was to end your life–*

– out of a warped, misplace sense of loyalty to we know not whom,

I completed for him.

You have a depth of understanding, David. I am impressed by your ability to look beyond the obvious, but, now I want to go over the ritual you underwent at Yeshe's behest. The rite is the only possible means by which I was summoned. It was the ritual which opened a portal. Either that, or I have always, since your own birth into this world, been a part of you, and the ritual merely advanced my emergence. Perhaps I was meant to be you, or you me, and some anomalous event caused the incarnation to stall? Whatever the answer, it would be useful to determine, would it not?

I agreed. Since that potent experience I had wanted to put it behind me. Perhaps it had frightened me? It certainly disturbed me. Perhaps there was an element of shock which caused revulsion and an unwillingness to retrieve the memory of it? It was unusual for me to avoid dissecting something so illuminating.

I went over what I recalled of the ritual: the pungent elixir; the arcane passages recited so lyrically, taken from the ancient tome, my consciousness being carried away upon the mesmeric ululations in Yeshe's droning voice; the vision of immense radiance, ethereal light I had interpreted as a kind of cogent, universal power; my feeling of being in the presence of an authoritative intelligence, angels, perhaps; a feeling of witnessing omnipotence in the only manner the human mind was able to interpret it. The recalling of the experience to mind had the curious effect of obliterating all that had recently occurred, with an eminence sapping the past of all importance.

These things were merely the capricious and insignificant actions of small-minded beings with little understanding of what surrounded them, with so very far to travel in attainment of that which we have come to name enlightenment.

None of this was meaningful; not our escape from prison; not the bush trip; not Yeshe's sad little clique of a community; not the machinations of a corrupt Buddhist brotherhood and not the possible interference of a power obsessed Chinese Communist Party. It was all suddenly and entirely laughable. My mind distanced itself from all of it. From a distance I was able now to see the insignificant little human drama amounting to virtually nothing.

There was no control, imagined or otherwise; no power, however these self-deluded people imagined their world to be structured, and in the instant I saw the whole of human endeavour as no more than a dream of glory and purpose pursued yet never gained; only imagined self-importance because there was no ultimate purpose; there was no great fulfilment, a perfect world filled with love, contentment, richness beyond imagining or an existence that would deliver an ultimate state of being. Not for us humans, the way we presently were. Perhaps in millennia, if we worked hard at it.

Bliss was the invisible goal, and the province only of those able to see beyond all illusion, acting as a reflective veil, mirroring ourselves and our imagined world back at us in some crazy, kaleidoscopic way, obscuring the truth for as long as we continue to deceive ourselves with beliefs more rooted in ego than in the cosmos; that which gave birth to it all.

There was nothing here to be concerned with. It might all be a theatrical production, written by a second rate playwright, staged and performed by mindless drones being controlled by invisible hands. But those hands were our own and we are blind to the fact of how deep our self-deceit goes.

It was with such clarity that all this was revealed. I was overtaken by the feeling of existing within the personification of perfection; a universe so beautifully precise, delicately poised and self-sustaining that what I had once understood as being either supreme order or chaos was revealed to me as opposing facets of the same dream in which I, myself, existed as yet another dream. It was all a dream: a dream within a dream within endless dreams, and all constructed according to that which the participants projected from within their own mind; believing in their own counterfeit existence; an endless diversity constructed by mere human perception, leading nowhere but to more of the same until the circle is broken.

It was this I had felt by instinct alone from my earliest days. A need to break the cycle, but not realising the cycle was there, and certainly not knowing how to break it but by throwing confusion and chaos into the mix, hoping that by acting out of accord with the invisible web of predictable cause and effect events which rule our every action, I might find the flaw—the chink in the armour—the means by which God might be knocked off of His pedestal and forced to reveal to all what lay beyond the great conjuring trick.

11

— Realization & *Thank-you* Chapoc —

As I woke the following morning I knew that Chapoc had departed. Everything I had absorbed from that remarkable dream had been a parting gift. Chapoc had unlocked for me the mystery of my own aberrancy. He had shown me what I might eventually have discovered for myself, but only through many more pains taking years of bumbling through life, bouncing from one situation to another, all the while questioning, guessing, performing mental gymnastics in trying to account for everything in this convoluted life experience. He had saved me a lifetime of chasing an answer I might never have discovered this time around.

Nature had, in me, and, I suspected, in many like myself, produced a component mechanism of analysing a not entirely perfect virtual machine, if reality, so-called, might be called such, with my own function and connection to the all enabling self-correction; a means of dissipating minute but ever mounting accrued errors.

Somewhere within the vast complexity—the interwoven plexus which is the all—there needed to be a balancing, self-correcting equation. Intelligent life are a vital component of the all, needed to minutely adjust discrepancies and maintain harmony between one facet of reality and another, which, paradoxically, are the product of imagination projected outwardly, and without which the beautiful equation would fail, resulting in the near impossible balance of the enormous energies at work being lost, resulting in instant oblivion. The key was to realize the near-impossible foundation on which the cosmos was built; the billionth of a degree of mathematical offset upon which all was poised; incalculable potential between *is* and *is not*, plus and minus, where zero is the intersection at which everything in creation was able to be.

Such abstract notions had for decades circled one another within the theatre of my mind, but without resolution. Upon waking this morning the beauty of it held clear, firm and knowable; a snapshot of the unending circle of foreverness visualized within the mind: crystalline and perfect. *The all* could be no other way than it was, an endless tapestry of virtual realities supporting one another through manifold unrecognised dimensions as a single enormously complex creation. Created by what? I had my notions, but so far removed from my own personal reality, it was beyond relevance to such a creature as I.

'Existence is the way it is because it can be no other way,' I said it to myself.'

Abe stirred in his bunk, an arm appearing, dangling from the bunk above, and I shifted my mental focus in his direction, receiving, *What are you mumbling about? I want to sleep.*

Had he said that? It had doubtless come from Abe, but did I actually hear him say that or was it something else?

'Did you just speak?' I asked him.

In response, I received a long groan. His arm disappeared upward as he repositioned himself above me. 'Mmm? What? No.'

— but what followed came not as spoken words. They came to me through my mind: *Please shut up, David.*

There was no mistake. There was a modest but unmistakable difference in tenor between speech and thought. The weirdness was going to continue, it appeared. And here was I thinking that with Chapoc's departure my life was about to get a whole lot more simpler. *Fat chance of that!*

Well, if Abe wanted to sleep, I would leave him to it. The light through the window suggested it was early; around six, perhaps. I rose, dressed quickly and left the cabin to explore what else had changed in my world since hitting the sack last night.

The sun was low on the horizon and shadows stretched across the landscape. With birds chirping their morning song, the atmosphere clean and clear, the dampness in the ground I walked suggested a light shower had occurred before dawn, producing that lovely earthy scent.

Wow, I thought to myself. *Beautiful.* I loved mornings like this in surroundings like this. It had been too long.

As a much younger man, my friends and I would drive out deep into the unspoilt countryside, take an acid trip and spend the entire day wondering around, admiring Nature's handiwork, luxuriating in the vital, magical quality of the atmosphere generated by the natural world. I was reliving that experience now. The world seemed fresh and new. No one else had yet emerged from the scattered buildings on the property, leaving me to stroll about alone, recapturing those feelings I had so long been separated from, before I had somehow strayed into the mayhem of human society and so gradually been corrupted by it.

Serene: the word fit perfectly. In my mind I went over all I had been gifted during the night. If this was a product of my own outward projection, a reflection of my personal, separate reality, I loved it—loved it from the core of my being—and I resolved in that moment that I wanted to be surrounded with such as this for the rest of my life. God, I had been so stupid. I had wasted so much of my life raging against the world I had come to occupy, when all I needed to do was to remove myself from those things which caused me so much perturbance. I could not, and would not, ever, be able to assert influence enough on the rest of the world to make them see that the path they followed was the road to ruination. And, in any case, that was *my* take on the world. It was true for me; it impacted on me. If they could not see what I saw and try to rectify all the wrongness... What was so for the rest of the world would be near impossible to change. I could no longer waste my life attempting to reflect their shallow views back at them in hope of sanity prevailing.

I had been playing an unwitting, unwinnable, though entirely necessary game, looking for fractures in, for lack of a better description, God's perfect creation: Trying to prove what? That there's no such thing as perfection? And so what if I was right? From what I had gathered, I *was* right; creation was not precisely perfect, it was nearly perfect; nevertheless, creatures like myself somehow identified those imperfections in the virtual machine, allowing for tiny corrections to be made, rerouting within the all encompassing connecting pathways which acted as a nervous system, and, too, the incomprehensible sentience of which we, small yet far from insignificant creatures, are a mere component of, playing, no doubt, a vital role, the function of which completes the sum of the whole in a manner I could only guess at. The cosmos was complex, and, okay, not quite perfect, but how could it possibly be? And the things with which I had been busying my mind were undoubtedly a minor fraction of the incalculable depths, all beyond the capacity of a human imagination to wrestle with. I had my own patch of reality, and I was overjoyed to have it. I would, I promised myself, cease from meddling with it any further, and extract from it what joy I knew existed, if I only allowed it to come to me. The rest of mankind could continue as they wished. It was no longer my concern; and, in fact, never was. I was handing in my resignation and going to ride off into the *dawn*, which felt perfectly appropriate right now.

Adios, I told the human circus, and *Thanks Chapoc!* —laughing inside. I continued my stroll into the totally revitalized landscape under a blue sky, made more enjoyable by the warmth of the rising sun, symbolizing perfectly, for me, the fresh new start which was already beginning to formulate as I wondered over the landscape, reviewing all that had brought me to this surprising juncture. I was freeing myself from my past. All that had gone before were the building blocks upon which the now David Aaron Harrison would step forward into the future.

In the strangest of ways I had been reunited with the child I once was, before contamination. That boy believed in magic—the magic of the natural world. Even then, my entire being had connected with the ubiquitous energies, surrounding and all encompassing. I recalled the day I stood motionless in a field, on just such a day as this. In the stillness there was the hum of life as insects, birds, animals small and large went about their lives, doing what their nature dictated they do. I recalled the way the breeze would rise intermittently to rattle the leaves in the tree-tops, adding to the great symphony of life abounding, with the sun shining down and the beautifully fresh air breathed in to the lungs, filling the body with a wonderful vitality, but which seemed to ebb as the years saw my inner being evermore corrupted and contaminated by entering into a world increasingly misshapen by our incessant meddling—a world we had so misguidedly constructed, thinking of taking control of it all for ourselves. Such clarity filled my mind and I was transported back in time, to again inhabit that boy. He had been right to be suspicious of the future. He had seen all the signs of approaching disharmony, even then! As he grew, he hung onto childhood with all his might, knowing that to lose such innocence—an innocence enabling the ability to connect with the natural world on so basic a level—was something to be desperately fought for, lest the connection be broken and lost forever.

There were many subtle indications of the connection back then. Animals instinctively understood; wild animals, especially, who shared the association. Magpies, crows and even shy starlings had often come down from the sky and walk over, inquisitive of the odd attraction, putting aside their instinctive fear. The world sang in a language of its own, lifting my spirits so high I felt I lived in a magical realm, yet I had thought little of it then. It was the connectedness of all living things; the way the world was; there was harmony and affinity linking life of every kind, with even the tall, ancient trees I climbed as a boy emitting their presence and deep connectedness in a way that transcended the more ephemeral things, standing with an authority which comes only from age, and a permanency, soaking up the many years and constantly cycling seasons under sky and wind and sun and rain.

How right I was to hold those ancient wooden giants in reverence, sensing from them their aloof presence, like regal sentinels standing guard over the less permanent, more fleeting life forms scurrying about beneath their reverend countenance.

It was a variety of magic beautiful to behold, and it filled that child's heart with knowing, unsurpassed respect, and a wonder which never left, only growing as does a seed sewn on fertile ground and nurtured under the right conditions. That had been the problem. Stony ground. The stony ground of mankind's realm of consciousness; the world created and born of shortsightedness, inability to see beyond instant gratification; self-serving, self-righteousness, ignorance and lack of forethought in failing to seek knowledge in areas outside of what would gratify and make life simpler, easier and more comfortable. Being immersed in such a culture had stunted my own growth, and it near drove me crazy, setting my feet on the path of exposing the fraud I had erroneously recognised as a flaw in reality. The concept of reality and the disease inflicted upon me by a culture of greed and destruction must have confused the mind to the point of near insanity. If it had not been for this whole crazy chapter in my life, the path I had been on was destined for certain self-ruination. But now things were changed. That ritual had open a door. My connection to the world had been changing of late, and those changes were accelerating.

Chapoc had blessed me with a parting gift, which, if my hunch was correct, I had not yet experienced the full capacity of. The surrounding events of past weeks were not worthy of further consideration. Such things were of the other world; the world of man attempting to assert dominance over Nature; a foolish, inequitable world, and doomed to extinction. A world, as of this moment, I was resigning my membership from. Let them keep *their* reality. There was no way for me to alter it anyway, and anything I did in fighting against the foolishness was only going to see me in a rubber room, ostracised and running foul of the law for the rest of my life. If that's what they wanted for themselves, on their own heads be it. Let them reap whatever the hell they sow. They could live in any world they pleased, but as for me, I was, as of this moment, most definitely *out!*

Trouble was, our realities were still merged. As long as I wore this face and had these fingerprints, I was open to being plucked out of my world and dumped, unceremoniously, right back in prison. In separating our worlds I had to compromise, just a little longer, and to untangle myself from the lunacy surrounding me. It wouldn't take much more than attitude. That, I decided was the key to it all. . . and had always been!

12

— Choosing —

On my return, I discovered Abe, sitting on the edge of the small verandah out front of our cabin. Barefoot and wearing the track suit pants and singlet he slept in, he looked as though he had just risen, his shaggy hair ruffled and generally disrupted about his head and face.

'Good morning, comrade,' I greeted cheerily. 'Sleep well?' He gave me one of his *are-you-kidding me* looks.

'Are you kidding me?' he replied, sleepily. 'How's a bloke supposed to sleep with you rummaging around and muttering incomprehensibly all flamin' night long?'

'Oh, dear,' I responded, at once realising what an annoyance I must have been. 'I'm sorry, buddy. Actually, there's a very good explanation.'

There was no response, only continued annoyance. Then, having forgotten my new trick, I was surprised to pick up on his thinking:

I'm hungry.

Was I going to let him in on my secret? I had to decide. Perhaps, not yet. I would need to consider the pros and cons of letting anyone know. I had only just put a foot on the path to my new future. I was not going to make the mistake of *not* thinking ahead. Not this time.

'Where you been?' he asked.

'It's such a nice morning, I thought I'd start the day with a constitutional. And now,' I said, attempting to raise his obviously low spirits, 'I could actually eat a *mung bean*. Come one, buddy, let's get some breakfast.' But he stayed put.

From a pocket he produced an envelope, extended it toward me. 'This is for you, apparently.'

'What?' I looked at it, baffled as to how I could possibly be in receipt of a letter. . . *here, off radar.*

I took it from his extended hand, turned it once to reveal scrawled handwriting, depicting, "David A Harrison, Esq.,"—and looked back to Abe, disbelieving.

'I found it just a moment ago, lying on the table.'

He watched with immense interest, not to mention disquiet, as I tore it open, slipped from it a sheet of paper on which was scrawled:

> David. . .
> I found a portal left open by the
> ritual performed by Tenzin Yeshe,
> who, by the way, had no hand in
> your attack. I have decided to take
> my leave. You might have made a
> good Dalai Lama. Too bad things got
> messed up. The problem, as you must
> know, is insurmountable. The present
> Dalai Lama will not be budged. The
> political fallout within the inner circle

would tear it apart, so forget it. It's not
your destiny in any case.

Your destiny is what you make it.
In answer to your personal quest for
understanding, this may help: îxis-
tence is the way it is because there is
no other way it can be. It's all a dream,
my friend.

Chapoc PS

Your mind is an interesting place, but
I wouldn't want to live there. *Ha-ha!*

I chuckled mirthfully. It was the very phrase I had
spoken to myself as I climbed out of my bunk, earlier.
Chapoc must have engraved it into my mind before leaving. 'Well?' Abe asked.

'I will explain over breakfast,' I told him.

The rostered cook had just set things in motion, but
after a wait scrambled eggs, toast, juice and coffee were
available, and consumed with gusto.

I had the urge for a cigarette and dashed back to the
cabin to scrounge for them, returning after a few minutes
to find Abe chatting with Tenzin Yeshe. Other's were
beginning to file into the dining area for their morning repast, and I thought it best to lure Yeshe and Abe
out into the garden to talk, without fear of being overheard. What I had to say was not something needing to
be transmitted, made the subject of gossip. From here on
in my life would require a level of privacy; secrecy, in fact,
until one or two things had been sewn up.

The ideal location for our discussion was right outside, where cane chairs had been placed around wrought iron tables on the grass, taking perfect advantage of a mild, late summer's morning. Oleander and hibiscus were in bloom, along with the well tended natives which gave a wonderful perfume, attracting all kinds of insects which could be heard buzzing about, fulfilling their life's contract with *the all*. With juice, mugs of coffee and my cigarettes brought along, we settled ourselves, and I took a moment to compose my thoughts.

'I will be leaving. I have, during my stay here, had something of an awakening,' I told them, and allowed a moment for this to be absorbed. I was about to continue when Yeshe responded:

'I'm not convince that is wise, David. For several reasons.'

Abe gave a derisive chuckle, saying, 'Do you forget who you're talking to? The secret agent of disorder and mayhem? I've been waiting for this to happen. I'm surprised it took so long, frankly.'

I regarded Abe's demeanour to see that he was joking, and affected a mock expression of pain. 'You wound me.'

He laughed. 'Yeah, but it's true, isn't it? Is this about your propensity for implementing chaos, again? I hoped we had gotten past that, by now.'

'We have, Abe. And it's mostly thanks to you. You have been incredibly patient.'

I turned to Yeshe. 'And your involvement. I cannot tell you the changes brought about by your hand,' I told him, honestly.

If only he knew what changes he *had* wrought. But to reveal that I was reading his thoughts and emotions with such ease, he would be intimidated, and left feeling ambivalent about his role in unleashing someone such as I upon the world.

The problem, I imagined, was that if knowledge of my growing abilities were to become known, the effect on my life could quickly become catastrophic. I had not become enlightened to the point of being naively trusting. Human nature was human nature, and even though Tenzin Yeshe, carrier of light and a servant of reason, had been the fluxing agent, I was not about to risk my one chance at retaining anonymity. Should my sudden development become known. . . Well, what hope of a natural progression through life would be left to me?

'I have absorbed as much as I am going to from your influence,' Yeshe. I have changed.'

'You are the rightful heir to the position of Dalai Lama, David. Forgive me, but you are a young man and do not see the ramifications of your decision. I have much to teach you, but first you must be centred, taught many things. You cannot possibly allow yourself to imagine that you have absorbed all there is to be understood under my guidance. It takes years. And you have a home here. Where can you go where the atmosphere will ever be as safe, as conducive to growth?'

His words were reasonable, perhaps even compelling, but behind the words I felt that humanness which so many will never shed themselves of. There was in him that unsavoury emotion, *need.* People can be so damned needy, and I have never much warmed to the emotion. Yeshe, despite all of his superficial best intentions, needed me in fulfilling his role as pedagogue, to be regarded by all his acolytes, preferably those who sat at his feet, while he dispensed wisdom and enlightenment to all the lost sheep who would look to him for guidance and with lasting devotion.

'I can only thank you for opening a door for me, Yeshe. Between yourself and Abe, I have been forever changed. I honestly wish I could say more,' I told them, regarding both with much warmth.

'But where will you go?' Yeshe asked, still bewildered.

Abe contributed with, 'You go back out there and you'll be back in prison before long. On your own, fellah? You won't last long. Why not hang on a bit longer while we try and find somewhere off the map, where you might start afresh?'

'No need,' I responded. 'But there's one thing you might do.' 'Yes?' replied Yeshe.

'Call the Department of Corrections. Tell them to clean out my old cell for me.'

13

— Ever Rotating Mechanisms—

The circle: a commonly occurring motif in life and in the mechanisms of creation itself. While galaxies, the stars and the planets follow vast circular planes of travel, so do we small and seemingly insignificant creatures tend to follow these endless orbits ourselves, but to what degree this observation applies, I suspect that few people have sufficiently investigated, and therefore are rarely aware of. In circles are we ever drawn. It is true for our larger life cycle too. We will live, die and be recycled until we begin to fulfil our full potential and our destiny. For some it may take many more rotations than for others. Some may, by trusting to instinct and the basic understanding of right and wrong, logic and illogic, justice and injustice discover a shortcut, thereby circumventing many wasted incarnations in reaching enlightenment, and thereby the gaining of wisdom. I apparently fall into the group, who, through pig ignorance, hardheadedness, believing in gut feeling and sheer, dumb luck managed to cheat nature to arrive at a higher plane of existence merely because I did not much like the idea of falling into step with the rest of the world. And in a way it makes perfect sense that this is so. Following a bunch of blind people, groping about, constantly arguing and fighting with one another, walking over the less fortunate in order to snatch the lions share of whatever is on offer, this is patently not the path to enlightenment, and one is far better off in striking out on one's own and trusting to instinct.

On weekends, two days which are spent away from working in the laundry, after queuing for a plate of food outside the kitchen and consuming the meal in the B-Division mess, we move out into the yards to wonder about in the rain or the sunshine, sating the desire for forward motion and exercising the lower limbs. That or sitting, play cards and having a chat. On Sunday afternoon there is a movie in the assembly hall, but Abe and I like to work off some of that stodgy, overcooked prison food by playing a few games of handball in three-yard. Three-yard is exclusively for exercise in the afternoons. Seldom are there more than half a dozen inmates in there at one time. After our game, we like to sit, relaxing and shooting the breeze, talking about anything that comes to mind. It doesn't much matter, so long as it aids in luring the mind away from present surroundings. But that is okay too, because both of us got lucky and didn't have long left to go. We handed ourselves in, and were fortunate in finding an intelligent, Law Society, Legal Aid lawyer who took us on, *pro bono*. We, each of us, received a paltry six months on top of our original sentence. For Abe, who was very close to being paroled prior to our little jaunt, it meant he would be out in close to a year, provided he kept his nose clean meanwhile. For myself, it meant I would be out in around seven months. These sentences we could both do *"standing on our heads"*, as prison lingo describes.

I still had not let on to Abe about my recently discovered and still burgeoning abilities. Anomalous curiosities were popping up as time passed by; things that I was not at all expecting. The mind reading trick was coming along a treat, and I could turn it on and off at will, for the most part. There was also, now, telekinesis. I had recently butted heads with a particularly arrogant thug of a prison guard by the name of Wentzel. It was he who had gone out of his way to ride me every time he saw me, even before the escape. Upon my return he took enormous delight in rousting me, turning my slot upside down, just before lights-out. I would be left with a tremendous mess, with books, study assignment papers and other items strewn over my bed and across the floor, just at that time of night when all cell lights were extinguished. It would leave me attempting to clear up in pitch darkness before I could retire for the night. There are always lowbrow, vindictive screws in any prison. The job attracts particularly dull witted men with power issues, I have noticed, but, naturally enough, with a few exceptions. I have, in my time, met truly nice fellows who were simply desperate for income, usually newly wed chaps who had guessed wrongly that a government job such as this, offering medical insurance and job security was a good, long-term deal. Unfortunately the intelligent ones see the truth of what goes on within the system and soon have trouble sleeping at night. They last around three months, tops.

This Wentzel fellow had been transferred from prison to prison and state to state. He was a natural sadist in the making, and I had heard stories that made the skin crawl. He had just pulled the cell roust routine on me when I reached out with my mind, thinking, *How would you like to be deprived of sight and have to clean up a mess like this?* when I heard a frightened utterance from out in the passageway, and the sound of what clearly was someone falling down the steep stairway adjoining the tiers. I heard through the grapevine, a couple of days later, that my nemeses had suddenly lost his sight, just as he began descending the stairs at speed and taken a frightful tumble, and breaking a collar bone. His sight did return in only moments.

The revelation came as a shock, and, I must admit, with just a small measure of satisfaction. After that, I began experimenting. I could produce an itch and watch people scratching at themselves. I could whisper into someone's ear from ten metres off, and watch as they reacted by casting their gaze about the room in search of the mystery offender. Physical assault was possible, and I must admit to tripping one or two people as I learned the new trick. But further things of that nature I regarded as being particularly unsporting, and stowed the practice of physical interference to my slowly emerging arsenal of *magic.*

Telekinesis; books, spoons, pannikins and things commonly discovered about the big house. I amused myself by practising, alone in my cell and out of sight. Whatever had occurred in the wake of Tenzin Yeshe's spooky ritual had apparently put me in touch with a whole new dimension of possibility, and I swore to myself that I would keep my activities in this field down to an absolute minimum. There was a glaring responsibility attached to these things, I realized, and I was not going to allow myself to turn into something unsavoury. Choice, I had learned, was perhaps the most powerful of all things given us in this life.

Prison life is not, generally, as bad as people make it out to be. Movie writers love to pad out prison movies with violence and sexual perversion. Such things may be more pervasive in particular prisons, but this place was, with the odd exception, a fairly tame place; and, as all old lags know, it depends entirely on the class of criminal contained within. The trick is to keep your mind occupied with positive pursuits. Never allow time to be stolen from you. Use it to your advantage and come out a much better educated, fitter delinquent than you were upon arrival. That was my thinking, and it served me well enough.

Time inevitably flowed by. My release date had been set and so had Abe's. I had just a week to while away, and he had in the order of five months. My belongings: stereo player, accrued reading material, tobacco pouch and other odds and sods had been promised to assorted characters whom I had come to call friends, and I would soon be walking out of those gates, beholding to no one. The whole idea of coming back here to finish my time, my so-called debt to society, was entirely necessary. I had learned that it was *impossible* to live within the confines of one's own singular reality. Reality, among people, was shared; a shared reality constituted the larger reality for us all. That was the way the cosmos decreed it in our small portion of *the all*, and that, for most of us, was the way it was.

I had a long path to navigate with all I had learned and all that was coming increasingly to light. Yeshe had extended an open invitation to us both, upon release, but I had other destinations in mind. Abe had become as much like a brother to me as it was possible to be, and I told him I would welcome us both hooking up again on the other side of the wall. He would have his parole tying him down, including the usual conditions entailing a consorting clause, outlawing any association with convicted felons. Happily, that did not include myself, having escaped being convicted of a violent crime, but it would be difficult for my friend to move about freely while seeing out the end of his parole period. He would be dogged for quite a while to come, having to report to his parole officer regularly, and having to prove how he was making a concerted effort to secure employment and all the rest of the jumping-through-hoops palaver the Department of Corrections weighted one down with after locking you away from the world for any length of time.

But there was Henk, aka Evo. Evo had come and visited me after my return to the big hose. He had seen in the papers how we had been *apprehended by police*, which was, of course, a lie. We had both marched into Cop Central on Angus Street, Adelaide, accompanied by a willing lady parole officer I had enlisted in order to witness our *self-designated* return to penal servitude, just in case some glory seeking copper wanted to pull a gun, claiming our scalps and in the manoeuver a medal to pin on his manly chest. Henk agreed to us using his mailing address, so that Abe and myself might keep in touch when at last the path became clear for reunion. Until that time I had another destination in mind.

A man who has travelled the convoluted path on the quest for awareness and wisdom eventually will come to a crossroads. Unlike a certain blues guitarist purported to have sold his soul to the Devil for the ability to play the guitar wonderfully well, to thrill audiences and become well heeled in the bargain, my own crossroads was in the choosing of whether or no I would continue concerning myself with the interrogation of reality and the journey to ultimate wisdom; attempting to untangle the endless tapestry of creation, woven by unseen hands of gossamer threads, drawn from tangled skein, given shape and form despite impossible odds, a mighty dream born of want for expression of itself and nothing more; mystery of mysteries. . . Or would I simply accept what the universe had gifted me, and be grateful; find a comfortable nook, a female companion, there to live out my days, satisfied to have put behind me, forever, my formative and tumultuous years?

Ha! Who am I kidding? There is no getting off of this ride.

end

BEYOND THE RIM

FOREWORD

The eco-war lasted ten years, from October, 2022 to June, 2033. Hostilities escalated across the globe between those that could afford to turn things around regarding carbon emission and pollution generally, and those who could not keep pace, including the third world and the still developing countries who did not stand a chance in hell of investing in what became known as The New Economy. Embargo and tariff hikes were the first weapons, and weaker economies soon began to feel the pain, but before long it turned into a shooting, bombing war—a war of survival for the millions being forced beyond their means to toe the line of the new ecological imperative. The speed with which this severe socioeconomic climate swept the globe resulted in hunger and deprivation, finally pushing countries into a desperate struggle for survival at all cost.

When the smoke and dust of destruction had settled, Earth was a different place. The old economy had fallen, to be replaced by the new, eco-conscious, fiscal and political formula for the future. The human population had been decimated during those ten years, as much through warfare as by impacting natural disasters brought about by mankind's negligence, including flooding on a scale never before witnessed, famine, pestilence and want for adequate shelter, resulting in deaths from exposure.

Because man had witnessed the nightmare of near self-inflicted extinction, the *New Order Watch* was devised; a watchdog organization with teeth, demanding that any industry with the potential to cause damage to the biosphere must migrate off world. It seemed a crazy and tyrannical action to many, and sure to send us back to an agrarian based society, but we found a way. In the aftermath there was discovered an abundance of untapped fiscal wealth which the *New Order Watch* rapidly plundered with impunity. Space programs and off world settlement projects, which had been abandoned over a decade previous, were reinstituted and augmented with vigour, and before we knew it the dream of zero impact existence seemed within reach; an actual possibility.

Our moon became the industrial centre for our future. It was discovered that the moon held vast quantities of metal ores and raw materials essential for Lunar habitation and heavy industry alike. Low gravity engineering and production revealed many previously overlooked advantages and the mineral rich moon became a miracle of modern industry in short time as technical problems were tackled and solved, one at a time. We committed vast financial resources and what remained of manpower to the dream. It was often said that the period compared to the era of the pharos, with its far ranging harnessing of labour and resources, and the single-minded focus on the primary goal, to be achieved at any cost. The resulting accomplishments inspired the concept of creating an even further reaching scheme of acquiring raw material for future needs and planned rapid expansion after such a terrible setback. The plan became known as the Far Reach program.

The Rim is what spacers call the Kuiper Belt, the ring of asteroids and accumulated debris left over from the formation of the solar system billions of years ago. The term applies to anything in that general area, including the recently completed Niven Space Station situated four point eight billion miles out from Earth, just inside the path of Pluto's orbit. Niven Station is companioned by another, nearby platform, financed and constructed by my employer, Universal X, an abbreviation of Universal Mining & Exploration. The platform is named *Far Reach-A*, suggesting that there are already on the drawing board the plans for another, similar structure. As big as *Far Reach -A* is, it is entirely the domain of the company, providing accommodation, life's necessities, services and supplies, as well as providing housing for the many mining and exploration machines, vehicles and maintenance personnel to keep them functioning. From it are launched frequent expedition craft, manned by a highly motivated and particularly hardy breed of spacer whose job it is to search out, conceptualize, compute logistics and evaluate profitability of mining primary and exotic minerals from the vast number of asteroids, passing comets and anything else out there drifting in the vacuum.

Travelling the distance out to *the rim* once took three years, nine months, and nineteen days. That was a mere twenty seven years ago. Today, with the advent of the plasma pulse engine, that time has been cut down to eight months, with a good proportion of that time being consumed in the deceleration portion of the trip. Fortunately, there is the option of medical assisted stasis, allowing one to sleep throughout the journey. This option is preferred by most and avoids the possibility of passengers becoming stir crazy. The well heeled, those who can afford the expensive, first class option, experience much the same as first class ocean liner passengers once enjoyed, with all the opulence and pampering entailed with that manner of travel. Naturally, the company flipped the bill for my medical assisted stasis and I arrived in reasonable mental state, keen to get on with the job I had been commissioned to perform. It seemed like an opportunity at the time. A change from the usual grind.

As an undercover operative for Universal X, I have been posted here to discover where the company's missing consignments of hardware, food supplies, spare parts, tools and other miscellaneous items have been disappearing to. With Niven Station being fully operational only these past few months, already a quite well organised criminal network has sprung up in the sector.

Anything brought out here to the rim increases in dollar value by at least five hundred percent, depending on the item in question. It isn't difficult to see how conditions are ripe for criminal enterprise. Brigands and chancers are setting up a network of black-market trade in anything from a can of beans and prohibited pharmaceuticals to weapons and expensive machinery parts—parts necessary to keep the wheels turning for the twenty-two percent of the human population who survived the war, a greater proportion of whom are the filthy rich and their immediate family members. The wealthy, for the first time in human history, now vastly outnumber the working class, and the working class are in great demand, especially out here. This place is the wild west on steroids, and a place where only the strongest survive, unless one is fortunate enough to have earned a position within the higher echelons of the company. That or knowing someone in the higher echelons where nepotism has become almost the norm.

Niven Station is well stocked and supplied, providing a commercial centre and a comfortable habitat for the many and varied walks of life; the lynchpin connecting Earth with the Far Reach platform and heralding a new direction for mankind's existence with its future firmly pointed toward deep space exploration and exploitation. These are the times I live in.

1

SNOOP, SNOOP, BANG, BANG

I disembarked the transport ship at the Niven Station terminus, a large, circular arena, it sat atop the station where ships arriving are hugged by giant mechanical arms to keep them secured to the landing platform. Hermetic, concertina like tubes were extended from the central dome and attached to the front and rear of our craft, allowing passengers to breathe an Earth similar atmosphere while gaining entry to the station.

I had hoped to have the time to take a bit of a look around Niven, but the ferry to Far Reach was due to leave just thirty minutes after our arrival and I had to make do with the view available through the triple layered *plexishield* scenic window in the café, as I sipped my large espresso in effort to stay awake for the last remaining leg of the journey.

It was a fascinating view. From a position near the hub of the immense multi tiered wheel of Niven Station, I looked out across its diameter into the pellucid depths strewn with an endless number of glistening points of light reaching beyond vanishing-point.

I had never ventured so far from Earth before. I had visited Lunar station on various occasions, but out here there was an indefinable difference. As tired as I was, the immensity and clarity of the vista seemed to dwarf the intellect and reduce the ego to zero. At that moment it had the effect of making mankind's endeavours appear ridiculous and meaningless. It was an uncomfortable feeling and I suddenly found myself questioning what I was doing here, sipping espresso coffee at a café, so very far from home. A quick glance at my wristwatch alerted me to the fact that I had allowed time to get away from me and I hurriedly made my way to the shuttle service at the opposite side of the concourse, presented my ticket to the guard standing at the gate, and joined the line of fellow commuters waiting on the platform to board the shuttle.

Sitting high on metal skids, the shuttle was rectangular, rounded at the ends, with a ring of manoeuvring thrusters bolted either end and powered by a single Dyson differential field engine. A thoroughly utilitarian design, assembled from stock standard parts and, no doubt, built with cheap operating cost and longevity in mind; totally in keeping with the way Universal X approached everything it did.

The two-hour journey felt much longer. The seats were reclined and comfortable enough. Four seats wide on either side of the central aisle. The passengers were employees returning from a short leave on Niven; most of them hung over and exhausted from kicking up their heals in the privately owned pubs and clubs, of which there were ample. Many entrepreneurs hade rushed to invest in the off world business boon, many catering to the highly paid mining and exploration workers, being by far the most lucrative. These guys worked hard and played hard. With fat pay packets at the end of each work cycle, and starved for entertainment, women and anything which would relieve the stresses of living and working in one of the most dangerous environments imaginable, they were only too willing to pay through the nose and indulge themselves, often to excess, in anything that would serve the purpose of allowing them to decompress for a time. Their faces reflected the harsh lives they lived, and, to a man, their eyes, staring blankly ahead, betrayed thoughts turned inward. Perhaps they called to mind the faces of loved ones; those left behind in order that they earn the big money needed to support and ensure a better existence for all. The older men were here for that reason, I knew it well enough. The younger men had come primarily for the adventure. Young men always chose adventure over financial reward, but here in this place both were available. It was a curious fact how quickly the visage of young men who worked in environments such as this came to resemble those of the older men. The adventure gives way to endurance of the gruelling routine. Youthful energy slowly and surely transforms to dogged determination. Working amongst men of this calibre, newcomers will very quickly find themselves falling short of the strength and resolve required for the task, or succeeding in digging deep enough to find the resilience needed to survive the indoctrination process. That process is achieved within the first month. The line of work such as these men perform has the tendency to quickly identify and target the slightest flaw in one's character and physical strength. I have seen men slowly erode away to nothing rather than admit not being up to the task. No, youthful enthusiasm counts for little on The Rim. It is one's metal, the strength of will that counts out here.

Then comes the bonding of men committed to a common task, the emerging brotherhood, mutual respect and reliance which, in some indefinable process, provide what is necessary to survive and succeed in the jobs worked by these men.

In the pocket at the back of the seat in front of me I noticed a pamphlet. Opening it I discovered a 'You Are Here' map, beginning at the drop-off point for arrivals at the platform, with a couple of pages describing what newcomers might need to know.

Far Reach Platform was a different kettle of fish from Niven Station. The landing platform occupied a large area at the corner of the uppermost deck of the gigantic cube—a cube consisting of four flat tiers, each of which served a separate function. The topmost consisted of an administration block, landing field, warehouses for incoming goods and supplies, maintenance buildings and, tucked away in a corner, what I later learned had come to be known as the *Bastille*. It was the domain of company security. The nerve centre for the gigantic platform's network of electronic surveillance, and fitted out with an ample number of holding cells.

The next tier down supported further warehousing and a marshalling yard where transport ships loaded with equipment and paraphernalia in supplying exploratory outstations engaged in electronic detection and drilling for samples.

Below that, the entire tier provided accommodation; self-contained, two room utilitarian enclosures for the workforce, loosely resembling a residential suburb in miniature, including the occasional corner store, which, because of the size of the area, besides providing the general items one might expect from a corner store, also supplied a form of transport called zippers. The two-wheeled variety was nothing more than a scooter with a tiny motor capable of propelling a person at forty kilometres an hour. A four wheeled model, being a small trolley with seat and steering wheel, included a tray at the rear, large enough to carry a load such as a parcel of food items or a single passenger.

The lowest of the four tiers on Far Reach was a hodgepodge. Everything from bars, small amusement parlours, low-class, unregulated hotels and bordellos, workshops, repair yards, residential addresses, and more.

I woke, not realising that I had nodded off. The shuttle had landed and the last of the passengers were exiting, leaving me to hurriedly gather my wits and make for the exit, pushing the pamphlet into my rear pocked as I went.

I collected my luggage and wondered what to do first. I had intended to take a cursory look around a few of the compounds before settling into a room somewhere, but I needed somewhere to drop my luggage. The guy at the baggage collection counter told me he would hang on to it for me if I had nowhere else. The place never closed and it would still be here waiting for me when I got back.

A room was important, but, if I wanted to get to work, it would have to wait, so I dumped my bags under the counter, flipped the baggage handler guy a credit and got straight to it.

My watch had automatically adjusted itself to local time. It was 11:54 p.m. The place functioned nonstop around the clock, which meant that the time of day made little to no difference, if I wanted to observe how things ran. My body clock was a different proposition. The trip had taken its toll, regardless of the medically induced dormancy. In fact, the process had left me feeling enervated and not terribly sharp witted. I figured that the best thing I could do for myself was to find a room somewhere and catch a decent eight hours of *real* sleep; but, on the other hand, a stint of exercise might be just what the doctor ordered. I opted for the exercise and made my way to the bank of lifts beside the administration block.

According to the pamphlet, the marshalling of goods and major warehousing took place one level below, and that's where I headed. Stepping out of the lift I was struck by the size of the expanse. The place was massive, stretching perhaps a mile or more, square. Most of the activity was taking place a good distance away, with goods being loaded from warehouses onto a train of trolleys to be drawn across to waiting supply craft, no doubt to be ferried on to crew of outlying work camps.

The warehouse nearest was devoid of activity and lay in darkness, and it was as good a place as any to begin. The massive doors at the front end were drawn shut and bolted, but a side door provided unimpeded access, and immediately I entered the premises instinct took over as I went to stealth mode.

In barely adequate light to see to the opposite end of the building, I stepped lightly and silently, taking in as much of the interior as possible. Among the rows of packaged hardware, male voices emanated from about a hundred metres away. Conversational voices, and the smell of tobacco mixed with, if my nose was functioning properly again after the trip, the pungent sweet aroma of hashish.

I should have known better. I should have taken my own advice, done the logical thing and found a room where I could have made myself comfortable, eaten a meal, watched a movie, caught up on much needed sleep; but, no, I had to blindly stumble into where I was not wanted, walk into a section of two inch steel pipe protruding from a shelf, head high, causing a clattering din as the piled up and loosely stacked pipes rolled over themselves in reaching a state of equilibrium. But that isn't the best part. The best part of it is, this wasn't a case of a couple of warehouse workers skiving of, smoking a joint on company time. This was a case, I was informed later, of a half tonne of prime hashish changing hands. Black market hashish, worth who knew how much, being sampled by the buyer before the money changed hands.

I froze in my tracks, allowing the rolling clatter to come to an end. There was little I could do. My presence was established and the only thing I could think of to do was to speak up, as casually as I could manage right then.

'Don't worry lads,' I called out. It's only me,' I explained, continuing to walk towards the source of the aroma. And rounding the corner I came across a group of five silhouetted forms.

'Who the hell are you?' someone asked in a deep baritone voice, and before I could respond with a suitable answer, a flash and a spout of flame lit the shadows.

In that instant time actually did stand still. I've heard people tell how this is the case in life threatening situations, but until that very moment I never knew it to be true. At the first sign of a firearm discharging my body launched itself sideways; a leap any red kangaroo would be proud of, and in that warped and elongated frame, I remember thinking two things. First, what a damn fool I was to be creeping around a dimly lit warehouse, unannounced, at the height of criminal activity within these very warehouses. And second, did I remember to cancel my cable subscription before leaving Earth? It's funny how the mind works sometimes.

*

To be a snoop, and a really good one, I believe one must have the predisposition and a belief that the job is meaningful. I have never been able to leave a puzzle unsolved. I guess that imbues me well enough with the necessary predisposition component. The meaningful side is self-fulfilling. The solving of cases, for me, gives it meaning, and should I live a thousand aeons I would never find a job better suited to my makeup than being a covert situation manager for Universal Ex. That's me, Jack Hardin, situations manager for Universal Ex. I realise that just because the job has meaning for me, it doesn't necessarily hold that it is meaningful for anyone else. It's a matter of perspective, some would say; but one must admit, solutions, in and of themselves, are an absolute existential imperative. Without solutions... well, I hardly need finish the statement. Try living in a world without solutions.

*

I woke in a hospital bed, a transfusion line attached to my arm and electrodes attached to parts of me. A great lug of a cop sat in a chair against the wall at the end of my bed. A guy who apparently had trouble finding a uniform sufficiently large enough to fit his huge frame. The moment I came to he radioed in the news of my return to the living. To whom, I could not say. His immediate superior, one would expect, but for a run of the mill uniform cop, *superior* could account for just about anyone.

'What's the big idea?' I asked. Followed by my first stupid question for the day. 'What am I doing here?'

He smiled but did not respond.

I was still feeling a tad woozy. Without warning I vomited over myself, and it was ten minutes before a nurse came in to check on me. I had to remain covered in my own vomit all that time, with the plod ignoring me as much as he was able.

'Oh, dear,' the nurse crooned, approaching swiftly. 'Have a little accident, did we?'

I wasn't sure if she was referring to the bullet in the guts or the fact that I had thrown up over my hospital gown. 'No accident,' I told her. 'I always shoot myself in the stomach before turning in, and throw up over myself for good measure.'

I can be a real charmer sometimes, but I regretted saying that to her the moment it had left my lips. She was only trying to help. She finished cleaning me up and left the room without another word. I had spoken twice, and twice managed to make a dickhead of myself. I determined to try and do better.

I nodded off and was woken sometime later by the uniformed cop. He was accompanied by a large, overweight and middle aged detective. Beside him, a lanky, baldheaded young man, obviously his protege. The senior rubbed at the two day stubble on his jaw while he attempted to size me up.

'Sleep well?' he asked, his gravelly voice betraying weariness.

'Like a top.'

'The doctor says you're lucky to have survived. You've been topped up with five pints. A valuable commodity in this place, too. Universal X must consider you to be worth something.'

'They sent me *here*. That should tell you how valuable they think I am. What can I do for you—?'

'Detective Sergeant Emerson', he obliged. 'Saunders,' he added, indicating the human beanpole standing beside him, and the young man nodded in greeting. 'You can start by telling me what you're doing here at Far Reach. And how you managed to catch a bullet in the gut within an hour of arriving.'

'I'm sorry, Emerson. You know I can't do that. Confidential.

Company business.' 'And the slug?'

'An accident. Self-inflicted.'

'Your piece has not been fired recently,' he returned. 'Perhaps it was a stray bullet out of the sky?'

'Must have been,' I agreed, losing interest.

'You guys,' Emerson intoned wearily. 'If you're going to get yourself all shot up and hospitalised, you could at least do it without attracting goddamned attention.'

'Sorry.' I told him.

'Security staff followed the blood trail, if you're wondering. Found you with not a lot of blood left in you and called the medics. You slip in here unannounced, to do what? I have no idea. Within an hour of arriving you get yourself gut-shot and leave an awful mess. Really, Hardin? Now I have to act on it. Official like. What am I supposed to write in the bloody report? You tell me. Loose ends do not look good on my monthly efficiency rating.'

'It is a problem,' I sympathised, 'but seeing as I'm not here, and never was here. . ?' I let the statement trail off.

The young detective's eyes reflected mounting confusion. 'What do you mean, you weren't here? What do you take us for?'

His senior intervened. 'Can it, Andy. It's hard to believe, I know, but this guy's a professional. A professional snoop for *the company*,"— and he actually made quotation marks using the usual hand sign. 'These guys think they're above the law. Untouchable, ain't that right, Mr Hardin. Jack Hardin, isn't it? I know your mug from a classified report about a year ago. The Winthrop riddle?'

I nodded. Just enough to convey grudging respect to his barely adequate powers of recall. Or had he found my ID in my bag where I had left it at baggage collection? Done a bit of research, perhaps? No matter, he knew who I was and that was cause for concern. I guess he knew what I was thinking just then.

'Don't worry. I'd rather not document any of this,' he told me, 'and it's not unknown for reports to get lost occasionally. I guess this is one of those times. Lucky for you we're in the middle of updating our filing system. Shit happens.'

'You would do that?'

He gave me an odd sort of a look. One that told me I was missing something, but I couldn't quite put my finger on it.

'Call it professional courtesy,' he replied, and turned to his companion. 'Come on. Let's go find some real criminals—' and without another word the pair departed.

I guess the blood loss had left me somewhat light-headed, because I could not make sense of the visit, at all. Cops don't just drop by to check on your health and then leave. Not in my experience. I figured I would puzzle over it another time.

Apart from the blood loss the slug had not caused a great deal of damage. I was keen to get out of there but the doctor insisted I stay a further twenty four hours, which I did, mainly because the meals weren't half bad and I still needed to get over the effects of the voyage out from Earth. The next time I made the trip I would seriously be considering the first class assisted stasis option. It turns out I am not well suited to long duration space travel; but it's an unavoidable part of the job, so there was no way in hell I was going to let my superiors in on that delicate morsel of information.

2

THE OLD AND THE NEW

I was a little surprised to find my bag was still where I left it, behind the desk at the baggage claim. It made the most sense to find accommodation on tier four, amid the hustle and bustle of the pubs and clubs; exactly the types of places one would have to go to if they needed to purchase items considered not strictly cosher by the company.

My new digs was at a place called the Star Palace, a three storey combination hotel, gambling den, single star eatery and backstairs bordello to boot. This sort of cosmopolitan establishment was common on deck four. It was the name that appealed, and it was downtown, central, close to the action.

I took a corner room on the top floor—room 405. When the landlord departed I zipped open my bag and laid out the tools of my trade on top of the bed. I had brought along a tracking kit, consisting of half a dozen miniature tracking devices; wafer thin, about the size of a small button, self adhesive and activated once the backing paper was removed. Each had its own separate frequency, to be received by my communicator, enabling me to track six individual targets as far as the mobile network stretched. In my present position I wasn't sure how far that was, but I knew Far Reach had communication relay satellites of its own, capable of reaching Earth, and certainly more than adequately covering the temporary outposts where survey teams were dispatched to.

Another important item was my custom made handgun. I have never been a fan of firearms; believing that if a man had an argument it should be settled with logic, understanding and a sense of fair play, but I'm no fool. My philosophy is my own. I operate in a world where pulling a trigger is often the only manner of settling an argument or extricating one's self from an awkward situation. It's seldom I come across situations such as this, but here on the platform I am rubbing shoulders with some tough individuals, and it would have been unwise for me to have come here ill-equipped. Although firearms are outlawed, no doubt the black market had already found a way to arm those who have the required remuneration.

Lifting my weapon, its grip feels snug and reassuring in my hand. A short barrelled, compressed air shooter, capable of firing a six millimetre lead tipped iron slug at over three hundred metres a second, with no more than a whisper, and only five inches long. A concession made for me by the company, and without which I would not have agreed to taking on the commission.

The field kit included one last item, my *M.A.I.R.A.D.* or Mission Abandonment and Immediate Retrieval Alert Device. It's a mouthful, and necessary according to management.

Looking like a coin, and activated by placing it between the teeth and biting hard, it alerts the company to the existence of one of two possibilities. Either the premiss on which the mission was launched is found to be erroneous, and immediate extraction is required to avoid further damage or embarrassment to either party; or, an agent has been compromised to the point of possible, personal endangerment or loss of life. Although most of us in the field would never dream of pressing the panic button, any one of us who push too hard in what may turn out to be the wrong direction, illustrating to all that we have mistakenly gone after the wrong people and so caused a situation, would be so embarrassed by the error of judgement, the last thing we would want to do is advertise the screw up. Obviously those in charge are not yet aware of this fact, and because not a one of us would ever accept being transferred from the field into management, this little nugget is destined to remain forever a secret. We in this line of work, like it or not, are not the types to admit errors in judgement, and certainly not of such a magnitude. Mistakes are not acceptable, least of all to personalities unable to countenance failure. As far as being extracted in the face of mounting personal risk? For myself, I would rather take my chances. If there was no risk I wouldn't be here. That much I had learned about myself a long time ago. I'm sure psychologists have a term for the trait. Fortunately, a psych analysis is not a part of recruitment process, and one must wonder exactly why that is. In this line of work turning a blind eye is an everyday occurrence. No surprise there.

I changed into the clothes I had brought along in order to try and meld into the general tone of the place.

My cover was that I was nothing more than a general hand, recuperating from a work accident. Around here work accidents tend to be fatal, but with a bullet wound causing me real discomfort, I figured I could conjure a halfway believable story should the need arise.

My reflection in the mirror looked like a pretty typical roustabout; somebody who had relied on physical strength and endurance to bring home the bacon. Leather work boots laced above the ankles, heavy cotton jeans, thick flannel shirt, a well worn leather jacket with enough pockets in it to accommodate the tools of my trade, topped off by a woolen beanie over a military crew. Good enough.

The stomach wound was beginning to make its presence felt by throbbing painfully. I checked under the hospital dressing. It was red and angry looking, but there was little discharge, a symptom I was warned to keep an eye on. If it began weeping any more than it was, I would be impelled to go back and have it checked out for second stage infection. I gave it a quick clean up, applied the powder I was given and replaced the original dressing. Swallowing a dose of antibiotics and two painkillers, I figured I was good to go.

Passing through the front bar on my way out of the building, I noted the scarcity of clientele. That would surely alter with the change of shift, when the muscle sore and weary would converge for a copious dose of the amber fluid pain relief and whatever amusement could be found before the need for sleep impelled them toward their cheaply designed company beds.

My first port of call would be to the warehouse manager's office, up on the top tier. The top tier warehouse temporarily housed incoming goods, equipment which had been ordered by the various sections; spare parts, lubricants and the like. From there inventory was checked to see that it was all there and in good condition, before being routed to its final destination.

I went first to the administration building where a security pass could be issued. My presence here and my purpose was known to very few, for obvious reasons. Having it become common knowledge that a company snoop was here would only make my job that much more difficult. The guy I needed to find was the director, Joe Higgins. The woman at the reception desk directed me, two flights up, telling me his office was at the head of the stairs.

She had, doubtless, called ahead of me. A large man of perhaps forty years, with greying hair and piercing blue eyes, greeted me as I stepped out of the stairwell and into the hallway.

'Mister Hardin?' he asked, taking a step forward.
'Jack Hardin, yes. Call me Jack. You would be–'
'Joe Higgins,' he replied, offering his hand. The grip told me he was no mere paper pusher. It takes many years of physical labour to develop a grip like that.

'Pleased to meet you, Joe. I hope you are fully appraised of the reason for my visit?'

'I am. Please, come in and take a load off.'

I followed him into his office where we seated ourselves on opposite sides of a large metal desk. A quick look around told me nothing about Joe. The office was large, purely utilitarian. Maps of the complex site were pinned around the walls; a blueprint of a cargo carrier, a list of extension numbers. Nothing at all of a personal nature. Not a family photograph in sight.

Joe leaned back heavily in his chair, causing it to creak under the weight. 'I heard you stopped a bullet the other night. Are you okay?'

'Occupational hazzard.' I replied. 'I'm told I'll survive.'

He chuckled at this. Studied my face for a moment, while I did the same to him. I knew guys like this. A hard-arse, I knew it immediately. The sort of man who commanded the space he was in by pure force of will. Those who worked under him had to endure his bullying, but I had no doubt that he knew every inch of this platform; knew every person under his command, their strengths and weaknesses, their capability and worth on the job. He would also know every single package that entered *his* warehouses, who had ordered them, their cost and their intended destination.

'I have a list here of items that have gone missing,' he said, reaching into his desk drawer and retrieving the list, consisting of several pages.

I reached over and took it from him. 'Quite a list.'

'Two hundred items this past twelve months. It's pissing me off, big time, Jack. The dollar value is one thing, but the time it takes to ship out replacements... The downtime if machines are left standing idle?'

'Yeah, I get that. Can be very annoying, I've no doubt,' I sympathised. 'Which warehouses are taking the hits?'

'They all are. And it doesn't seem to matter, the position or the level of security. No real rhyme or season to what is being taken. Anything from medical supplies to crate engines and hydraulic hoses.'

There was no doubting Joe's annoyance. His blood pressure was rising and his face reddening.

'Do you have any suspicions? Anyone you think might be responsible, or in the know, perhaps? A starting point?'

'Quite frankly, Jack. No. I mean, I just do not see how this is possible. This is an airtight rig, security-wise. There's nowhere to hide the damn stuff that could not be found. Anything leaving the rig is subject to close scrutiny. The airspace is monitored around the clock. The stuff just seems to be vanishing. It's the damnedest thing.'

I gave the list a cursory eyeballing. The items certainly were wide ranging, seemingly random, but there had to be a pattern. I would study it with greater focus, later, I determined.

'Okay. Is there anything else before I go?'

'I wish there were,' Joe told me. 'In fact, if there was anything more in the way of useful information, you wouldn't be needed. I would have found these bastards by now, and they'd be deep space meat popsicles by now.'

I didn't doubt that. Joe took this personally, as a slight against his professional ability. 'I'll do what can be done,' I told him, standing. 'It's my job now.'

He reached again into his desk drawer. 'Your pass.' he told me, retrieving a plastic identification card threaded with a looped cord. 'It allows you unrestricted passage in all areas. It's valuable, so don't loose it, and hand it in before you leave.'

'Will do,' I replied. 'We done here?' I asked, moving toward the door.

'Just catch those bastards, Jack. This is a vital operation out here, and the people back on Earth deserve results for their investment. I'm not just talking about time and money, although that is the measure by which results will be measured. People's lives are tied up in this. Failure is not an option.'

As I walked away from the administration building that last statement echoed in my mind. I hadn't given it all that much thought when he had said it, but it was very true. Niven station and the exploration and mining platform, both were the culmination of a dream; the culmination of a great deal of effort and planning. They represented a huge investment in the future and of our continuance as a species. Success overall depended on every area of endeavour being efficient, effective and completed. Accumulating cost blowouts were the sort of thing that could bleed us dry, bringing the entire enterprise grinding to a halt. But that was the concern of the bean counters. Personally, I didn't much give a damn. So long as the case was brought to a successful outcome and my payment was in my account, that was as much as I cared about. I am just a cog in a very large machine.

Seeing as I was up here on top deck, and not yet fully engaged in the hunt, I thought I should take the opportunity to visit the Bastille. The holding cells held no interest for me; it was also the hub of surveillance and I was very interested to see for myself just how thorough a job was being done.

Walking in the direction of the security building, a dark shadow was cast over the entire expanse of the platform on which I walked. Even out here, I realised then, the sun was able to emit sufficient light to cast deep shadows, and this shadow was the result of a massive cargo ship drifting high overhead, just beyond the geodesic dome encircling Far Point. The view stopped me in my tracks. It was something to see.

The vessel was enormous. Certainly it was too big by far to make a landing. As it slowed to a stop, many small vessels lifted up from the platform and began lining up at the transparent air lock. Evidently goods and crew were to be ferried in by the smaller ones. A procedure which would take a good long time, judging by the size of this behemoth.

A sentry confronted me at the entrance. My new identification card did the trick and I was ushered through. Immediately after negotiating the main entrance I was approached by a young woman dressed in navy blue skirt and jacket, light blue blouse and snazzy cap; security insignia attached here and there.

'Mr Hardin, how can I help you?' she wanted to know.

'The boss about?' I asked, continuing to make my way toward the elevator at the centre of the ground floor gallery.

'The boss?' she repeated, trotting alongside while looking terribly rattled and confused.

'Yes, the boss. The big cheese. He who gives the orders.'

I reached the elevator just as it opened its door to disgorge two personnel. I stepped in and waited for a reply to my question.

'Top floor?' I prompted.

'Top floor. Yes,' she agreed, nodding as the doors closed.

Department heads invariably reside on the top floor. Something to do with the size of the ego or the pay packet, I imagine.

When the concertina doors opened again, another woman, very much resembling the first, was standing there, waiting to greet me. It could not have been the same girl. How would she have gotten up here? The odd thought remained with me as she silently escorted me to a door halfway along the corridor—a door bearing the name, Chief Berringer—where she stopped and tapped softly.

'Come,' a gruff voice called from within, and I walked on through.

Berringer, a little man, stood at the far end of the room, staring out through the window with his hands clasped behind his back and watching the activity in the black sky above.

'I have been awaiting your arrival,' Mr Hardin.' He turned to face me, hooked a thumb over his shoulder, indicating the action beyond the window. 'I love watching the big ones come in. Really something to see, don't you think?'

I nodded, but I wasn't interested in the view any more. 'I would like to see as much relative footage, around the time of disappearance of the missing items, as possible. Can you assist me with that, George?'

'Straight to work, eh, Jack?' he countered. The years haven't mellowed you then?'

'Nope—'I grinned back at him.

Me and George Berringer had a history, you might say. We had lived in the same neighbourhood. He was a cocky little prick, always trying to prove how clever he was by pulling together one scam or another, making sure he got the biggest cut and paying those that did the grunt work a pittance. I didn't like him then, and nothing has changed. He always had an inflated opinion of himself, and he always enjoyed the fact that he had more money than anybody else, just so he could gloat. Fact was, the money always meant more to him than did people. I had heard that he became a big wheel somewhere out here. He was the head of security at Universal X's biggest enterprise, and that did surprise me. I had to admit that must have taken some talent, but I was here to do a job. Get it done and go home. No time for any of that *auld lang syne* shit.

'Well, okay then. I guess there's no reason pretending we were friends. Guys from the neighbourhood.' He moved to the end of the long table and jabbed at a button on the intercom. 'Alex, would you come and accompany Mr Hardin to the security video records library? You know which files.'

He looked up. 'Alex will assist for as long as you need her. This is no walk in the park, Jack. We've been puzzling over this for quite some time. Before we even considered getting outside help.'

The door behind me opened and a young woman stepped into the room. Pretty. Well groomed and with one of those bright-eyed, eager expressions on her face.

' Alex, this is an old acquaintance of mine. Meet Jack Hardin. Jack, my very capable assistant, Alexandra Jordan.'

'But please, call me Alex,' she responded, offering her hand and a quick smile.

'Pleased to meet you, young lady.' I really didn't need anyone getting chummy, right now. And I had good reason for that. 'Shall we begin?' I suggested.

She led me downstairs to a well lit basement where a number of consoles and work stations occupied the central floor space, with work tables here and there, and cabinets of memory banks standing against the perimeter walls.

'We have many hours of video memory, Mr Hardin,' she told me, walking to a workstation and activating the screen.

I grabbed a chair and sat in beside her.

'It's very peculiar,' she continued. 'Our inventory reveals the loss of a considerable number of items, but how or when the items were taken, we just do not know.' She brought up on screen the list of items gone missing. A list numbering some two hundred items.

I scanned the list, occasionally reading aloud as I did so: 'A one mile long roll of five ply nylon cord. One bobcat mini earthmoving machine. Two hundred instant chicken dinners with vegetables. A Christmas tree. One two hundred metre roll of canvas. One geological chemistry test set. Fifty kilos of powdered milk. Ten patio umbrellas. Twenty kilos of protein concentrate. Twenty bags of expanding polycrete building foam. A box of rubber gloves and one kilo of boiled sweets.

'An interesting array of items,' I commented. 'Almost tending towards random. It doesn't quite make sense. I don't see how there could be a black market demand for hardly any of this.'

'Boiled sweets and a Christmas tree,' Alex reiterated.

'There are no children on this rig. And what the hell would anyone need a bobcat for? Why would someone who lived out here want that? Where would you hide it? Personal space is at a premium out here. A two hundred metre roll of canvas? How do you conceal something like that?'

'Maybe it's being taken to Niven station.'

'How?' I asked, incredulous, and to which she only flushed and remained silent.

'And how the hell is this much stuff disappearing without security detecting the presence of these thieves. It could only be done with the complicity of security personnel.'

'That's not possible,' Alex countered, exhibiting the effort of containing her indignation. 'No one of us would be an accessory to any of this.'

'Perhaps you don't know people as well as you think you do,' I goaded. 'Everyone is corruptible, despite what you think you know. It is entirely dependant on the price.'

She looked at me as if studying an insect, but did not reply. I knew exactly what she was thinking. To have that particular opinion one is virtually admitting to being corruptible, themself. I didn't give a damn. I knew my estimation of people was spot on. This girl had a lot of growing up to do.

Avoiding the subject, she suggested, 'The only sure way to find out who is stealing from the company is to view the hours of stored video surveillance files, from the time we know the goods are in place to the time they are found gone.'

I chuckled without meaning to.

'What's funny?' she wanted to know, indignant again. 'The phraseology you just used. "...*found gone.*"

She made a comical face. 'Oh, yes, I see what you mean. Found to be missing,' she corrected herself.

'Don't mind me,' I told her. 'My mind, I think, tends to work differently than most.'

'No, I like things like that,' she responded, smiling now. 'Most of the people I work with would never pick up on the little things like that. It's amusing, isn't it? The little things? People, modes of speech, routine, the *illogic* in our daily lives that we never notice.'

I hadn't meant to spark a conversation, but I found myself liking that she got it.

'How many hours of surveillance video is there?' I asked, needing to break this needless chitchat.

'I would need to focus on the relevant time spans, during which the theft likely took place. Rough guess? Thousands of hours.'

'Thousands of hours,' I repeated. 'Honestly? There must be ways to automate the search. I am not viewing thousands of hours of footage.'

It was Alex's turn to chuckle. 'You mean, data.' 'Do I?'

'Yes. These are digital video files. The term footage is a relic from when video was recorded on actual film. So many feet of film. *Footage.*'

'When you're right, you're right,' I agreed. 'Find a way to search the footage for anomalies. Light intensity anomalies, I would suggest. Unless these guys work in the dark. And contact me when you have found what we want. *Vis-a'-vis,* crooks stealing stuff.'

I left her to it; walked away without having to see the look I knew was stuck to her face. She had thousands of hours of *footage* to view in order to find the odd few minutes heist. Relic? I didn't much appreciate the term, and I would use whatever damn word I pleased.

It was now time to play on the other side of the fence, I told myself. Perhaps an ale at one of the many inns and pleasure houses on level four; and while I was there I figured I might enquire as to how one might procure certain items not readily available through the usual channels.

I took my now established route to the elevators beside the administration building, alighting within the protective steel cage on level four. Judging by the sudden upsurge of foot traffic, I figured that it must be change of shift, a time when hostelries, public houses, barrooms, and not to forget the odd café, were sure to be starting to pack them in.

A place called the Event Horizon caught my eye. A public house in a singular state of dilapidation. Odd considering the platform had only been up and running for a short while. Its owner looked not to have outlaid a fortune on its exterior, but upon entering within a transformation occurred. The interior walls were brick constructed, and with what looked to be actual wooden rafters running across the ceiling, supporting the upper structure. The bar was a continuous arc, circling the interior and passing through the walls of every room adjoining, making a perfect circle. Newcomer though I was, I knew expense when I saw it. Timber from Earth? The expense must have been colossal. The place was a paradox. A ramshackle exterior and a plush interior, complete with a brass rail on which to place a hoof while drinking at the bar; and comfortable furniture, too. Perhaps its outward appearance was contrived to throw tourists and non residents a curve? I considered.

Workers milled around in every corner, engaged in loud conversation and raucous laughter. The bar and tables were likewise populated, and those lacking a place to sit, stood, exhibiting obvious weariness from a shift which had sapped a good deal of energy from their bodies, but that would change. Given time the alcohol's ameliorative effects would begin to apply its design purpose, loosening taut muscles and purse strings alike.

I ordered a beer, or at least the chemical contrivance which, nowadays, passed for beer. It was cold, which I did not expect, and a surprisingly close approximation of the real stuff. My opinion of this place continued to rise beyond expectation. It was the sort of place I never expected to find on a rig like this. From around the corner the recognisable rattle of an eightball pool table releasing balls into the tray could be heard. The perfect opportunity to make contact.

Rounding the corner I found three guys at the table, a couple of credits resting on the edge of the table, signifying their intention to retain the table for two games. Acknowledging the men with a nod, I added a coin of my own and stepped back to view the game.

Halfway through the frame the odd man out turned to me, saying, 'Not seen your face around here before, mister. You new to Far Reach?'

'Only arrived a couple of days ago,' I obliged. 'Haven't been assigned yet. Some sort of foul up with Central Data finding a glitch in my personnel file.'

'Tell me about it,' he said, smiling. 'So now you're expected to wait with your thumb up your arse while they take their time sorting it, right?'

'Right. And meanwhile I'm millions of miles from home and have sweet *eff ay.*'

'That certainly sucks,' he sympathised. 'That would mean you can't eat at the company cafeterias. You gotta pay to eat until you're on the payroll.

'Yep. Today's choice is to pay through the nose for dinner, or have a few ales and get to know some of you guys.'

'Hey guys,' he called to his pals. 'Another guy here having to pay his own way while the office sorts out their fuckup.'

The guy taking a shot lifted his head, shook it, expressing disgust.

The other spoke up.

'Bloody typical of those bastards.'

The following rack I was included in a game of doubles. We drank and played for a couple of hours, during which time I was introduced to their friends as they entered the bar and joined us in beer, pool and conversation. I must admit to enjoying the interlude, although it was an entirely necessary ploy to establish myself on the lower rung of the labour force hierarchy. The lads even chipped in and bought me a meal, which we ate together at a table upstairs, insisting that it was protocol for guys in my position. Apparently my story was not in the least uncommon. It seemed that the working man's code of brotherhood was still very much alive and well out here.

At the end of the day I ambled back to the Star. The landlord, Pietro, caught me at the bottom of the stairs on my way up to the room, wanting to know if I was in need of clean linen or towels. Today was that day of the week, but I declined and headed on up. My stitches were beginning to irritate and the wound was becoming ever more uncomfortable. All I wanted was to wind down for a while and catch a few hours nap. I was on my bed and snoozing for barely a half hour when my communicator woke me.

Miss Alex Jordan, the assistant Berringer had assigned to assist me, had done as I asked and ran all the relevant security files. Assuming the thieves needed light to perpetrate the theft, the editing software had been set to identify the presence of light within the warehouse outside of scheduled work times, and run at high speed it did not take too long before irregular instances of illumination were identified. She had done the job I asked for a little too efficiently. Just a few hours longer would have seen me rise from my bed, refreshed and in an altogether better state of mind. In light of her success, I advised myself to try not to take my ill disposition out on the keen to please miss Jordan, and grabbing the essentials, I headed off to see what she had discovered.

The elevator delivered me to the basement of the security building. As I neared the work station at which Miss Jordan was bent assiduously to her work, she turned, smiling.

'Mister Hardin,' she greeted.

'You must be tired,' I speculated, chuckling inwardly. 'Once you've shown me what you have, you can go home, grab some rest.'

'Not a bit.' She pointed to an assembled camp bed recently installed in the corner. 'Once I had set the parameters of the search, I was able to lay down and rest while the computer ran it through. Easy.'

'Half your luck,' I muttered under my breath, and if she caught that, she showed no sign of it.

'Okay. What have we got? I asked.'

'Several instances of brief illumination. Take a look at this.'

I moved up beside her to get a better view of the monitor. She had isolated a good many instances, but it was not at all what one might have expected. I had to ask her to go back several times, in order to clearly identify what had taken place. In each instance there had been a flash of brilliant light, during which time inventory simply disappeared from view. In the end I had to refrain from asking her to replay the event; the unlikely occurrence was not going to be made easier to understand for the number of times it was viewed.

'Is this some kind of hoax?' I wondered, aloud.

'It's no hoax,' Alex replied earnestly. 'I wondered the same thing. I have studied the time sequencing of every incidence and the file has definitely not been tampered with. I will bet my reputation on that. These things seem to just. . .' she baulked in continuing.

'Vanish,' I finished for her. 'How the hell is that possible? She looked up at me. 'And who has the technology?'

'Do me a favour and note the exact locations of these events.' I would normally never bring anyone along with me when inspecting the scene of a crime, but this was different. An extra pair of eyes might prove an advantage. 'And when you've done that, maybe you wouldn't mind accompanying me to inspect the scene? That is, if George doesn't have any objections?'

At the mention of an outing, her face had brightened, until she realised her boss would not permit it. 'I'm afraid he wouldn't like it, Mr Hardin.'

'Tell you what,' I said, feeling suddenly magnanimous, 'You find those locations and I'll sort it with Berringer. Okay?'

'Okay,' she beamed.

I found George in the staff lunch room making himself coffee. 'If you have finished with my girl,' he told me, 'I need her back. This is *her* job. I have better things to do than waste my time making coffee for myself.'

'Really?' I watched as he overfilled his cup, splattering the counter and his expensive clothes. There was no way I was going to ask his permission. He could make his own bloody coffees for a while longer.

'A while longer, George,' I told him, and left him dabbing up the spill with paper towel.

Warehouse-A dealt with appliances, motors, transmissions and spare parts for the same. Alex led us to the spot where we had witnessed a crated air-conditioner disappear. The position was still empty. There were no recent scrapes, no telltale black streaks where rubber souls had marked the surface as labourers struggled with the weight of it. For the next two and a half hours we dragged ourselves through warehouse after warehouse, viewing the sties where these events had taken place, and I was becoming more and more annoyed at the total lack of evidence of any kind. Not until, at the twenty second site of the day, a metal fastener was found, which had been used to secure the crate in which a stolen motorised cart had been. A puny piece of evidence which would probably amount to absolutely nothing, but it was something. It would, to my mind, tell me if some kind of powerful device had been employed in snatching the item, or if I was the butt of an elaborate hoax intended to waste my time and sully my reputation. At this point, anything was possible.

I had Alex accompany me to the science lab. George would just have to learn to make his expensive coffee without making a mess; and I didn't like to see her potential squandered by the arsehole. Besides, if it annoyed him, I was for it.

My opinion of miss Jordan was beginning to reform. In her early thirties I judged. A bright disposition, which, at her age, I might have expected to have eroded after spending time playing second fiddle to someone like George. Attractive too. No wedding band, intelligent, and as an off world employee of the company, probably without children.

While we waited for the analysis of the fastener I searched out and found somewhere to sit and talk for a while. A bench seat in the foyer served the purpose, so we grabbed a soft drink from a machine, seated ourselves, and I remained silent, waiting to see what she would do with a chance for conversation.

She seemed nervous at first, sipping the soda and glancing around at the first sign of movement. There was concern over a few pieces of lint on her navy dress, but after a couple of minutes she piped up.

'Are we believing what we saw on the video file?'
'What do you think happened?' I replied.
'It could have been doctored. An elaborate method of leading us in the wrong direction, but who would go to such trouble over a few odd items? Everyone here is

so busy with their work-a-day existence. Who could be bothered?'

'You said yourself that the videos were authentic,' I reminded her.

'Yes. Of course.'

'Consider for a moment that someone did exactly what we witnessed, and they were able to dissolve matter into nothing.'

'I didn't see it that way,' she admitted. 'Again with perceptions. I was thinking the objects were taken from one place and delivered to another. Not destructive, just a theft. Why would someone want to simply destroy these things? A demonstration, do you think?'

'It's a possibility.' I pulled a cigarette from my pocket and lit up. 'So, assuming what we saw was real, the possibilities are that it was done as a low key demonstration of a powerful tool, or a weapon, or it was as we first assumed. A bizarre robbery, pure and simple.'

'And if they can take things like that, they can just as easily help themselves to items of great value. So why everyday items and not precious metals, valuable stones?'

'That's an excellent question,' I responded. 'Do you think we would know about it if such a heist had taken place?'

'It would be embarrassing for the victim. Anyone entrusted with or owning highly valuable merchandise and having it swiped so easily? It could be devastating if news got out,' she correctly pointed out.

'When you're right, you're right. Now we have a wider field of speculation. If a moderate case of pilfering with such a small chance of being caught in the act is possible, the same applies for theft on a major scale.

Human nature dictates that the thieves would not risk detection for a smalltime job, not when big money is as easily obtained. They only need strike once, and be set for life.'

She made a face expressing puzzlement as she thought on it awhile. 'So. . . Someone is toying with security? Maybe a demonstration? Or are they just dumb?'

'I don't know,' I admitted, 'but the possibilities are what we have just mentioned. Dumb crooks with insufficient imagination to go for the big money. Someone far from dumb who is toying with us and demonstrating their technology. Or the somewhat incongruous situation of someone in need of the items they selected and unable to acquire then by other means.'

'This is fun,' she announced with a smile. 'Isn't it for you? Like a *whodunit*, using nothing but deductive reasoning. It's like one of those paperback novel detective stories.'

The remark surprised me. 'You don't read those things?'

'Of course not,' she responded indignantly. 'Chewing gum for the intellect. No. I only mean I enjoy the challenge. You must enjoy it. Why else would you do this work?'

'Why does anyone devote most of their life to jumping through hoops at the behest of others?'

'Is that how you see it?' she asked.

'Is there any other way? I suppose you're out here on the rim, working for the company for the joy of it.'

'Everyone has to work,' she retorted. 'Life is not a free ride.'

My communicator buzzed, indicating a message had arrived. The lab had finished the analysis.

'Hold that thought,' I told her. 'We can philosophize about life another time. Shall we see what has been learned from that fastener?'

The guy in the white lab coat said that what we had was a standard, hexagonal, metal alloy, boxing crate fastener. Nothing unusual. I had been hoping for something more, thinking that anything touched by a dematerializing energy field would leave its signature, but I was wrong about that and we were back to having nothing to go on, except for our theorizing about how and why these thefts were occurring. I organized for the areas where the items had been seen to disappear to be likewise analysed by the science boffins, but I held out little hope for anything like a result. For the remainder of the day I suggested to Alex that she go back to the office. For myself, a nap was in order, after which I intended going back to the Horizon, and to ascertain if my new chums could tell me anything about how one might obtain certain items otherwise precluded through normal channels.

It would be interesting to try and get hold of something from the list of stolen items. If the order came though, it was then just a simple matter to track it back along the supply chain to the source. Trouble was, it was an absurd list, and there was not a single thing on it which would make a blind bit of sense for me to order. Why were these items taken? I made myself comfortable on top of my bed and studied the list yet again.

One bobcat mini earthmover. Okay, so somebody wanted to shift a bunch of dirt. It has been known, but there was nothing around here coming close to terrain.

This was particularly interesting. Besides the fact that it would be next to impossible to hide a stolen bobcat anywhere on the platform, it was obviously intended to go somewhere it could be used. It had to be transported off of Far Reach, but how do you transport it when every craft into and out of the platform is company owned and under the gaze of company security? I struggled with that particular dilemma until my head began to hurt, and moved on, looking for some kind of pattern.

Two hundred chicken dinners with vegetables? Everyone eats.

No clue there. Next. . .

One Christmas tree. Why does one have a Christmas tree? To celebrate Christmas. A Christian holiday. One, single Christmas tree. Pass. . .

A two hundred metre roll of canvas. At least that made sense. Sort of. Canvas is useful. It can be used for various purposes. A ground sheet. To cover stuff, protecting it from weather etc. To provide people with temporary shelter from the elements, in the form of a tent. Canvas was eminently useful, and expensive. Especially out here. Next. . .

My alarm woke me. It was time for me to make my way to the hotel.

On the way over to the Horizon the absurdity of this whole situation impressed itself on me like a great weight pressing down. I was wasting my time with this meeting, I told myself. Nothing would come of it. I would insinuate that I was in need of one kind of contraband or another, and in the event of the deal being made I would find myself treading water while waiting for confirmation and eventual arrival of the goods. It would then be an uphill battle to convince these men to betray the supplier. It was a grubby plan and I wondered at my loss of perspective for ever having thought I could go through with it. The notion only augmented the sense of creeping self-doubt which had been dogging me since arriving on this pile of scrap iron. I had actually deceived myself into thinking it was okay to rope those guys in this way. There was a time I would never have hatched such an unimaginative and underhand tactic, let alone considered playing it out. Such tactics were the province of brutish and lazy coppers who were willing to step on anyone in the way, without regard for their circumstances.

Maybe I had been in this game too long. I had only gone this route because I had a natural talent for sniffing out fraud and outright brigands, and because of my intense dislike of those who saw themselves as being above the rest of us; somehow special, able to do and take as they pleased, with the cost impacting on the little guy, and without earning what they had because the system greased the wheels for those in position and with privilege while putting the screws on those doing the grunt work. All this was for nothing, it dawned on me then. I had strayed so far off track with this case. Gone totally in the wrong direction.

'Blast!' I growled, pulling up in mid stride, and in the process drawing unwanted attention to myself as those around me glanced to see what was up.

3

UNEXPECTED

Eight hours later and I was sat on a packing crate, concealed in the near total darkness of warehouse-A, where the majority of the thefts had occurred. In my mind I had been running through my previous conversations with Alex. She had noticed these occurrences tended to fall within a particular time frame; during the third work shift, and significantly so. Sheer frustration had lead me to come here and sit in the darkness, watching for anything untoward. It was definitely a symptom of my frustration with the lack of progress, but it beat the hell out of twisting my brain, trying to reason my way to an answer with far too few threads of information and not even a good working hypothesis of what was going on here. It may have looked like clutching at straws, and the odds were astronomically against the chance of me witnessing anything useful, but it was something; and, hell, if nothing else it served to reduce my ever growing sense of futility and mounting frustration.

The hours oozed past like molasses on a cold winter's day. I thought about Detective Sergeant Burt Emerson;

whether he was making any effort to track down those responsible for the increasing discomfort in my abdomen. With so little to go on, I figured the incident had already been pushed to the back burner. Apart from the pieces of lead they had cut out of me, there was precious little else to go on. Another cold case, but at least there was no corpse this time. That was the single positive, so far.

I thought about junior officer Andy Saunders, Emerson's offsider. He was at the beginning of his career; a baby-faced, no nothing beginner; a greenhorn with no idea how much the job would change him as the years slid implacably by. If I gave a damn I would sit him down, warn him of the relentlessly long hours of tangled and conflicting emotions which turned a man to stone while his family gradually learned that the acts of violence and human degradation he dealt with, day in day out, were slowly but surely going to take precedence until nothing recognisable remained of the man they once knew as husband and father.

I thought about Joe Higgins, head administrator. The boss man and king of the heap. A man who had worked his way up from almost nothing at all through focus of will and dint of hard work. In the end he knew more about this place than those who envisioned, designed, financed and built it. It was he who breathed life into it, made it function by precise coordination, careful distribution of power and responsibility, by the planning of interrelated, co-dependant ancillaries from exploration, mineral ore testing and cost assessment, retrieval, refinement, delivery and all in between, including allocation of man hours and overall expenditure. That men like this existed at all, to me seemed a freak of nature, but without them places like this just would not function. And his reward? Satisfying his need for control and the pursuit of perfection, and doubtlessly culminating in an early grave.

I thought about Security Chief George Berringer; an egotistical arsehole who thinks life is a competition, thereby missing the point entirely. When he was young, for him it was all about who was the cleverest, who made the most money, who had the prettiest girl, the best car. Bragging rights. We were friends, once, but it was he who pulled away, considering me to be below par as far as friends go. He was so caught up in trying to prove himself superior in every way, he never really made a single, meaningful connection with another human being. Poor George. I actually pitied the man more than I ever resented his intolerable superciliousness.

How much time had passed? I wondered. Looking at my watch would either disappoint or surprise. I would avoid the disappointment. My experience was that time moved faster in the dark than in the light. I had been here a couple of hours, I guessed. The alarm would alert me when six hours had elapsed and I would decide whether or not to stay longer then.

I recalled suggesting to Alex Jordan that everyone was corruptible, depending only on the price, and the look on her face the comment had provoked. In that very moment I had considered if I wasn't saying something about myself, that I too was corruptible, and for the first time in an age I had felt uncomfortable under another human being's gaze. Why the hell would I care what she thought? Someone like her would have very little life experience by comparison. I had seen things that had made grown men reel; experienced situations so far removed from what everyday folk had to confront or would believe possible, it had forever eclipsed in me whatever faith in human nature might have existed. I had once believed in the existence of beauty and meaning in life, but that was long ago. We had almost killed our planet, and ourselves. We were no different now. We survived because we were too frightened to die, not because of any altruistic revelation we may have experienced. Even now, who's to say we have made it. Our basic nature has not changed; it still exists, and it will corrupt and infect whatever place in the cosmos we come to occupy.

What was that? Did I hear something? Perhaps not.

I pulled a cigarette from my pocket. When the lighter ignited a face appeared up close in front of me, startling me so much that I nearly fell off the crate I was sitting on.

'Holy shit!'

Alex stifled a giggle. 'I didn't mean to catch you unawares. Sorry.

I brought you some coffee.' 'How did you find me?'

'Simple,' she responded. 'It's what I expected you do after being shown the cluster of occurrences.'

'And you reasoned I would be here, this exact place, now, tonight,' I stated dubiously.

I couldn't see her face in the darkness, but if I could I would have expected to see the nervous look of someone caught in an untruth. There was slightly more to it than she was admitting. She had gone to some trouble to home in on my whereabouts, but I let it go. There were several reasons why she might have done this, and none of them sinister.

'Are you terribly annoyed?' she asked in a small voice.

My internal radar flashed, *warning*. Was she coming-on to me? 'Did you bring two cups?' I replied, avoiding. 'And keep your

voice low, if you must talk.

This was the absolute last thing I would have expected, but she had been enthusiastic about the case right from the start. The endless routine of assisting someone of Berringer's calibre would cause anybody to crave a distraction. I guessed she found it to be a pleasant change from the dreary norm.

She had indeed brought two cups. I lit another cigarette and we sat in silence for a time, sipping, peering into the darkness. In a moment she reached for my wrist, causing me to flinch, but she only wanted to check the time.

'Is there somewhere you have to be?' I asked.

'No.' There was another long silence, until she asked, 'Could I have a cigarette?'

'You smoke? I thought I was the last person in the universe who smoked. Cocaine addicts get more respect than smokers.'

'Nicotine. It's an excellent stimulant,' she replied, 'and relaxing at the same time. It also helps to focus the mind. Tell me of another substance which does all that.'

'I agree,' I told her, pulling a cigarette from my pocket and holding it out in her direction. She located my hand, took it from my grasp, and I lit it for her.

'You never told me you were a police detective before coming to work for the company. Did Universal X recruit you?'

'I quit the force, then quickly discovered it was all I really knew. This job seemed a good fit. What about you? Have you always worked for Berringer?'

'God, no. The very thought of the idea. He doesn't know it yet, but I'm about to move on.'

'Really? Where to?' I asked.

'My first love was anthropology. *Xenoanthropology*, now. But I'm interested to know more about you, Mr Hardin.'

'How about we move to first name status? Call me Jack, why don't you?'

'Jack is a twist on John, or Jonathan, isn't it?'

'Not this time. Jack is the name on my birth registry. Jack Hardin.

No middle name.'

'I'm plain old Alex. Alexandra, actually, but Alex is preferable.

Why did you quit the force?'

'Why *xenoanthropology*?' I returned. I was not going there. 'And does it mean what it seems to imply? The study of other than human culture?'

'That's right. The study of alien culture.'

'Not exactly in high demand, I would imagine.'

'Not yet,' she answered. 'What time is it, please, Jack?'

I looked at my chronometer. 'It is exactly two minutes since the last time you checked. What's the obsession with time, tonight? You have a hot date or something?'

'Actually,' she replied with humour in her voice, 'you're not far off the mark.' She switched on a torch she had brought along, aiming it at the floor of the empty storage compartment beside us. With her other hand she reached into her pocket, withdrew something I couldn't make out. Then there was the distinctive click of a hammer being cocked into firing position, and things became quite tense quite quickly.

'Please step into that spot—' and she indicated where by moving the beam in a circular motion.

I then noticed how fuzzy everything seemed to be getting. I was becoming unsteady on my feet. She had put something in the damn coffee. How stupid could I be?

'Why don't you sit on the floor before you fall, Jack? I don't want you hurting yourself. And, please, don't worry. Everything's fine. There's something I want you to see.'

I moved to lower myself to the floor as she suggested. 'I don't get it,' I said. 'Why?'

As the question was given voice the air around us began to glisten and tremble. Alex moved quickly to sit on the floor beside me, and a second later a brilliant white flash filled my world.

*

Trans-spatial Migration is a technology humans had dreamt of for hundreds of years. All I knew was that it required the understanding of mass and energy being fundamentally the same thing. Only the scientists of my time familiar with temporal field dynamics and quantum reciprocal action duality ever pretended to understand the basic theory behind the phenomenon; but that was to be in the future.

The experience of *travelling* by this method is much the same as being put under general anaesthetic prior to an operation. A great black void opens up, swallowing a person whole. There is no sense of being, no sense of time, only the unsettling feeling that this must be what death feels like. A wholly disquieting experience, and I always hated travelling that way; but then travelling is not quite the appropriate word.

When I awoke I was on my back and staring vacantly upward. Sky, I guessed. Was that blue sky? I could not see anything clearly. My mind would not connect in any meaningful way with a single thing at that moment. An odd-looking creature was leaning over me, babbling something absurd and unrecognisable even as words. My eyes were capable of rolling about in their orbits, which they did to the great distress of my stomach, which felt as if it hadn't taken food in over a week.

I was in a white room which might have passed for a ship's medical treatment room; sparsely furnished and containing three narrow metal cots fixed to the wall, illumination coming from all around but nowhere in particular. On the bed beside me lay Alex. On her face she wore what I presumed to be an oxygen mask, and not until then did I realise that I did too. I was extremely enervated and beyond even thinking of climbing to my feet.

The second time I woke I was feeling much better. Alex was recently up and on her feet, swaying slightly and regarding me while holding on to a metal rail for support.

'You drugged me,' I stated accusingly, suddenly remembering what had occurred prior to my turning up here. The mask over my lower face muffled my speech, so I removed it and said again:

'You bloody drugged me, woman. Are you deranged?

An opened, arched doorway behind her presented a view of outdoors; somewhat desolate looking, with a clear, pale blue sky overhead, and what looked to be low, scrubby vegetation in the distance.

'I had no real option,' she replied. 'I know your reputation and you would have found out eventually anyway. I couldn't allow the company to become aware. And the transportation process required that you be still. I didn't know how you would respond, and the last thing I wanted was for you to be hurt during the process. Are you alright?'

I explored that topic by sitting up, letting my legs dangle over the edge of the cot as I located and tested the rest of my extremities.

'I seem to be all here,' I told her. 'Wherever here is. I'm not sure I *want* to know the answer to that right now, though. Is the answer likely to piss me off even more than I am already?

'What?' I replied to the coy expression on Alex's face.

She sat on the edge of the cot and regarded me thoughtfully. 'I'm actually taken aback by how well you are taking this. Thank-you for not exploding. I was frightened. I thought for sure you would react far worse than this.'

I managed a thin smile. 'Why? Would it help? She shrugged. 'No.'

Right then a tall, blue skinned, humanoid creature appeared in the doorway. It stood there regarding the two of us with mild interest for a moment, and ambled off unconcernedly.

'What was that?' I asked, as evenly as I was able to.

'You mean, *Who was that*? That was Dortl Karp, Fernac's offspring.

I remained silent awhile, processing. 'Where are we and how did we get here?'

'How did we get here? They call it something totally unpronounceable, but if I had to translate, and I've thought about this, I call it trans-spatial migration. It's kind of a clumsy name, and doesn't describe the process well, but it's the best I can do. They tried to explain it to me and I didn't understand. These are incredibly intelligent people, Jack, with aeons longer gene pool than mankind. Their brain is far a superior. I cannot communicate with them in their way. They have a basic language structure which they can use, but it is beyond me. They quickly learned to communicate with me by learning my language in short time. They communicate with one another telepathically, but they can communicate with us using a mixture of words and what telepathy can be filtered through our encephalon, or central nervous system. It works sufficiently well to communicate most things.'

'I still don't understand how I got here, but I'll put that aside for now,' I relented. 'Where am I? is more important to me right now.'

'A little known world called Ki Kassini, and that is only an approximation of the name they call it. It's an unnamed planet on the extreme outer edge of our galaxy. I mean, little known to them, and totally unknown to us. They're marooned here.'

'They're marooned here?'

Alex nodded. 'Something vital broke on their ship. Serious enough so that they had to land and try to make repairs.'

'How the hell did you end up befriending them?' I asked. 'We're a very long way from Far Reach.'

'When the missing inventory first came to my attention, I did as you did. I staked out the warehouse. They were actually entering the warehouses, personally, taking what they needed to aid their survival. In all the confusion of the unplanned confrontation, they brought me back here to explain, hoping to avoid frightening the wits out of me and gaining my confidence. I guess they were lucky. They gained an ally. I would never jeopardise their desire for anonymity.'

'Bringing me here was your idea of concealing their existence?

Are you sure this was your smartest move?'

'No, not entirely. I could see things getting way out of control, though. If you had reported back to the company that things were disappearing—I mean *actually* disappearing!—there would be no way of putting the genie back in the bottle. Things would have gotten way out of hand. These people do not want to be humanity's introduction to extraterrestrial life. They just want to be left alone, to make their repairs and get off of this barren, inhospitable planet. They're such shy creatures.'

I raised my hand, halting the flow of information. 'You must know how difficult it is, trying to take all of this in. It's actually making my head spin.'

'No. That's the atmosphere here. It happened to me, too. It takes a little while to get used to the lower oxygen content of the air. I do appreciate how difficult it is to swallow all of this. It kind of shakes one's foundations. It did with me.'

'It does put a new slant on things,' I admitted. 'There's a sort of pervasive unreality, right now. And before you say it, no, it's not oxygen deprivation. It's more the same feeling as when you're told at age seven that your parents are getting divorced. Like that. World altering.'

'That happened to you?' she replied, almost sympathetic. 'No. It's just a analogy.'

'Oh, right. Yes, I see what you mean. Good analogy.'

'So, are you going to show me around this place? Introduce me to your friends?'

4

THE JHAI

The craft comprised a large, dome-topped, flat-bottomed cylinder as a central hub, circled by seven similarly shaped dome topped cylinders of slightly smaller volume. I've seen jelly moulds of similar shape. Some of Alex's *friends* gathered around as we left the confines of the craft via the opened archway, and we all stood, facing one other.

They were, I thought, aesthetically pleasing to the eye: light-blue, of slender build and a half metre taller than myself; baldheaded, three fingered, cloven footed and with all the usual sense organs and orifices incorporated into the head and face, as it is with us, though significantly smaller and less prominent, making them appear friendly and innocuous. The eyes were almond shape, black and large, pupils circular with green irises, shrunken extremely small in the brightness of the day. Their demeanour was nothing beyond calm, relaxed and curious as Alex presented me to the small gathering, waving her hand in my direction and saying, 'My friend, Jack Hardin.'

That was it. Introductions made, the circle parted to allow us freedom of movement.

'Come on,' she said, 'and I'll show you around the place.'

The encampment was situated atop of a rise, with a flat, wide expanse surrounding. What vegetation there was grew low to the ground. Shrubs, miniature trees, a kind of purplish grass that snaked over the compacted, dry, brown earth.

A series of jerry rigged sunshades encircled a large open fireplace. The shades, constructed of rope, canvas and steel poles were the obvious proceeds from the great warehouse caper.

'Starting to make sense now?' she asked.

'It is,' I answered, and pointed to the Christmas tree standing in front of one of the makeshift shelters. 'But hardly a necessity.'

'The children like pretty things,' she explained. 'That would account for the kilo of boiled lollies.'

'Actually, no. the boiled sweets are a favourite of the adults. The children don't like sweet things. I had to warn the adults of possible damage their teeth, but they appear to be impervious to tooth decay. Tooth decay, bacterial and viral infection, run of the mill illnesses as we experience are unknown to them. They have an incredible natural resilience to such things. Their immune system is a wonder.'

'Half their luck,' I replied, aware that my wound had begun throbbing painfully once again. 'Let's sit for a while,' I suggested.

Over the edge of the hill I caught sight of a construction site. A large quantity of earth had been gouged out and sealed with polycrete; the bobcat earthmoving machine parked alongside. The sides of the hill had been fashioned into tilted terraces in hope of channelling rainfall, directing it into the newly constructed dam with barely three inches of water contained.

'How badly is their ship damaged?' I asked. 'It looks to me they expect to be here for some time to come.'

'A vital component,' she answered. 'Do you know what a bio data processor is?'

I shook my head. 'Never heard of one.'

'Apparently there are several of them throughout the ships nervous system, like small brains that monitor and regulate the vast number of systems and energy flow. There are a number of small ones that maintain running temperatures, engine functions and like that, but it's their guidance and astronavigation bio processor. They cannot navigate without a replacement. They would quickly become lost among the stars.'

'That would be a problem,' I accepted. 'But I'm surprised to find they're so in need of water. They have a craft capable of interstellar travel. Distances which, presumably, would take considerable time to travel, and they don't have the necessary water aboard? I remember protein concentrate being on the list of stolen goods. Why would they be so ill prepared?'

'Don't ask me,' she responded, studying me closely. 'Why, you're not suspicious, are you? Questioning their sincerity, why they're here? Why they're raiding our supplies? Because, it's obvious, just looking around, to see that these people are in a bind.'

Until Alex asked the question I was only allowing my mind to follow its natural trajectory, as is its nature.

But there was merit in the asking, I had to admit. It didn't add up terribly well, that a space faring people would so easily get themselves marooned on a backwater planet, finding themselves so ill equipped to deal with a not completely unforeseeable event such as a breakdown. Just how intelligent were these *people*?

'Exactly how well do you know them?' I asked.'

'I've been visiting for maybe six months, bringing a few supplies every so often. I've been here probably twelve times and I've gotten to know them quite well.'

'Hence your little joke about being an exoanthropologist?'

'Xenoanthropology, actually,' she corrected.'No joke, and I'll be able to write one hell of a paper on the Jhai.'

'That's what they're called. The *Jhai*? I thought they wished to remain anonymous? In any case, you must be aware of the risk you would be running.'

'What risk is that?' she asked.

'The most obvious of them all. The risk of you being branded a fruitcake, unless these guys don't mind you taking a few happy snaps for your scrapbook. And that I somehow doubt.'

She turned away from the view to regard me anew. 'You are one cynical man, Jack Hardin. How did that happen?'

'People are shaped by the lives they lead,' I answered.

'Yes,' she responded, thoughtfully. 'That is very true. I would give anything to escape the life I currently lead. People get trapped, I think. by their own inertia.'

'Pithy.'

'Pithy?!' she repeated. I couldn't tell if she was offended or amused.

'What?' I responded. 'You don't like *pithy?* It is. What you said was pithy. An accurate and weighty observation stated in few words. Is that not pithy?'

'I thought you were making fun of me, the way you do. You weren't?' She regarded me with obvious suspicion.

'No. Honestly, I wasn't.' The incident suddenly struck me as funny. I began laughing, which didn't appear to help.

She jabbed me in the ribs, hard, enough elicit a painful cry. 'You really have no idea how to be a human being, do you?'

She regarded me angrily, but I had no idea why. I also had no idea why I was feeling the way I did or what that feeling was; why I felt anything at all, and for the moment I became distracted by the anomaly.

We resumed walking the circuit of the settlement. On the far side of the encampment, the aliens, these Jhai, had attempted to implement the growing of basic food crops, sowing cereals such as corn and wheat; the seed, no doubt, obtained from Far Point, but nothing had survived to harvest. What small amount of seasonal rainfall there was had been far too minimal and all their attempts at farming had failed. The small amount of available rainfall had necessarily been retained for personal use.

By the time we arrived back where we had begun, a couple of the group had returned with a batch of freshly killed small animals, not dissimilar to rabbits. We were invited to sit near the fire pit, on a mound of earth covered with soft grasses bundled and loosely tied, providing a comfortable position to sit. A pair of the adolescents busied themselves with preparing the kill, and then placing the prepared meat, suspended in a rack, to cook over the searing heat of the coals.

Alex turned to me, saying, 'We have been invited to share the meal and stay the night. Would you like to?'

I hadn't camped out since I was a child. The idea quite appealed to me, and how many could say they had attended a barbeque hosted by extraterrestrial aliens?

'Why not?' I answered, after thinking on it a short while. 'I've nothing special to do, and I must say I'm not exactly keen to make the return trip.'

'Don't worry. I should have told you, the body quickly adjusts to the method of travel. The next time won't be nearly so bad. After that, it's nothing at all.'

'When did we receive this invitation?'

Alex nodded to one standing within the group. 'Maja, the elder,' she replied. 'I receive the invitation telepathically as we returned from your tour.'

'Am I to be subjected to this mind reading lark? I don't much like the idea.'

'No, Jack. You have to remember, they're born with the ability.

It's not the novelty it is to you and me. They could care less what is on your mind, and common courtesy forbids encroachment on your privacy.'

'Very glad to hear it.' I said, relieved. 'I can only imagine where my mind might stray if I thought I was being read like a book. You know what I mean?'

She nodded, smiled broadly. 'I know exactly. They were quick to reassure me that no such incursion on your privacy would take place, and they are as good as their word. Lies are as foreign to them as calculus to is a chimpanzee.'

When the *rabbit* was cooked it was shared among all, along with an assortment of indigenous nuts and berries, and washed down by sweetened, instant coffee, once again courtesy of the company. We were left to our own devices throughout, and I found it a pleasant departure from the human norm, where mealtimes are often full of needless chatter while trying to eat in peace.

The air did not become chill as I had expected with the loss of daylight, but remained comfortably warm; and as the evening progressed our hosts dutifully cleaned up the area before silently wandering away, presumably to their beds and a good night's sleep. For myself, I was far from tired. The day had been full of puzzles and surprises which had served only to stimulate the mental processes to a level of heightened activity. Sleep would be difficult after a day like this.

With the gradual loss of illumination from our local star, starlight from the more distant sources gradually strengthened until the night sky fairly blazed. In addition, a pair of small moons popped up, one after the other, augmenting the soft, milk-white illumination over the entire landscape. It was quite a site. Enchanting even, and with every shape being silhouetted by the light pouring down from above, the overall effect reminded me very much of something one would find in a children's fiction storybook.

'This is too good a night to waste,' Alex. 'If you're up to it, how about another stroll? If you're tired, it's okay. I'm happy to-'

'Don't be silly,' she cut me off. 'I agree. It's a beautiful night. It would be a crime to waste a night like this.'

I would have been disappointed if she had declined. There were simply too many unresolved questions circling in my mind; and damn it if there wasn't something else simmering there—simmering like a cauldron full of secrets and delicate, tantalizing morsels which could not have been better contrived to elicit a response from someone such as I. It takes many years of effort and repeated failure to insulate a human heart; a lifetime of struggles and disappointments before a man at last wises up, finally telling himself that the pursuit of happiness is only for fools who are prepared to lie to themselves and buy into the illusion that we are all worthy of love and fulfilment, and that one day it will come. If I had been honest with myself I would have seen the signs and turned away in time, but even I am susceptible. Something within deceived me, blinding me to the subtle indicators, somehow causing me to ignore the hard lessons I had learned and thought I had learned well. I can only take solace in the fact that it was Nature's primal edict that brought me undone; it was not entirely my own fault. Nature leaves a chink in the armour of all men. The genetic imperative will not be ignored, but all this is revealed now as a matter of hindsight, and far too late to alter the flow of events as they implacably unfold along the endless chain of cause and effect.

It is true that the human brain is especially adept at recognising emerging patterns in nature and the environment in general. For me, the ability is augmented for some reason, and this is specifically why I have become so proficient at my work; but it is also my curse. My mind has always sought to recognise and distinguish order, structure and meaning, from the truly exceptional to the countless occurrences of seemingly random everyday events. I was once told, by company psychologists, that this was my talent; those who were ultimately responsible for my being hired some several years ago. Patterns and repetitions emerge when the human brain has observed its environment over a sufficient span of time, and before too many years have passed there is so much that has been detected and accumulated, eventually there is *only* the continued repetition and the predictable patterns; imitation of form and event, as if life is intent on parodying itself, day after day, without end. For someone having such dismal expectations and a jaded world view as myself, the result is a kind of slow descent into an absurdity beyond description; a kind of living hell where the future stretches interminably on without feature, without contrast, and without a single thing to suggest that any of this might conceivably undergo change.

Life just becomes predictable, and the same must be said of my view of human nature. I had reached something of an impasse long ago, needing to revisit what it feels like, the thrill and novelty of the unexpected, of finding something truly unpredictable—something new, surprising, pleasant, refreshing—something hopeful. Although I knew it not, the die had been cast, and my life, such as it was and had been, would be unalterably transformed.

'It would be a crime to waste a night like this,' Alex had said.

In this light I suddenly realised that Alex was an attractive woman.

Her shoulder length, auburn hair framed the well-formed and attractive features of her smiling face. The elegantly formed contours of her neck and shoulders presenting an eminently feminine package. How had I not noticed?

'There's a spot not far from here,' she said, standing, stretching out the stiffness in her legs, back and shoulders. 'Shall we?' she invited.

We covered a considerable distance while she told me what she knew of the Jhai. Their species had also reached a crisis point in their development. A situation not dissimilar to ours, but they had been smart enough never to allow their population to grow so ridiculously large so that it would endanger the biosphere to the same degree. Forward thinking allowed them to plan well into the future, and the populating of exoplanets presented itself as a perfect solution, both to providing impetus for scientific advancement and relieving pressure on planetary resources. In just a few generations space travel had become almost mundane; their already highly advanced sciences striving and providing every amenity until the species became much more the itinerant, space oriented travellers than the sedentary planet dwellers of their beginnings. It was a fascinating story. The revolutionary change had been made thousands of years ago, and since then, their species had been able to devote all of their lives to exploring and expanding their knowledge of the cosmos. The lifestyle had also expanded their concept of existence and their philosophical nature. I must admit to being impressed, but also more than a little ashamed. By comparison we were fools. I guess I had always considered us that, but to be confronted by a race who, by all reports, had handled their affairs so much better than we had, it augmented my already heightened sense of human beings being dull-witted to the point of near extinction.

'What must they think of us?' I commented, as we skirted the top edge of the hill overlooking the moonlit, blue veldt.

'They consider us to be children,' Alex replied. '*Spoiled* children, in fact. In their travels they have scarce seen a planet as abundant in the variety of life and of natural resources combined on a single planet. They see the fact that we have despoiled what we were given, when our only responsibility had been that we cherish and safeguard its value and rarity.'

'Yes. That's exactly it, isn't it? They must be angry.'

'Not at all,' Alex replied. 'Not at all angry, but certainly saddened. They very much prize and appreciate individuality. They have a strong appreciation for beauty. An artistic sensibility, do you understand? There's not a bit of resentment—not a single negative facet to them, as best I can tell. Perhaps saddened isn't quite the word. Disappointed, perhaps.'

'Is there a difference?'

Alex shrugged. 'A little, but my point is, there's no animosity about it. No resentment. Not that I can detect, anyway. I don't think they know what resentment is.'

I nodded. 'It's to be expected, I guess. It would be difficult to be small-minded when the universe is your backyard.'

'That's true,' she said, halting as we neared the campsite once more. 'Why don't we sit here awhile?' She indicated the grassy embankment beside us. 'My legs are getting a little weary,' she explained.

We reclined on the slope, taking in the view. In a moment a soft, warm, breeze arrived, its progress was marked by the movement of gently rising pockets of dust across the plain. In the far distance was heard a raucous screeching noise.

'Some kind of night bird,' she answered, without being asked.

I continued to soak in the pleasant atmosphere of the night. The twin moons were high in the sky now, their radiance soft and easy on the eye so that I could easily make out peaks and valleys etched into their surface.

'It's pleasant here,' she said, quietly, and her voice was as soft and warm as the lambent light filtering down from the moons in the sky. My senses felt heightened, as if perfectly attuned to this world, and there was a clarity of mind seldom experienced. 'It is,' I agreed. 'Very peaceful. Very pleasant.'

Her scent was in the air, and her proximity began to impress itself heavily on me. I wondered if she was feeling it too.

Her hand reached out and touched my own, and the current flowed with a force too great to offer any resistance against it.

'Jack,' she almost whispered, her voice laden with something resembling desire and poignancy.

In her eyes I saw reflected the flame of passion I felt rising in myself, and she came to me, an exquisite angel wrapped within the balmy softness of the night—a long, warm, wonderful night which wrapped us both inside its powerful, timeless spell.

We woke some hours before dawn, at the bottom of the slope, still wrapped together, and in the remainder of the night Alex lead me to her quarters; a compartment within the ship the Jhai had made comfortable for her, with an bed of ample girth to sleep in. There we once again entwined until sleep overtook us.

5

SMOKE AND MIRRORS

I woke feeling as good as I could remember feeling for a very long time, and I was in no particular hurry to climb out of bed, especially when lying beside me was this gorgeous creature. How had I gotten so lucky? I was forced to ask myself, but the question evaporated the moment her eyes fluttered open and she beamed that smile at me.

'Is it the morning already?'She moaned softly, and extended an arm across me. '*Hmm*, what a night,' she purred.

We lay that way, me on my back, her on her side, cuddled up close with her arm over me, and at that moment the world in which I lived seemed so alien to me. Why was I doing what I was doing? I was the *fix-it guy* for the company; I had been the fix-it guy for as long as I cared to remember, and I had no real identity of my own beyond that. Should I cease being a part of Universal X tomorrow, what would I have? No home, no real place of origin even. I would be adrift as much as it is possible for a man to be. At nearly forty years-of-age most men had a family and were happy to have one, putting

[212]

their energies and resources into keeping them safe from harm, fed, well educated, enough at least to prepare them for the world as it is, equipped well enough to squeeze the most out of what is left to enjoy. But then, perhaps having children was not such a wise thing. Society was not like it once was; the pressure is on from an early age to slot into the positions society has earmarked for every individual from the moment they are assessed at age five. Not like it was when I was growing up. At that time there was still the chance of determining one's own future and pursuing whatever it was that gave the most joy and satisfaction. It was possible just to follow a direction for the amusement value of it, to experiment and find one's own feet, unlike today. If things change—if we make it past this period of great urgency—then would be the time for raising a family. A man should have a son, I figured. A son to carry on the bloodline. An old fashioned notion these days, but what did life add up to if the genetic line were to end? A life should count for something. There should be a legacy, something positive left behind to say, *I was here and this is my mark. The world is a better place for my having existed.*

'What are you thinking about,' Alex asked, eyes still closed. 'What makes you think I'm thinking about anything?'

'You're very still, and I know you are still awake. What are you thinking about?' She pinched me. 'Come on, spill it mister.'

I pulled her to me and we were both laughing, until she locked her gaze to mine, as if attempting to stare into my inner being. Her eyes were brown, flecked with gold;

pools of loveliness and longing. 'Something is troubling you, Jack. I can tell.'

I wanted to lie to her, tell her, *nothing in particular. About you, about last night,* but I couldn't. Something had happened last night and it was continuing this morning. Something special, and I didn't want to ruin it.

'I was thinking about who I am, and that I am little more than the job that I do. How, suddenly, it's not enough any more.'

'Don't you dare go thinking any such thing, Jack Hardin. You're something very special and don't you forget it. You are a highly respected man and your reputation causes people to take notice whenever they hear your name mentioned.' She wrapped herself around me and planted a kiss, long and so full of wonderful that it made my head spin.

'I think I'm oxygen deprived again,' I told her, rolling my eyes affectedly.

Again she hugged me more tightly, and sighing, said, 'I don't want to get up. Let's just lay here in bed together, and let the world pass us by. We owe it nothing.'

'That would be nice,' I agreed, saying nothing to counter the notion. If only that were possible, I was thinking. If only both our whereabouts weren't the business of the company and we were able do as we pleased.

We pretended that time didn't matter and made no mention of obligation or commitment, tacitly agreeing to make this blissful hiatus last as long as we dare.

We continued to talk, for hours, getting to know one other as best we could in what time we had. Alex came from an academic family. Her father had been a professor of physics and astro sciences, in Geneva, Switzerland, no less, with her mother, a high up in the medical profession, leading the latest, cutting edge round of testing for cancer antigens. A cure for cancer was still the holy grail of the medical world. Alex had not specialised in anything, making sure she got as broad an education as she was able to, until she discovered whatever it might be that she found the most interest in. Coming to work out on the rim was just another stab in the dark. She thought maybe working out here in space would provide the spark of certainty she was looking for, leading to something she could sink her teeth into. She discovered exobiology by chance, but there was no chance of pursuing the subject professionally. Xenoanthropology had presented itself by sheer fluke, and she embarked on a singlehanded study of the Jhai after she had met them for the first time.

My own history was not nearly as gratifying. My father had been a cop; an overworked cop with a drinking problem, who took his endless grievances out on my mother. He was shot and killed by a teenager when he accidentally walked into a robbery in progress at the corner store. My mother died a year later, when I was fifteen, and I have been making my own way ever since. Not an impressive legacy, but with whatever natural talents I possessed, at least I had cut out a path for myself.

Time inevitably began to run short. We emerged to find a few of the Jhai hauling a machine into the belly of their ship and I figured the least I could do in return for their hospitality of the previous evening was to pitch in and help.

Upon enquiring what the machine was, I received a pictorial display flashing through my mind. The sensation caused me to start, a reaction the Jhai seemed excited about. Back-slapping apparently is a universal gesture, and I received a thorough pounding. The image I received suggested that the machine drew energy directly from the ether. I asked Alex to translate for me. She obliged by calling it a dark energy converter.

My interest in their vessel incited an impromptu guided tour. The one called Dortl Karp, who I had learned to be Fernac's offspring, took it upon himself to do his best to describe what I saw. There were such things as stasis chambers, where, on long voyages, they could place themselves in a sort of suspended condition where somatic activity could be slowed to avoid the passing of time while another function provided direct input to the brain. This provided input to the mental faculties, allowing data on any subject to be uploaded and ready for referencing upon arrival at whatever destination. There were the expected navigation and piloting consoles, food preparation areas and a few creature comforts. The engine bay, however, was a totally sealed unit and impossible to view. Cracking the seal of the engine incasement was not a wise action, I was informed by a mental depiction of humanoid figures being blasted by some form of radiation.

They were particularly keen to direct my attention to the topic of something translating to *bio data processing*. The Jhai used DNA sequencing breeding techniques to grow actual organic neurons to regulate ship functions, just as the brain and connected nervous system run and regulate the human body. The ship was part machine, part animal, with neural processors acting as a self-protecting system. It was capable of taking total control of a long range, beyond light speed voyage without any need for a Jhai pilot to lift a finger. A destination was simply chosen and the bio processors would handle every facet of the voyage, including course corrections, using star recognition and pulsar triangulation. Bio processors were also employed in handling any emergency which may arise. At beyond light speed, processing any correction or initiating collision avoidance procedure needed to be lightning fast, involving intuitive, preemptive action, I was told. Only bio-processors were up to the task, and they were installed in many vital positions around the ship, similar to the plexus or nerve clusters of an animal body. The ship taught me that we humans had a very long road to travel before safe and sufficiently speedy navigation of astronomical distances would be within our reach. In short, it was a technological marvel. It turned out to be a damaged one of these bioprocessing plexus things which had necessitated their making the emergency landing on Ki Kassini; and they were not going anywhere until a replacement had been found. Where they would find such a thing was beyond me, but they seemed confident that one was about to become available. With their faculty for genetic engineering I supposed they were in the process of growing the replacement.

Alex tugged at my elbow. 'Come on, Jack. I hate to say it, but we're probably stretching our luck. Perhaps we ought to be getting back.'

'This is incredibly interesting,' I told her and our hosts, 'Thanks guys. This has been a blast. I can't tell you how fascinating, but I'm afraid we really must go. I'm looking forward to coming back, if that's okay?'

I received another round of back-slapping, which I assumed meant that my returning was fine with them.

We travelled back to Far Point. The second trip, as Alex had promised, being appreciably easier on me than the first time, but now I had a problem. From my standpoint the case was solved. The mystery of where the missing items had gone and who was responsible for the thefts was no more, only, I could not report a word of it. Not without revealing the Jhai's existence; and not being able to resolve the situation for the company would result in a sizeable black mark being placed on my record. I would not have come back here except for the fact that my absence for any appreciable time would produce curiosity, especially in the mind of the security boss, George Berringer. I decided I could keep him at arms length for as long as I needed to. He knew how I worked, but raising suspicion in his mind was not a good idea right now. When I am assigned a case, I am generally left to my own devices until a resolution is reached. I simply hand in my detailed report, *on high*, scribble a rough outline to whoever needs to know, locally; aside from George that would only include Joe Higgins at Administration, and then I would be clear to get the hell out. That was not going to happen this time. Things had gotten suddenly quite complicated. I had never not concluded an assignment, not in all my years of service. How I was going to account for the loss of goods and materials, I had no idea, and the question was going to plague me until an answer was arrived at. I knew that much, for sure, but it wasn't the first time I had found myself in a spot. I could mope around in my room puzzling over it, or I could get out and about. From experience, getting out and about is the best option. Interacting with the world provides both the necessary distraction I needed to distance myself from the problem for a while, and it exposes one to myriad esoteric bits of information and random stimuli from which a glimmer of a solution might be discovered. To that end I showered, redressed my wound and set off toward the centre of town. Besides, for some unknown reason I had woken with the desire for chicken chow mein.

The place felt different, no doubt in light of what had occurred over the last twenty four hours. Just being here, the pretense of it, made me uneasy. The chef at the Horizon sated my desire for chicken chow mein, which I washed down with a beer at the front bar.

On the spur of the moment I decided to book a room here, and so I made my way around to the office to do just that. It was often a good idea to have somewhere as a fallback in case of things going unexpectedly awry, and being in possession of an alternative identification card, courtesy of the company, it was a shame not to put it to good use. After enquiring if there was any unobtrusive way of exiting the building, should the need to leave unobserved arise, I booked under the name Patrick Dempsey, paid for a week in advance and asked the grey-haired lady behind the counter to hang on to the key until I arrived to claim it.

That done, when the two men who had befriended me on my first day walked in, we greeted one another in the accustomed, blokey manner and moved to spend time in the side bar, shooting pool and the breeze, but when a brawl broke out, occasioning company security to be summoned, my growing sense of uneasiness got the better of me, and making my excuses I bade them farewell, leaving the Horizon without really having a destination or purpose in mind. What was worse, not the faintest hint of a solution had presented itself to me.

I found myself wandering back towards my room, my mood darkening with every footfall. Whatever was happening, it was something I hadn't experienced before. My mind kept slipping back to thoughts of Alex and of last night. That woman had found a way of burrowing under my skin. Why? I didn't know. I've had my fare share of steamy one-nighters before, but this girl. This girl

—

As far as the job went, I needed an out. Its whole complexion had changed, altering the situation far beyond anything I could ever have expected or even envisioned. I had to find a way of closing it down without affecting my standing within the company. It was going to take some doing, but I didn't see an option. To expose the Jhai would cause an uproar I had no wish to be a part of; and they wished to be kept out of the picture in any case, a position I felt it was important to respect. I could only image the repercussions should they catch me taking a sly snapshot of them. Alex's relationship with them would likely be destroyed. Why she had mentioned writing an anthropological study, I couldn't fathom. Perhaps a joke; but, no, exposing them was not an option. I had to find reason to present an argument in favour of us cutting our losses and convince the company that the pilfering had ceased. I think whey would accept that, but in order for them to swallow such an argument, they would have to believe there was no hope of retrieving the stolen goods, and likewise no chance of prosecuting the culprits responsible. No problem. *Damn. . .* I was in a bind.

My communicator sounded. It was Joe Higgins calling; the head administrator.

'Yes, Joe. What's up,' I enquired nervously. 'Haven't seen you around in a day or two, Jack?' 'Snooping,' I explained.

'Ah, yes. Undercover,' he deciphered, musingly.

My radar was *pinging!* What the hell did he care what I had been doing? He was administration. If Berringer had asked, it would make some sense. He, at least, was security.

'Something like that,' I hedged.

'I would like you to come over this afternoon, Jack. Something here of interest. I think you should see for yourself.'

I checked the bedside chronometer. It was close to change of shift, and close to the end of a normal work day; but this was Far Point and I was talking to Joe Higgins, someone for whom such things meant next to nothing. The man was his job and he was never off the clock.

'Half an hour?' he invited, and hung up before I was able to respond.

'Son-of-a-bitch,' I cursed bitterly, but I would have to go and see the prick. Everything rolling along nicely, I would tell him. A waiting game. Too early to expect anything resembling a result. Patience is a virtue, Joe.

After killing time by wandering the streets for a while, I was once again greeted at the front desk by the smiling face of the bland female functionary inside the administration building, and climbing the stairs I propped at Joe Higgins' closed door, tapping twice.

'Come on in Jack,' he called.

I discovered him walking the perimeter of the office, griping what I instantly recognised to be a bug-detector; a high-end model, too, waving it over the walls, around electrical outlets, light fittings and under his desk.

'Take a seat,' he offered, continuing the exercise. I did as he asked, remaining silent until he appeared satisfied with the outcome of his search.

'Mice?' I asked, as he finally seated himself behind his desk. 'Rats, more like,' he answered gruffly. 'Cockroaches even.'

I nodded knowingly. 'Comes with the territory, Joe. I'm glad to see you're staying on top of it.'

He stood and walked over to the fridge which stood in the corner. 'Beer?' he offered, reaching in and pulling out two before I had answered.

'Thanks,' I said, accepting. 'How's everything running? Smoothly, I hope?'

He rounded the desk and lowered his considerable bulk into his chair with a sigh. 'Not bad, actually. Not bad at all. An exploration team have reported a fresh deposit of nickel and silver. A big one. It should be in production in a month or two.' He took a swallow from the bottle and plonked it down on the desk. 'I didn't know you and George Berringer were previously acquainted, Jack. Tell me about that, why don't you?'

I was intrigued by the question. Was this idle conversation? I wondered. 'George and I grew up in th same neighbourhood,' I began. 'There's not much more to it than that. I guess there was a small amount of competition, perhaps animosity. I don't know, but mostly on his part. He's that sort of a person. He always seemed to be trying to one-up everybody, even as a teenager. We don't particularly care for one another.'

'Okay,' Joe replied. 'I've got something a bit interesting to show you. It's something George brought to my attention.'

He lifted a remote control from his desktop, pressed a button and swung about in his swivel chair as a large screen descended from its compartment within the ceiling. 'Watch,' he said, as the screen came to life.

I tensed as I recognised the interior of a warehouse, comprehending immediately what was about to play out. The camera zoomed toward a pair of figures in the gloom. It was Alex and myself, from two nights previous. As I watched, one figure approached the other sitting beside a storage bay. The figures were difficult to recognise, but clearly, one was a man, the other a woman. The woman poured something from a flask and offered it to the man. Conversation ensued; a cigarette was lit, but fortunately the face was downward turned in the lighting of it. In a while the woman produced what looked to be a firearm, directing the man to move into the vacant bay, then to sit. The woman moved to join the sitting figure and a moment later a blinding flash caused the screen to white out. When vision returned, the figures were gone.'

'What do you make of that?' Joe asked, casually.

'Incredible,' I answered. 'I'm not really sure what happened. Did those people disappear? Is that even possible?'

A thin smile accompanied by a look of amusement moved across Joe's features as he held back his reply for affect. 'Seeing is believing, isn't it?'

'I don't know what I saw, Joe. Has the video file been messed with, perhaps? People can't disappear. It looks like a prank, to me.'

'No prank, Jack. Your old pal George inspected it thoroughly. It's genuine.'

'Why are you bringing this to me?' I wanted to know. 'Security.

This is George's province.'

'I run this rig,' Jack. You know that. I told him a while back to send me anything interesting as soon as something was detected. And you have to admit, this *is* interesting.'

Just then there was a knock at the door. Joe released me from his gaze and called, 'Come!'

To my amazement, Alex entered, carrying a package. At the sight of me sitting there, the hint of an unsettled expression flashed across her lovely features. 'The report from Mr Berringer,' she explained, and crossed the room swiftly to present the item to Joe. She turned to me, her eyes not quite knowing where to settle. 'Nice to see you again, Mr Hardin. Is everything going well?'

'Well enough,' I replied, conversationally. 'And it's very nice to see you again, too.' I smiled warmly.

'Oh, come on, you two!' Joe was standing now. 'Really? Do you think I don't know what is going on?'

Alex feigned a startled expression.

'What are you talking about?' I responded incredulously.

Joe remained motionless, critically regarding the both of us. 'Like that wasn't the pair of you in the video file? Are you honestly denying it?'

I turned to Alex in explanation. 'Joe was just showing me some warehouse security footage from...' I turned to Joe. 'When was it taken?'

'Two night ago,' he growled.

'I've seen it,' Alex replied insouciantly. 'I helped compile it. What is going on?' Her manner was perfectly calm and controlled as she stared Joe down with her questioning look. 'What was meant by that remark?' Her manner became indignant, and I could not help admiring her nerve under fire.

'Alright,' Joe responded. So you're gong to play it that way. You've made the delivery,' he said in dismissal, and Alex left the room without further comment.

'You're wrong, Joe.' I told him. 'Way off the mark, this time. If we're done here I have better things to do.'

He leaned back heavily in his chair. Sighed. 'Sit down, Jack. Finish your beer. I had to test the theory. You, above all people understand that. I had to know, and you two fit the description. Tell me I'm wrong about that.'

It was my turn to hold his gaze unwaveringly, pondering the situation for an extended time. 'Okay,' I said, at last. 'I guess I do see it...but it doesn't mean I have to like it.' I took a sip from the bottle and sat back down. 'Quite the charade,' I observed.

I left Joe's office, furious at the turn of events. We hadn't fooled him for a minute; he was just unable to take it any further, and he had attempted to defuse the situation by pretending we were in the clear. I needed to know what George Berringer knew; how much he actually knew or what he *thought* he knew, and upon departing administration I made my way directly to the security building.

When the girl at the help desk in the lobby recognised me she reached for a phone. No doubt she meant to alert Berringer of my presence. The elevator doors were closed, the lights above showing both cars already ascending. The way my wound was beginning to throb, I didn't like to take the stairs, but I was in a hurry.

At the head of the stairs I entered the hallway to observe a man standing beside Berringer's door. A tall guy wearing a black suit, hat, dark glasses. It appeared he wore the hat over a shaven head. There was something altogether not right about the guy; he did not even acknowledge my approach until we were standing toe to toe.

'Excuse me, you're blocking my way,' I told him, at which point he turned his head slightly to regard me.

'Engaged,' he said, and turned away.

Who was this dude? I asked myself. From within George's office came the sound of muffled voices, and through the frosted glass I could just make out two figures standing in front of his desk. Nothing distinguishable could be heard of the conversation. 'Then I will wait,' I told the taciturn object, and seated myself in one of the pair of vacant chairs opposite the door.

I had heard of these guys. If my guess was right, this was *a 'man in black.'* A ridiculous term applying to sartorial ineptitude. The dress code tended to make the guy look ridiculous, rather than, as was doubtlessly the intention, to instill something akin to discomfort, apprehension and impotency in their presence. But what were he and his cohorts doing here? I knew their reputation and what their perceived function was meant to be.

'What's up?' I asked the door guy. No response, predictably.

The cat was out of the bag, doubtlessly. So who had spilled the beans? Or was it a case of who had been watching the watcher? And how would things proceed from here? I could be getting ahead of myself, I then realised. Best not to jump the gun, they might be on a fishing expedition, having picked up on rumour, speculation and second or third hand information. Scuttlebutt in other words. Although, where had they come from? Would they have travelled a vast distance to check out a rumour of alien visitation because of some gossip coming from a space platform millions of miles from Earth? Perhaps these dudes were posted out of Niven Station. It would make the most sense.

After a few minutes the door to George's office finally opened, and the pair who had been talking to Berringer departed without even a glance, the door guy following behind.

'Nice talking to you.'

Without waiting to be summoned I let myself in, hoping to catch George even more off guard than usual. His blanched face caused me a moment's regret, however. Those bastards had shaken him pretty good.

'Jesus, George. Are you alright? Let me get you something. Water okay, buddy?'

I poured him a glass and offered it to him. He took it from my grasp while loosening his collar with his free hand. 'Thank-you. Give me a moment, will you?'

I rounded the desk to sit opposite. 'Sure thing.'

I watched as he sipped twice at the water. A little colour began to return. He sipped again and placed the glass on the desk.

'Do you know who those people are?' he asked me. 'Have you ever had to deal with them?'

'I know who they are,' I told him, 'but I've not had to deal with them. Don't let them get the better of you, George. Two-bob thugs in dress up. The two of them trying to put the frighteners on you, were they? Real heroes. Comic book characters. Well fuck 'em, buddy. Have another sip of water.'

He took a last swallow and attempted to compose himself.

'I appreciate your support right now, Jack. But there's something–' he stalled; baulked at the hurdle.

'What is it George?'

'Nothing—nothing at all. Why did you come here, Jack?'

'I came here to shake you up, find out what bloody game you guys are playing, but too late by the looks. Someone beat me to it.'

He affected a wan smile. 'Yeah. Look, Jack. . . I know we've never really been friends. In some way I suppose, that's my fault. I want you to be careful. All I got from those guys just now was veiled threats and accusations. They seemed to think I knew something. Something about something. They never said what the something was. They just pumped me for information, but I haven't the foggiest idea what they were on about. "Don't think you can keep secrets affecting global security," they said, and there's something creepy about those fellahs. They're not normal, you know? Something creepy, Jack, and I don't much like it.'

'There is something funny about them, and that's a *cert*. You really don't have any idea what they wanted from you? I find that fishy, George. You're telling me you were just pressured by experts and you don't know why. . . what about?'

He looked to have suddenly taken full possession of himself once again. He squared his shoulders, pulled himself upright in his chair and looking at his watch, telling me, 'I appreciate your concern. I do, Jack, but there are some things I cannot talk about. You understand, I know you do.'

I allowed myself a rueful chuckle. 'Funny,' I said, 'you're the second person to tell me that in less than an hour.'

He did not respond, except to make a show of inspecting his watch one more time.

'Okay George. I get it,' I said, standing, preparing to leave. 'You know I have always been able to get more out of your silence than all your bullshit over the years. And, you know? Nothing has changed. I'll be seeing you, George. And a word of advice, buddy. The less you know, the better off you will be. Trust me on that. Keep your head down.'

It could not have been clearer, I told myself, entering the streets below. The way I was being kept out of the loop it only went to making it clearer than ever to me that I was currently *a person of interest:* cop speak, meaning that I was being closely watched because I was being linked to whatever the secret something was; the secret something George knew nothing about and had almost warned me about but chickened at the last moment, and what Joe was on my hammer about. Only, it was no secret. An alien connection. So goddamn what? Big deal. Why the need for all the cloak and dagger secrecy? What happens to the adult mind when they achieve positions of power or go to work for clandestine government agencies? They lose all sight of reality; they start seeing conspiracies where there are none, *danger* where there is none. They start banging on about national security, threats to civilization and God only knows what else. They become obsessed, delusional and paranoid, and because they're surrounded by like minds, the whole thing becomes plaguelike—*a contagion*—and very, very dangerous. Why did the human race almost fail? Mass insanity brought about by a total lack of honesty. When honesty retreats, there is no more trust left, everybody mistrusts everyone, every*thing,* and there we go, straight down the tubes. The human race is totally mad and it's just too bad we are still viable and now on the verge of being able to spread the madness among the stars.

Look out cosmos, the lunatics are loose!

6

CIRCUMSTANCES

I noticed that foot traffic had thinned as I negotiated the way back towards my room and a couple of hours of downtime. I recognised how surrounded by events I had become, and even though I had not yet formulated my next move, the one looming thought in my mind was that I no longer wanted any role in this ridiculous game that everybody was playing. Whatever it took, I was *out*. Let the cards fall where they may, I did not care one iota. I was cashing in my chips—taking my ball and going home, wherever the hell that was.

'Mr Hardin?' The voice came from over my left shoulder as I came up to a quiet street corner. From my right came a punch to the mid section, immediately followed by a crashing blow to the head, producing a shower of stars behind my eyes as the pavement rushed up to meet me.

I woke in a chair, tied, in a darkened room with a single, brilliant light beaming down on me; and I remembered then, being knocked cold on a street corner.

'Mr Hardin. Thank-you for joining us.' The source of the voice I could not identify. Disembodied voices. What next?

I looked around my immediate surroundings. Beyond the spotlight there was nothing but penumbral gloom and shadows. 'It's true, you know,' I said, addressing the emptiness. 'One really does see stars when being clonked on the noggin.'

Someone stepped forward a single pace in front of me. All I could make out was the silhouette. Tall, medium build and wearing a hat.

'Funny man,' replied the dark figure. 'I apologise for the tap on the head, but if we had merely asked you to come along to this meeting, I know what your response would have been. And I thought it was important to impress upon you that we are not playing games here.'

'You actually thought knocking me senseless and dragging me here was the way to go? Huh. You guys.'

'So you would have me believe that you would have come along voluntarily?' He laughed derisively. 'Don't give me that. You want to pretend you're a reasonable guy and *we* are the brigands? You should know we've seen your psych profile, and your *handiwork*, and, having seen it, I have to wonder why the company has kept you in their employ as long as they have. You're a violent man, Jack Hardin. Your profile lists you as being incorrigible, irascible and antisocial. That's some profile. It's no wonder the force sent you packing. You cost them a fortune in legal fees with your heavy-handed methods.'

'Results are results,' I argued. 'Nobody takes issue with my success rate.'

'Nor do I, but shall we talk about your new friends?

'Could this be any more cliché?' I asked, attempting to keep this superior bastard off side. I was pissed off at allowing myself to be taken so easily, but I was not going to let them think they owned me. My guts were giving me some grief, though. Someone had slugged me pretty good in the solar plexus and they had likely opened up a stitch or two.

'The old methods are usually the best,' the voice replied calmly. 'But this is more your friendly chat type situation. Which way it proceeds from here is completely up to you, understand?'

I understood alright, but to hell with them. I was in no mood to cooperate.

'Let's talk about your new friends.'

'I don't have any friends,' I responded, and got a laugh from someone in the darkness—a weird, false kind of a laugh, as if laughing was not usually in the man's repertoire.

'That doesn't surprise me. You've never been very popular, have you?'

'Get to the point, why don't you? I can't abide idle chitchat.' There was a moment's silence until another voice joined in.

'I think that's fair enough, Mr Hardin.' This voice undoubtedly came from an older, and therefore a more experienced operative.

'We have a task for you.'

'Why would I want to do you any favours?'

'Because you will find it to your advantage, but you haven't heard what it is, yet. Don't be too much in a hurry. Hear us out first.'

It seemed a reasonable request and there was little choice, but I was quite sure I wasn't going to like anything they had to say.

'Okay then. Let's hear it.'

'We have been monitoring transmissions in this sector for some time. Strange, one might even say *alien* transmissions. A kind of powerful, modulated energy signature sort of thing.' He paused for a short while to see if I would respond, and continued. 'These signals have been heavily concentrated around the warehouses where items have been disappearing. The last time we detected one of these phenomena, it coincided quite inexplicably with your unexpected disappearance. Not just your disappearance, either. A miss Jordan was present. Miss Alexandra Jordan. I thought I heard you say that you didn't have any friends?'

'What are you talking about, disappearance? Nobody around here has disappeared. Who the hell are you anyway?'

'I'm asking the questions, Jack. You know the game. Your job is to answer them. Where were you? What happened in that warehouse? Where were you teleported to?

It was my turn to laugh derisively. 'Teleported? Can you hear yourself? Teleportation is science fiction bullshit. Really, you guys must live in a fantasy world. Perhaps you've been there so long it has softened your brain. I always knew you lot were full of shit. I suppose you believe in leprechauns and hob goblins.'

The following pause contained a modicum of tension, telling me I was beginning to get to him. Someone I had not detected had been standing behind me during this exchange, and I received a slap in the back of the head. I have a knack of irritating people which comes in handy during sessions like this. *Rattling one's cage*, I call it. Always effective, but it has been known to backfire on occasion.

'What's the matter, shadow guy? Grasping at straws here? You're on shaky ground and we both know it. Why not stop wasting your time. More importantly, stop wasting mine. Unlike you, I have constructive things to do with *mine*. You and your mickey mouse club members. Your mommies will be wondering where you are by now.'

He responded with a chuckle—the worrisome, self-assured, rug from under the feet kind. 'Oh. You're going to work with us, alright,' he said, and our little *tet-a-tete* was suddenly at an end.

When I awoke in the very same hospital bed I had occupied only days before, I knew my last remark had hit the spot. Very *deja vu*. Even Detective Sergeant Burt Emerson and junior officer Andy Saunders were in position, as per the first time, when my eyes eventually opened.

Emerson wore a crooked, *I-saw-this-coming* kind of a smile.

'I thought I told you to stay out of trouble. I can't keep making paperwork disappear forever, you know.'

'I'm fine. Thanks for asking,' I retorted. 'Ooh. . . let me rephrase that. Would your press the morphine button for me? I can't raise my arm. Give it a few pumps, Burt, would you? There's a good chap.'

To my immense surprise, he did as I asked, and he even waited until the pained expression left my dial before continuing.

'You're playing with fire, Jack. You must know that. I only hope you know what you're doing. Do you?'

Hearing him speak the words, it dawned on me for the first time in a very long while, that I *did know* exactly what I was doing. Or, more accurately, what I *would* do… as soon, that was, as I could lift my sorry arse out of this hospital bed and walk out of here. Unfortunately, I didn't think that would be anytime soon. A crack on the scone like that can put a crimp on one's day. And my knee hurt like blazes, the bastards. One of them must have given me one for good measure while I was out.

'Those mongrels really did a number on you, pal. What did you do to piss them off? Actually, there's no need to answer. I can imagine.'

The comment tickled me, but the laugh reflex was quickly stifled by a bolt of pain.

'Jesus,' Saunders responded. 'They went too far.'

'Yeah? Well I appreciate the concern, lad, but they knew when to stop, at least. Well practised, I imagine, and they want my cooperation. Can you believe that? For that they need me alive. Just as well, eh? Trouble is, I don't know what the hell it is they expect from me, and it didn't seem to matter to them that I refused to lift a finger to aid them. God only knows what they have in mind.'

Emerson lifted his tired frame from the chair he had occupied. 'I just wanted to see you were on the mend. Listen, Jack… you have my number. I have to go now, but if there's something. You know—'

'Yeah, sure Burt. Thanks. I appreciate it. A friend in need is-'

'A pain in the arse,' he finished for me, allowing us both a moment's grim reflection. 'Okay then. Well?' He turned to his offsider. 'Come on. Lets see if we cant catch some bad guys. Later, Jack.'

'Later,' I agreed, watching their departure while wondering at the sudden display of giving a damn. Wondering also if there wasn't a microphone secreted somewhere in the vicinity, or if one had just been planted. Such was the level of my growing sense of mistrust and outright lack of confidence in everybody around me.

I heard George laughing in the hallway outside my room as he retreated. Five seconds later a matron entered, carrying a bowl of streaming hot water, a wash-cloth, soap and a towel, and I realised immediately what the bugger had found so funny. I would have put up a fight, but I was far too week and too tired to protest the indignity of what followed. Mercifully, the drugs and the injuries allowed me to fall back into the comfortable, lulling arms of oblivion. Who knew for how long? But when I awoke, some of the old vitality had returned, and I even found I had an appetite again. The following couple of days were spent resting, eating and cogitating.

Life can get pretty simple when one has been pushed into a corner, but I had pushed myself into this one. The choices do become simple. Perhaps they had never been complicated and it was nothing more than my stubborn disposition and hardheadedness complicating matters. Maybe it had been that one night with Alex that was needed to put things into perspective? The pain didn't matter any more. It was easing by now anyway. My mind had begun to see things clearly for the first time in a very long while, and things were becoming exceedingly simple. It was life that mattered. A quality of life, and maybe even a sense of purpose. I had been chasing illusions for so many years, practically all of my life, and none of it made any sense when reviewed from this hospital bed. Who the hell had I become? *What* had I become? The question continued to bother me.

On the morning of the third day, I woke to find Alex, sitting at my bedside, her chair pulled up close. Her presence was entirely unexpected, intoxicating, and to my mind a dangerous thing to do right now, but I was pleased as hell to see her all the same. I had been unable to get the girl out of my mind, and seeing her here right now answered the foremost question on my mind.

'How do you feel,' she asked, softly. 'I can't tell you how worried I have been. Are you alright? They hurt you pretty bad, didn't they.'

'Much better this morning,' I replied, honestly. How did you know I was here?'

'That policeman. Emerson, is it?' 'Yes, Sergeant Emerson. *He* told you?'

'He called me. And I'm very grateful to him for that.' Her face became a picture of concern. 'Jack, I had no idea things had gotten so out of hand. Look what they have done to you. What's it all about?'

'They're telling me they know about *'My new friends,'*I told her. 'I don't know what they have planned, but they wanted me to cooperate and work with them. But before you say anything, I told them I didn't have a clue what they were talking about, and we best stick to that. And, yes, they tried to involve you, but it's me they're really interested in. They will use you to get at me. Just remember that we have no clue what the hell they're on about. Okay? We'll ride it out, for now, and decide what's best as the situation unfolds.'

I studied her face during the telling, watching for signs of weakness as the wheels turned in her mind. She showed no sign of panic, only calm, clarity, and rapid analysis of the situation. 'That seems best,' she agreed. 'There's little doubt that they'll be

keeping close tabs on us both, so... I think you're right. We just go about our business and give them no reason to intervene.'

'That's my girl,' I responded, smiling. 'I'm pleased to see you. I was wondering, you know, about everything.'

'*I* have,' she replied coyly. I couldn't stop thinking about you, but I just didn't know—you know?' Again the coy smile. 'It's been driving me mad and you just disappeared. I didn't know what to do

— what to think! I've been so worried.'

I reach across and took her had, 'Well you can stop worrying. I'm right here, I'm in the pink, and I'm so glad you came. That's one big concern off my mind too. Thanks for turning up, kiddo.'

She squeezed my hand, tightly. 'Of course,' she said, 'How could I not?

We spent a quiet minute watching one another until she broke the silence. 'I really have to go now, Jack. Work, but I'll be back as soon as I can. Okay?'

'Okay, but I'm going to see if I can get out of here as soon as possible. I'll be good to go in a moment.'

'You do as the doctors tell you,' she told me, affecting scorn, and broke into a gorgeous smile. 'I really have to go now. I'll be back.'

'Alright,' I consented, and she bent to give me a kiss before parting. As she did so, I slipped a piece of note-paper into her pocket, in the hope she would discover it in time for her to meet me where and when the message indicated, and I watched as she made her way out, disappearing into the corridor, the scent of her perfume lingering long afterwards. I had it bad, and I knew it. But I could not fight against the one single good thing in my life. My years of solitude at last threatened to turn against me. A situation I would never have thought possible. I figured I was beyond all that.

It occurred to me how large a problem I had. For so many years I had been the lone wolf, with no responsibility but to myself. With Alex being implicated, all that had suddenly changed, and what made my situation insurmountably worse was our location. Out here on the rim was no place to be when contemplating a disappearing trick. There were so few routes out of here, and most, if not all, were under constant surveillance by the company, as well as these black suited hard cases. I had copped a beating, but it wasn't the first time. My ability to recover quickly from something like this had always been an asset. Resilient; the word was even in my personal file. I was stiff and sore; a rib or two may have been cracked but I knew, if I needed to, that I could drag myself out of here and manage to do whatever needed to be done. But it wasn't just me anymore. She was bright, and I figured she must be realising, by now, what was on the line. She would be analysing and formulating possible moves, as I was. The safest thing she could do for herself would be to cut me loose, distance herself and allow me to deal with circumstances. I could, of course, play ball with these pricks and betray the trust of these Jhai, but, as I said to them at the time, why the hell would I want to? The Jhai had done nothing but trust me. I had never betrayed a trust in my life, and although they weren't even the same species, I had no intention of ratting them out. Imagining what might become of the Jhai should these clowns get their mitts on them, it hammered my conscience even to contemplate it. Of course the Jhai might be way out of these guy's league. Probably were. The thought made me smile. Somebody would get their arses kicked very badly, but it would be on me. I did not want to be responsible for something like that. What a stink it would cause, and the blood would be on my hands. '*No,*' I determined, aloud. The black suit brigade had to be kept out of the frame as far as the Jhai went. I would not betray a trust and the black suits could go to hell.

The human mind is a curious thing. All this contemplation, pretending to myself that I could find a perfect solution to the problem when there was, during all this time, only the one obvious escape route now. But would Alex want to play along? Would she be willing to leave it all behind and embark on a jaunt into the complete unknown with the likes of someone like me? Perhaps she was, even now, coming to the same, inescapable conclusion. Would she choose her career, the future and the familiar, or could she possibly determine to launch into the realm of the unknown for the sake of adventure, a life together, dare I say, *love?*

Damn it all. Did I have the nerve or even the right to ask the question of her? It was times such as this that human nature seemed dead set bent on killing the organism rather than preserving it. When logic and human nature collide, the odds most always favour logic. Unfortunately, and without exception, logic becomes the first casualty. For me it seemed completely within the realm of possibility. Nothing tied me to Earth any more. Not emotionally, not physically, not in any way that would give me pause once the decision had been made. The proposition began to shine in my mind's eye as the most desirable of outcomes. It solved the puzzle of my life; the perfect solution to escaping the corner I had been painting myself into all of these years. Jack Hardin the misfit. Jack Hardin the antisocial, the misanthrope, the square peg in the round hole. I cared nothing for the human race. I would not miss them and they wouldn't miss me. If Alex was game, here was the obvious, perfect solution.

Nighttime on Far Reach was, of course, an outmoded term. The language here retained the use of words denoting a time of day only for convenience sake. The sky was an eternally star-sprinkled depth of darkness, but the rig remained lit up like a jewel against the spangled backdrop, more so during a twelve hour period designated daytime, with a gradual diminishing over a two hour period in simulating evening and eventual nightfall. The ploy helped the diurnal body clock of the human animal to assimilate conditions.

At three in the morning, when the hospital was at it's quietest ebb, I pulled on my clothes, having to tear open a trouser leg to accommodate the cast on my left leg, the result of my left kneecap having been cracked with the butt of a handgun. I pulled the walking stick I had procured earlier in the day from under my mattress, and slipped out quietly into the sublime tranquillity of the night; quite beautiful in an eerie kind of way. The reduced and sporadically placed night lights cast strangely elongated shadows across the uneven deck. The silence, as I set of, was complete, bringing to the fore all those instincts that millions of years of evolution had equipped us with; nerves singing in heightened anticipation of the slightest detection of danger.

My intention had been to return to my room, there to gather what belongings I deemed necessary and make my way to the Horizon Hotel, there to claim the room I had pre booked and to remain for the remainder of the night, keeping off the streets and out of sight from those who had become more than just a thorn in my side.

Upon entering my room at Star Palace, it was at once apparent that someone had been here during my absence. Drawers had been pulled and rummaged through, the bed upturned and my closet rifled, with the pockets of my clothes turned inside out. I could only see the humorous side. Those lugs had wanted to advertise their presence, appearing untouchable, able to disrupt my life at will and with impunity. It made no such impression on me and I had to chuckle at the mental image of full-grown men in alike costume getting their rocks off in this manner, like willful children throwing a tantrum. As far as I was concerned, this would be the last night I would spend as a member of society and the *rat* race of man. Nothing they could do to me, barring capture and detainment, mattered any more, and I would have to make sure I avoided that particular scenario at all costs.

I pressed the night bell at the rear entrance of the Horizon. After a short wait, a middle-aged lady wrapped in a blue nightgown came to the door. She inspected me briefly through the frosted pane of glass until she recognised me as the man who had pre-booked the room for a week, and she set about pulling bolts and opening locks.

'Patrick Dempsey,' I told her as she cracked the door open a few inches.

'Yes, Mr Dempsey. I remember you. I am Myra.' She pushed the door ajar and stepped back to allow me entry. 'Goodness. You've been in the wars,' she observed, indicating the leg and facial bruising, which by now had turned into a lovely mixture of blue and yellow.

'Occupational hazard,' I told her. 'I'm sorry to trouble you at this early hour. 'Lovely night, though, isn't it?'

'No trouble,' she replied. 'Who sleeps anymore? If you're hungry I can bring you up a sandwich, if you like?'

I declined the sandwich, but I spotted a bottle of *synth* whiskey on the shelf and had it charged to my room as an afterthought. Having left the hospital unannounced I had forfeited access to pain medication and I would soon be in need of a substitute. At the office she handed me the key to my room and bade me good night.

The room was snug, which is to say, small, with a window, a double bed, a dresser, a closet, a single chair at the bedside, and a bathroom wash-basin installed in the wall; somewhere I could freshen up in the mornings. It would do in a pinch, I decided.

The journey from the hospital had been a painful one. Not so much because of the beating I had received, although it didn't help, but the exertion had caused the old belly wound to begin throbbing once again. It really didn't feel good, and I was beginning to sweat. I really did not need the thing to be infected; it would be a real spanner in the works, and I had to wonder if leaving the hospital without at least a bottle of antibiotics to keep the infection in check was such a brilliant idea. I made a mental note to do something about that and moved on to other concerns.

A glance at my watch told me it was almost four in the morning. If Alex had read my note, and if she had decided to come, she would be here in a half an hour. If she was being followed it would make things awkward, but not impossible. I had taken the possibility into account. The black coat and dark glasses brigade would not intercept her, but they would follow to see where she led them. It was how they worked. They depended on their quarry being dumb enough to tip their hand so that all they needed to do was to move in and mop up.

I found a shot glass in a cupboard and swallowed a couple of doses of synth whiskey, found an opened packet of cigarettes in my bag, climbed onto the bed and lit up, there to wait for the tap on the door which I was afraid would not come. Moments like this always felt to be saturated with portent. In my career there were many such moments of waiting, alone in a room, just like this one, swinging wildly between optimism and doubt, the mind racing through one possible scenario after another, making contingencies for each possible outcome and knowing that, in the end, it was as much dependent on sheer dumb luck and random timing as any brilliant, mastermind planning.

I reached over and retrieved my weapon from my bag, felt its weight, checked that the compressed air cartridges were firmly slotted into their recess, inspected the lead tipped iron slugs which would flash through the air at over three hundred metres a second with little more than a whisper. The perfect weapon for a circumstance like this. I rested it on my lap and took a good, long draw on the cigarette. I was ready to see this thing through to the end, come what may.

I must have dozed for a minute. What had woken me? There came a soft tap at the door. Yes, it must have been what woke me, so I climbed off the bed and quietly sidled up to the door.

'Who is it?'

'Me—' and I immediately recognised Alex's voice. 'Me who?'

'Are you going to let me in or do I have to thump you?'

As I opened the door she threw her carry bag into the room and flew into my arms, wrapping herself around me, kissing me gently, being sure to avoid the worst of my bruised face.

There was nothing else for it but to succumb to the moment, and be damned with the circumstance. I locked the door and carried her to the double bed, where we let loose our passions. The both of us, it seemed, knew that the next couple of hours might be the last chance we might have in which to avail ourselves of each other. There is something about the presence of impending danger, the looming spectre of peril, that precipitates the basic sexual imperative of ensuring continuance of the species. It is a fact which anyone who lives in a state of unrelenting fear for their life will acknowledge, and it makes for a most intense sexual encounter, completely bereft of reason and an almost indescribable experience when the ego is dissolved into something far removed—

far exceeding—any mere sense of self. It is a combining of souls, a complete surrender, and a heightened awareness of that difficult to explain experience often described as ecstasy, and more often than not, love. For me, it was a phenomena I had only heard about, and, until this moment, denied the existence of—but now? I could only lay, exhausted, stunned and confused, in attempt to make sense of what had just happened. This, for me, was revelation, verging on the divine.

We lay in the grip of a spell which had taken us beyond mortal concerns, and at this hour there was total silence. Nothing stirred; there was only the sound of our breathing, our hearts beating, blood coursing through our bodies in a moment without end in a capsule of timelessness and bliss. It was a memory I was destined to carry with me throughout eternity, only, I did not know it yet.

7

BEYOND THE RIM

I had planned an early start to the day but by the time we had gathered ourselves, and our thoughts, the initiative was lost. It didn't much matter, I told myself, and explained to Alex:

'We could be a little conspicuous making our way to the warehouse so early in the morning. The streets need to be filled with people to aid our movement without detection.'

'How about a disguise?' she suggested, with the glint of girlish humour in her eyes. 'It will be fun.'

'I was thinking along the same lines, but where would we get what we need?'

'What would you do without me?' she replied, and nodded towards the carry bag she had brought along.

'Disguises?' 'Yep.'

'Clever girl. What did you bring? Let's take a look.'

When she bounced from the bed in moving to fetch the bag, a bolt of pain shot through my insides, causing me to stifle a cry of intense discomfort.

'What's wrong?' she called, dashing back to me.

My insides felt suddenly gripped by fire, causing me to curl up, clutching at my stomach, and for the moment unable to speak.

'What is it, Jack. Tell me,' she demanded desperately.

The pain eased, but the cramping persisted, and sweat began to bead on my brow. 'Goddamned wound,' I replied. 'It's giving me some trouble. And the treatment handed out by those jerk-offs didn't do any good. The infection has started up again, I think.'

'What are we going to do?' She knelt down beside the bed to try and comfort me. 'You should be in hospital.'

'Too late for that. Maybe the Jhai can help out. We'll just have to carry on as intended until then.'

'Yes,' Alex assured. 'They'll be able to fix this. We'll be fine.' 'Of course we will. Let's have a look at what you have there.'

The bag contained a few items Alex had pilfered from inside the security centre building where she worked. For me, there was the navy uniform of a security guard, complete with a poncy cap and torch. For herself, coveralls. The type worn by those involved with goods handling, storing supplies in the appropriate areas ready for dispatching. To cover her face and hide her locks, she employed a bandana, the sort commonly used by employees to cover the mouth and nose whenever the rising dust became too severe, and on top, a leather, peaked cap.

'Very good,' I commended. 'The very items. This should be a synch.'

'It's exciting, isn't it?'

I had to smile at her enthusiasm, but this wasn't over 'til it was over. A thousand things could go wrong between here and there, but I didn't want to worry her more than I already knew she was. She was putting on a brave face for me and I didn't have the heart to tell her I knew how scared she was. I would be worried if she hadn't been. If we were discovered, the jig was really up. Both our careers would, doubtless, be over in a moment, and that was serious. The black marks against our names would ensure a life of struggle. Finding an employer willing to take either of us on after something like that would be very unlikely. We had talked it through. She seemed certain that the Jhai would gladly let us tag along. They were a nomadic people who lived their lives roaming the galaxy, making a home here and there, utilizing wherever resources were rich enough to support an easy existence. The technology they carried with them ensured they had everything they needed, when it wasn't broken down, as was presently the case. But they also knew of several civilisations scattered about who were welcoming to itinerant strangers and who would have no qualms about letting the pair of us settle in amongst them. The Jhai, themselves, were such a race, and according to Alex we would have no problems fitting in while she continued her study of them in preparing her planned scientific, anthropological paper. A paper she figured would eventually make her a celebrity and very wealthy to boot, when we finally returned to our own race. As far as that was concerned, I was not entirely sure it was what I wanted, but that was far enough away in time as to cause no immediate problem. And thankfully it didn't seem to be of major relevance to her right now. Like she said to me many times since agreeing to the idea, 'It's exciting.' About that, she was not wrong. In fact, I viewed it as an adventure beyond comparison. We were about to embark on perhaps the biggest adventure of all times, depending, I suppose, on one's point of view. All we had to do was make it to the warehouse this evening and initiate the Jhai transponder she had been given. Until then, the day needed to be dealt with as best we could manage.

In talking the situation through it was obvious we would need to clear a path for our entering the company compound, enabling entry to the warehouses. I figured I could call George Berringer regarding that.

I told him I needed three things. First, to significantly lower the number of guards within the compound, and to make sure people were aware of the reduction in security. Secondly, in the same period to take security cameras offline from 23:00 hrs to 03:00 hrs, but not to make a secret of it. Last of all, to enlist a squad of his best men and station them within the compound, ready to jump to whatever location I needed them when I gave the word. To him it would appear as if we were about to spring a trap on our thieves, and I felt sure he would be pleased to play along without protest. In reality it gave Alex and myself complete freedom to walk in there and depart without anyone lifting a finger. There would be some red faces, I mused with some satisfaction. When he realised he had been employed to facilitate our final departure, the only thing poor old George could do would be to keep the whole matter hushed up, lest his superiors decide that his head should roll. I almost pitied him, but bringing him down a peg or two could only teach the man a much needed lesson in humility. I wasn't going to lose any sleep over it, that was for sure.

Our real problem lay with the boys in black. They were outside of anyone's jurisdiction here on Far Reach.

It was likely they had a coven on Niven Station but they were a secretive bunch. It would be handy to be able to find a way of diverting their attention for a short time while we made a break for it, but at this juncture nothing came to mind as a bonafide great idea. They were well aware I had gone to ground, and doubtless, even now, they were beating the bushes pretty hard in attempt to flush us out. Their only option was to keep eyes on the streets and places I had frequented since arriving. Checking hotel registers and the like would not provide what they needed. It was why I had thought to book this room well in advance, and under a bogus name. I suppose that if they checked every single name of every hostelry they might find that Patrick Dempsey was a registered pressure vessel welder and fitter, but nothing about the identity would arouse suspicion. For these reasons I felt reasonably comfortable holding up here at the Horizon with Alex.

The die was cast in any case. George had agreed to the measures I stipulated without too much fuss. Lowering the numbers of security personnel made him nervous, but as soon as I told him he would have his thieves by morning, he was only too happy to oblige. After all, he would be the one to catch all the credit. I knew he would find a way to put the spotlight on himself. He probably planned to mention how the plan was his own invention. I could only smile to myself at the thought. If he pre-empts the setup with a word to his superiors, the whole weight of this event will be on his head.

'What are you smiling at?' Alex asked, rolling over and throwing an arm over my chest. *'Machinations?'*

'Of a sort,' I replied. 'Just thinking this through.'

'That's my little strategist,' she mocked, playing the coquette. 'They don't stand a chance—' and she hauled herself up on me, began nibbling my ear as she sniggered playfully.

Show me a man who is invulnerable to an attractive, desirable female behaving this way, and I will show you a man made of stone. Needless to say, we found an enjoyable way of filling in the afternoon. By the time we heard the siren for the afternoon change of shift, we were both ravenously hungry, and it made perfect sense to eat a good, hearty meal before going into action.

I contacted Myra, the proprietress, on the house phone. Asked if it was possible to have two meals brought to the room.

'For you and your lady friend?' she enquired. When I was slow to respond, she added, 'It's alright, dear. Nothing gets past Myra. Remember? I don't sleep well. I told you that. What would you like, Mr Hardin? I'll have the chef send it up.'

We ordered big. It would likely be the last meal of this kind we would be having for quite some time. It was something neither of us had really considered until now.

A rig on the outskirts of the solar system does not have the greatest cuisine, but we were happy to settle for soup and a plate of meaty stew containing unfamiliar ingredients, which I wolfed down with considerable delectation. For the remainder of the evening we were happy to simply enjoy each other's company until it was time to make a move.

With perhaps thirty minutes remaining before time, we donned the apparel Alex had selected. Reversing the original plan, I dressed as the navvy and Alex dressed in the role of the security officer. My wound continued to cause discomfort though, and it was taking more of an effort than I would have liked in order to ignore it. I could not allow Alex to see just how much effort. If the need to make haste should arise, I feared I might be in some trouble. There was nothing else for it but to push on.

I poured a good measure of the remaining synth whiskey into a tumbler. 'Will you join me?' I offered.

'Why not? What shall we drink to?'

I poured hers, passed it across. 'To success. What else?' 'And a new beginning,' she added, cheerily.

'Success and a new beginning,' we chorused, and downed the fiery liquid in a single gulp.

Alex pulled a face while trying not to breathe. 'Rocket fuel.' 'Has a kick to it, doesn't it?' I agreed. 'One more?'

We drank another and stood, looking at each other. 'Is it time?' Her voice was steady, but diminutive now.

'It's time,' I affirmed, injecting as much confidence into the two words as possible.

Alex pulled the device the Jhai had provided her with from her divested jacket pocket; the pencil shaped electronic beacon which she would initiate once we were in position, and primed it by giving the end a single twist. All it needed to start it functioning now was for her to push the tiny button on its end.

Outside, the lights were dimmed, feigning night-time, and with the sky ablaze and the temperature falling, tending toward a chill, we set off from the rear of the hotel, bracing ourselves for any eventuality. Again my senses were amped up, growing in sensitivity; the animal brain recognizing the nature of the game and attending to the job it was designed for. The job of self-preservation.

It was risky, under the circumstances, for us to exhibit any close personal attachment. Anyone looking for us would be looking for a man and a woman travelling together, but the uniforms we wore made us look like two men, so we could at least make conversation as if we were two old colleagues locked in routine and making our way to our place of employment.

We entered the compound via a side gate where a single gate guard was standing sentry, and we made directly for warehouse-A, a distance of around five hundred metres which put us out in the open without the convenience of surrounding foot traffic to conceal our progress, which the streets and thoroughfares had afforded us until now. It did at least allow a degree of unobstructed sight about us, but if anyone was standing concealed beside converging walls or in an unlit doorway, it was doubtful we could have picked them out within the shadows. But so far, so good.

At warehouse-A we took a last, quick look around before skirting the edge and entering through a small door halfway along the length. One end of the interior was in darkness, the end we proceeded towards was lit here and there where goods were in the process of being positioned into storage by men and machines.

'Take a break,' I said to Alex, halfway along the central aisle, and we halted to lean against a stack of pallets while I lit a cigarette, casually surveying the area for anybody lingering suspiciously, perhaps stationed as a lookout for the pair of us. We were well within the time period I had specified for the cameras to be switched off, but I had to admit that it didn't necessarily mean that they were. If the black suits had pulled rank on Berringer, they were, right now, watching our nervous behaviour.

'Alright, lets go,' I said, and we continued, her in her navy security uniform, torch in hand, and me, the warehouse worker walking down the middle of the enormous space, as vulnerable and as unprotected as it was possible to be.

As we approached the designated area I anxiously slid my hand under my coat to feel the reassuring grip of my weapon. Alex noted the time and nodded. 'Two minutes,' she observed, as we came upon the designated bay from where we were to depart.

'Are you alright?' she asked me, the obvious look of concern showing on her face.

'As a matter of fact,' I began, but then doubled over as an invisible hand gripped and squeezed my innards like a vice, causing me to double over and sink to my knees.

A hot flush came over me, my skin began to prickle as sweat beaded over my entire body.

'What is it, Jack?'

'Give me a moment,' I said, grimacing against the suddenness of the rising fever. 'Goddamn it,' I growled.

'We're here,' she soothed, squatting beside me and placing a hand on my shoulder. 'Soon we'll be with the Jhai. They'll know what to do. You'll see. Their technology and medical knowledge is well up to the task.'

'Going somewhere?' A man stepped out from behind a stack of boxes across the aisle from where I crouched. At the same time, every light in the building brightened to full illumination, and in the aisle either side of us appeared two sets of two armed men, their weapons levelled threateningly.

'What were you thinking?' he continued, in a mocking manner.

I knew this guy. It was him that conducted the brief but painful interrogation. I was sure of it. As the memory came back to me, I noticed Alex had ever so gradually slipped a hand into her coat pocket. She was activating the beacon.

The guy doing the gloating stood, hands in pockets, a grin on his fat face—a grin that would soon change to something resembling startled surprise, I devoutly hoped.

'Not you clowns again,' I responded. 'Don't you idiots ever take a break?'

His smile began to smear into something resembling displeasure. 'Stand up, both of you. And keep your hands where I can see them.'

Alex rose first, reached down to assist me as I pushed myself up, groaning.

'What's wrong with you?' the black suit wanted to know.

'He's injured,' Alex answered with venom. 'From what you bastards did while he had a bullet wound.'

'Oh dear. Were we playing too rough for you, Jack? Maybe you've always been out of your depth playing with the big boys?'

The snide prick wouldn't be feeling half as clever in a moment, I assured myself. 'You're so deluded that you see yourselves as that? You guys crack me up.'

'Stand down at once,' yet another voice joined into the discussion. It was Joe Higgins, chief administrator.

His large frame approached us from along the centre aisle. 'Did you hear what I said?' he demanded. 'Lower those damn weapons at once!'

We all turned our attention to him as he came to a halt between Alex and myself on the one side, and the boys in black on the other.

'You are interfering in company business,' he told the others, 'and you are on company premises. I have the authority here.'

What the hell was going on here? I wondered. How many people were going to turn up to our *secret* departure point?

The guy with the dopey smile stuck to his face and armed backup seemed momentarily nonplussed, but then snapped out of it. 'Do you know who we are? We override any authority and all jurisdictional concerns. We are in charge,' he proclaimed, and at that exact moment there was a colossal roar from overhead.

We all looked up in the direction of where the interruption had come from. The roof of the warehouse was maybe fifty feet above our heads, and on it a large diameter, cherry red circle began to appear. In seconds it began glowing bright red, then bright white as it melted, oozed downward and fell dangerously around in little explosions of molten metal sparks.

Everyone took desperate evasive action, but for Alex and I. Remaining together we adroitly stepped out of the molten metal's drop zone, to stand with our backs against the stack of wooden pallets.

'I'll leave you to settle this by yourselves,' I managed to call out above a high pitched whining noise which came from all around us, and a moment later we were surrounded by a circle of bright, white light, and the scene around us began to fade rapidly from view.

I woke lying on the exact same cot, looking up at the very same white, domed ceiling as the first time I had come here. Except, I was the only one lying down. Alex was at my side, gripping the side rail of the cot, watching over me.

My mouth was exceedingly dry, my body felt exceedingly heavy and there were drip lines attached to either arm.

'How long?' I asked in a raspy voice, and finding speech uncomfortably difficult. I tried again, 'What happened?'

'It has been two whole days,' she replied, her voice soft and soothing, which worried me immensely. 'The wound, she said. 'It's badly infected. The Jhai saved your life. If it hadn't been for them you would have lost your life, for sure.'

'I can't feel my legs.'

'It's alright, darling. Take it slow, you'll be fine.'

I smiled, remembering the last thing I had witnessed. 'Did you see the look on their faces? That was priceless, wasn't it?'

I began chuckling from deep in my chest; the look on those guys' faces was exactly what I had hoped for; and I thought for a moment she was laughing along with me, until I noticed the tears streaming down her cheeks. I didn't understand, but women are like that. Maybe all the excitement had been too much for her, I figured; but then she turned and fled from the room, making those squeaky, weeping noises women make when they cry and run at the same time. An odd response. A little overwrought, I guessed. A heavy and irresistible tiredness swept in to overtake my thoughts and I couldn't fight it. I had to retreat under the weight of it, to sleep. Two days? Why two days?

The weirdest dream came to me. *Stars*—millions, perhaps billions of stars in formations like whirling pinwheels, in clouds and clusters like floating islands adrift in the depths, each with its own distinctive character like fingerprints dabbed here and there within a three dimensional grid stretching beyond an eternity of space and time. It was wondrous, prodigious, limitless, exalting and exhilarating. A sense of freedom and peace; a flawless, harmonious existence I had never known—did not know was possible—uplifting and full of promise and joy; a place of belonging—belonging, for the first time, a feeling of belonging.

I woke an unknown span of time later, my mind ablaze, still, with the afterimage remaining and not wanting to depart.

'Jack. Jack? *Jack! Wake up Jack.*'

I was being gently shaken. Who was trying to wake me? It was Alex's voice. I had to concentrate, force myself awake.

'What is it?' I grumbled. 'Is it morning already?' I realised I was making no sense and opened my eyes to see Alex, again standing over me. A beautiful girl, I saw, looking over me. But no, not over me. I was upright and Alex was standing in front of me. Was I standing? How was I on my feet when I had only just opened my eyes? I couldn't feel my feet, and there were drip lines attached to me, still. *This was peculiar.*

Behind her the Jhai appeared to be working industriously with connecting lines to electrical switches, machines being connected up, conduits being strung up or sealed behind wall panelling.

My eyes came to perfect focus on Alex's features and I greeted her with an encouraging smile. 'This is peculiar,' I told her. 'Why did you run away crying? What is wrong, my dear? Tell me.'

I watched as Alex mentally braced herself. 'You were very ill,' she began, and took a deep breath before going on. 'The Jhai have been devoted to your survival. You are alive because of them.'

I moved my attention to those behind her, bent assiduously to a task, I had no idea what. One broke away from what it was doing and came forward.

'How are you feeling?' the words came clearly to my mind. It was asking me how I was feeling. I understood perfectly.

'I'm glad you hear us now. Are you comfortable?' It asked.

Before answering vocally I knew it had received my answer: *'I feel quite okay. Thank-you for helping me.'*

'We are please to assist,' it responded, and returned to whatever it was it was doing.

'That's amazing. I can communicate with them. In my mind.

Telepathy. Mental telepathy!'

'Yes,' she said, smiling warmly. 'There are differences now.'

I sensed there was something serious on her mind. And my legs.

I still couldn't feel them. And not just that. There was something about … how was I standing when I couldn't feel my feet? Something was much different. I felt it. I didn't feel right. Not right at all.

Alex saw that I was waking to the fact of the differences and intervened before my confusion grew and became unmanageable. A Jhai came over beside her, reached above my head in order to make some kind of adjustment. In response, my rising anxiety levelled, and diminished quickly, but I felt I had been sedated. My mind ceased racing and a calmness gently rolled over me like a wonderful, soothing balm.

The Jhai nodded to Alex and walked away, leaving us facing one another. All I could do was watch her face—her lovely face. I could stare at that face for hours and not grow tired of it.

'Jack. In order to save your life… ' She broke off, turning to the Jhai behind her. 'I can't,' she said. 'I can't do it. I just cant—' and turning back to me. 'Im sorry, Jack. I can't do this. 'Maja the elder will fill you in on the situation. I'm sorry,' she said one last time, and departed quickly from sight.

I would have followed her progress out of the room but discovered I could not turn my head. Something odd had happened, but what? I didn't feel at all right and I didn't understand what the hell was going on, and why couldn't I follow after her. Why couldn't I feel my extremities?

Another Jhai approached, or was it the same one as before? It communicated friendship to me; a belonging which I felt to the depths of my being.

'Thank-you for serving us,' it communicated. *'We honour you for your union. We are glad to aid your continuance as one with us and more than you were.'*

I was beginning to understand. I should have been beside myself with emotion of some sort; horrified, but I felt calm. This being was communicating something to me, not with word or thought or by some kind of logical sequence of information. It was a kind of osmosis—an osmosis of knowing. I was absorbing information, knowledge and awareness as if through my entire being.

The Jhai reached once more to make some kind of adjustment above my head, and as he did so, the entire sequence of events became known to me.

This whole episode had been a setup from the beginning: an elaborate ploy had been set in motion. From the beginning I had been the sacrifice and the only one not in the know. The information was flowing to me now. The company had never been told the extent of the theft of so much equipment and hardware. Higgins and Berringer had known before I came along who was stealing their precious stores, and they had made a deal with the Jhai, using Alex as the go between, and using Alex at the bait. The Jhai had broken down, that was certainly true, but they could not go on indefinitely taking as they pleased. They were in need of a biological brain to coordinate mechanisms within the craft's intricate guidance systems and to act as control servers and sub-servers. Biological systems operated throughout the Jhai's vessel, but the one which had failed was the prime system and could not be repaired or regrown, but only replaced—replaced by a delicate and complex nexus of switches and controls found within the brain of someone

having a talent. Someone with a talent for rapid problem solving. Someone like Alex Hardin who would not
be missed. Why? because a misfit like myself was totally
replaceable. I had been played from start to finish; and
Alex? She had done a superb job. What a piece of work
was she?

The Jhai in front of me, Dortl Karp, he was called.
He had been following my thinking. Apparently thoughts
here were not entirely private.

*'You are in error, Jack Hardin. The female was manip-
ulated as were you. She cares deeply for you and is ashamed of
her role in the method undertaken.'*

'I am here,' Alex intervened, returning now. 'I will
speak for myself, thank-you, Dortl Karp.'

The alien withdrew, returning to its work as Alex
came forward to stand before me.

'I am so sorry, Jack. I had no choice. I was threatened. My family back on Earth was threatened if I did
not play along. But I fell in love with you Jack, since that
first night with you.'

'What have I become?' I replied, ignoring the
attempt at gaining redemption. 'What am I? A bio-
server, a bio-system within a larger computer network?
What do I look like now?'

These questions should have been seething with
rage, oozing vitriol and desperation, but they were not.
No negative emotion remained withing me, but the positive ones? They remained still, and I could not help feeling the warmth of emotion I had felt for Alex since first
laying eyes on her. I felt nothing but calm as I asked these
questions which dwelt now only in the logic of the asking, and nothing whatsoever hinting of anger or the like.

'I had decided not to go along with them, Jack. I was going to risk it and refuse. Disappear if I had to, but you became so ill. You were dying, Jack, and I could not let that happen. We saved your essence, that which is you and I am glad for that. I am, Jack. The Jhai assure me you will have a rich and rewarding existence. You are now a part of a network spanning light years. You will adapt and thrive as an integral part of the whole. Have you not felt it already?'

I had. The dream I had must have been an inkling of what was to come. The thought must have been picked up by her, because she smiled. 'Is it good?' she asked aloud.

'Yes,' I replied, honestly. 'I think I am going to enjoy being a spaceship.' And one thousand years on, I can say that I was not wrong about that. For the first time in my life I felt happy, and that never changed. I have become so much more than I ever dreamed I might amount to.

Happy? The universe is my playground.

— end —

www.ingramcontent.com/pod-product-compliance
Lightning Source LLC
Chambersburg PA
CBHW050858130726
47900CB00013B/385